THE HAMILTON
BROTHERS

The Hamilton Brothers

Dria Andersen

www.driaandersen.com

Contents

The Hamilton Brothers

The Friend Contract
The Alpha's Affair

Dedication

To my husband who is my sounding board, my cheerleader, my critique partner, and all the things I needed to finish this project. I appreciate every hour, every word of input and most of all, your unwavering support.

To my family who had to deal with the random meltdowns and moments of frustration. Thank you for your patience.

To my sister Tina, who reads everything I write and gives me honest feedback and encouragement, thank you mucho mucho. I appreciate your continued support and cheerleading!

Also, to my Auntie Cathy who, probably unbeknownst to her, first fueled my love for reading. It's her bookshelf I raided for all things romance.

Thank you to every fan who continues to stick with me while I tell the stories playing in my head. I appreciate each and every one of you.

The Friend Contract

1...

Common sense told Gabriel Hamilton that sneaking over the fence of the panther compound would piss them off. But, once he weighed the amount of trouble it would take him to go through their front gate, it pretty much evened out for him. It honestly shouldn't take that much aggravation just to see his best friend, but he would do anything to see her, including slumming with panthers. It was well known that keeping a bear out of anyplace they wanted to be was near impossible, so really, when he thought about it, him sneaking in was the cats' fault.

He curled his lips at the scent markers the panthers had all over the place. The acrid smell of cat was on every inch of the property. A proper warning for shifters who had accidentally wandered too far onto their territory. The signs posted everywhere were for the humans. He bypassed it all, his steps light as he sneaked through their security. He growled in irritation as he sidled behind the pool house, keeping close to their fence, inching closer to the back door.

Why Naomi moved damn near across town into the panther's building when she had a perfectly great condo on the floor below his...okay, wasn't a mystery. But, still it was aggravating. She'd joined her family's prowl and was now safely ensconced in the apartment building where the panthers all lived close to the Alpha. Though...how safe was it when he'd easily gotten through their security measures?

He'd need to talk to her about that.

He popped the lock on the rear entrance of the building, cursing when the electronics shocked him. He hissed and shook off the bit of electricity as he worked through the lock. He took his time disabling it, putting the lock back in place once he was done to buy time before they knew he was there. He straightened and snarled in surprise as two females in panther form passed him in the hallway of the first floor. He walked past the lobby, hidden, thankfully by the large planters the cats insisted on having everywhere. It gave the whole space an exotic feeling, especially coupled with all the windows. It was perfect for him to slip past the security.

Now that he was in the building, it occurred to him, that it had taken longer to sneak in. But, riling the panthers was fun, so in the end, it would all be worth it. He ran a hand down the front of his dress shirt to smooth the wrinkles, heading towards the elevator. Excitement had his bear on edge. He'd not seen Naomi in a few weeks. Between his work and her traveling, they hadn't been able to link up. She'd texted him last night that she was back in town and he decided a trip to see her was long overdue. The amount of work on his desk should've prevented the outing, but he missed her.

Well, that, and he could no longer keep away from her.

He took the elevator up four floors and cursed when it stopped halfway. It didn't stop on a floor, no, it just halted, the jolt of the emergency stop shaking him slightly off balance. He sighed.

"Who the fuck are you?" Came a gruff question over the speaker.

"Gabriel Hamilton, here to see Naomi Rivers," he answered, irritated.

"Hamilton, what the actual fuck?"

This voice he recognized. It was that of the Beta panther. Second-in-command of the Ayala Panther Prowl, Derrick Lincoln was usually nicer to him. Gabe cocked his head in surprise at the tone. But then, he remembered...he'd broken in, so of course, the Beta was pissed.

"Sorry, I'm here to see Nay and I'm on a schedule." That last part was unnecessary, but...again, he did enjoy provoking the cats.

"Use the front door next time," Was Derrick's reply a second before the elevator re-started its ascension.

Gabe saluted the camera and flicked a bird at the security guard he knew would be watching the camera as he left. He walked down to Naomi's door and stopped, inhaling the familiar smells of mint, a hint of pine, and the slight chemical smell from her paints. Underneath it all was a scent, so appealing, and achingly delicious to his bear. That of their mate. He knocked on the door, taking a deep breath to calm his excitement.

She answered the door, a ready smile on her round face, her hair tied up into a scarf, the curls pushed up into a giant puff on top. Fresh-faced, her dark eyes went wide for a second before she glanced back over her shoulder. He looked down and growled at the large t-shirt she wore like a dress. It was his, one of many he'd left at her house over the years. The shirt emphasized their size difference and the caveman part of his brain got intense satisfaction from it. Her thick pecan colored legs were bare and he desperately wanted to feel them wrapped around his waist. He cleared his throat and blinked, hopefully clearing the lust from his eyes.

"Gabe, hey," She greeted him, going up on her toes and wrapping her arms around his neck.

He kissed her cheek inhaling deep, his longing for her a living breathing weight on his chest. His bear came alive, curiosity at the change in her scent. He grunted his greeting.

"You smell more cat than usual."

"I think it's because I'm fully in the prowl now." She backed away and let him into her apartment, a sheepish expression on her face.

He nodded at her answer but wondered why she looked embarrassed. Until he took in the scene around him. There were ties all over the place, tied to various surfaces from the base of her lamps, to the back of her dining table chairs.

"What's happening?"

"It's silly." She shook her head and walked away.

He blinked, waiting on her to explain. She didn't. His bear raised its head. Possessiveness—something he could never control around her—flared, his chest rumbled in a growl. She gave him a startled glance but went back to her project.

"Explain, Nay." He ordered.

Her eyes lowered, and he realized his bear was giving off dominant vibes.

"Sorry." He pulled back his power. "What are you doing with the ties?"

"Oh, well, I was watching a movie and she was tying her boyfriend's tie and I realized that I knew nothing about tying ties and if I want to get married, maybe I should know how," She said in a rush of words.

His brain malfunctioned for a moment so he shook his head. She had a boyfriend? Once serious enough to consider marriage to? Was he too late? Had he missed the chance to make her his? He had been busy at work, he knew that, but surely he'd not missed a boyfriend. He'd stayed in his lane, in the friend zone she'd imposed, content to be with her in any way. He'd been under the impression that she didn't want anything serious, now she was talking about husbands.

He should've learned from the first time. She'd been engaged, pregnant from a fox shifter Gabe hadn't trusted from day one. The relationship fell apart when she lost the child and he'd nearly killed the bastard for it. His brother had been the only thing between the male and death. Naomi had stopped talking to him for a couple of weeks behind that, so he was more careful when it came to her boundaries.

Her head was tilted as she stared. He realized he hadn't spoken.

"You've been dating someone long enough to get wedding ideas?"

She blew a raspberry and shook her head. "Of course not, I told you it was silly."

His phone rang and he growled, seeing the number for his office. He sent it to voice mail, knowing his sister would be pissed he was ignoring calls. He needed to clear up this boyfriend thing.

"So no boyfriend."

She huffed. "No, you of all people would know."

"We haven't seen each other in months, I could've missed something."

"Well, that's true. But you haven't. Missed anything, I mean."

He put his hands on his hips and turned in a circle, trying to understand. "The ties then, Nay? Make it make sense."

"I was just practicing," she muttered.

He moved closer to where she was stripping her lamp of a striped tie. "Where did the ties come from? You got one them bums you dated leaving shit behind?"

She sucked her teeth and threw a tie at his chest. "Excuse you, I don't date bums."

"The ties, Princess, where did they come from?" He tried to keep the irritation from his voice.

"I got them from Charlie and Savannah if you must know," she snapped.

"The hell your sister got so many ties for?"

She put a hand to her hip and scowled up at him. "Did you come over here for a reason?"

Her eyes were flashing in irritation, a deeper hint of an animal in their depths. He frowned.

"You're latent, how are you..." he sniffed again, the strong presence of panther all through her scent.

She pulled back her power, the scent fading. "It's part of my Zeta powers. Grandpa Harper says it's because a tribond leads our prowl." Excitement showed in her eyes. "I have a lot more power than I had before."

"Is that right?" He stepped closer to her.

Was she finally ready to be his? He hadn't crossed a line before because she had been adamant that shifters were off the menu for her. Her scent had definitely changed, the panther stronger and more prevalent. Would she be able to form a mating bond?

His phone rang again breaking into their silence. He sighed.

"Do you need to take that?" She asked over her shoulder as she turned around. She was pulling ties off the chairs.

He growled and nodded and went back into the hallway. He barked at his assistant and answered her questions. He came back in and Nay was out on her patio, a fresh canvas on the beat-up easel she kept at her house. It was much smaller than the one at her studio where she did her bigger pieces. She was humming and scraping paints out on her palate. She looked up when he leaned against the sliding door.

"I like watching you paint."

She smiled. "You sound busy, did you come over for something specific?"

He shook his head. He'd just needed to see her. It was nothing new to him. It was part of the mating, that need to see her. Early on in their friendship he'd tried telling her that she was his mate, but she'd dismissed his claim. The last time he'd tried had been after she lost the baby. It was one of the reasons she'd been mad at him. He'd been wrong to make his move at that time. She'd accused him of telling her she was his mate out of pity. He'd just wanted to try and take some of the pain from her.

He sighed and shook off the memory. The woman was stubborn and it seemed nothing he did or said had pushed passed her adamancy that she couldn't mate. He thought being her friend would be enough. His father hadn't had any advice about what to do. Latents were unpredictable. They all had different instincts. Her cousin Savannah had known her mates, but Naomi it seemed, did not. They spent enough time together that she should've. Hell, they'd been friends since middle school, something should've clicked by now. He'd kept back, not sure what do to.

But now, something had changed with this new Felix they had in their prowl. Would she be ready for him? She'd always told him she would never be a part of the prowl, and yet here she was, nestled securely in prowl housing, an official part of the hierarchy.

"So I take it, shifters are no longer off the table."

She gave him a startled look. "I still don't know if I can mate with a shifter. Grandmother says it varies with latents, but...I guess it's not off the table anymore."

Panic flared in his chest, would she overlook him again? He moved closer. "So you're just going to jump into the dating pool?"

She waved away his question. "You know me better than that."

"I do," he murmured, crowding her space. An idea was forming in his head. "You know, I am having an issue that I think you could help me with."

She gave him a droll look. He smiled and she narrowed her eyes.

"You're up to something."

He pulled her into her arms. "I need a favor."

She set the paints on the small table next to her easel. "You know I'd do anything to help you."

"I'm supposed to get married soon."

Her face clouded, her eyebrows lowering, "what?"

His mind was spinning, where the fuck was he going with this? "I…um…yeah, my parents set up a betrothal for me when I was younger and now it's time to mate. I thought I would be able to talk you into mating me by now, but since I haven't, my time is up."

She shook her head. "I don't know why you keep saying that," she griped, her face perturbed.

So, still in denial.

"You're going to bond with someone other than your true mate?" she pulled back to look up into his face, a hint of stunned anger swirling in her eyes.

He shrugged, she still didn't understand that she was his. He wanted to be frustrated, but panic was the more predominant emotion at the moment.

"That's where you come in."

"Okaaay?" she dragged out the word.

"We could marry instead, and then I won't have to go through with it."

She stepped out of his arms. "Wait…what?"

He bit his bottom lip, lucky that she couldn't scent his lies. At least she hadn't been able to over the years. Did her burgeoning panther change that? He crossed his fingers and hoped not. He tilted his head and worked to tie the strings of his story together.

"Yeah, if I say that I found my mate, then the betrothal is nulled."

"And it gives you more time to find your true mate?" She turned her back to him, wiping her brush on the palate to mix paint colors. The sharp, irritated flicks of her wrist belied her nonchalant tone.

Was she angry with him, or dare he hope...jealous? He clamped his lips shut to keep from telling her that he was looking at his true mate.

"I didn't know marriage contracts still existed." She declared at his silence.

"You know how small bear clans are." He said as an excuse.

She bobbed her head, "hmm, I didn't think about that."

"Well? Will you help me?" He pulled her back into his chest and settled his chin on the top of her head.

She was tense in his arms. He leaned over and nuzzled into her neck, dropping small kisses to test the water. Her body relaxed and she arched her neck. A good sign.

"But you..."

"What, princess?"

"We're—"

"Best friends?" he finished her sentence, spinning her around to see her face.

She nodded. "Won't your parents wonder what took us so long?"

"You're latent, everyone knows latents are different." He studied her mouth, need overtaking his normal restraint.

She pushed out a breath, "ain't that the truth."

"Just give it some thought." He said before giving into temptation and kissing her.

Her gasp of surprise opened her mouth. Her tongue dashed out, tangling with his, her hand clasping onto his arm. He closed his eyes, his heart racing at the first taste of her. His tongue coiled with hers, slow but hungry strokes. He took his time exploring her mouth. If it were to be the only kiss she allowed him, he wanted it to count. His bear moved through his chest, eager to claim what was theirs.

Gentle, he chanted to himself, fighting with everything not to overwhelm Naomi with his urgency. He pulled back, nowhere near satisfied, but he figured he'd pushed his luck far enough. Her eyes were dazed and the sweetest scent wafted from her. One he thought he'd never get to experience. His knees nearly buckled as her arousal scented the air between them.

Fuck, he wanted her. He needed to leave before his bear took over and she recovered enough to poke holes in his story.

"I have to go back to work, complicated case."

It was the truth, he was slammed at work.

"Ok. But, you know…" Her words trailed off and she licked her lips, staring at his mouth.

He stepped back. "Think about it. Me and you, Nay, marriage."

She blinked, seemingly tuning back into the conversation. "You really want me to marry you?"

Gabe fought to keep the smug smile from his face. "At the very least." Want was a mild word for it, really.

She studied him. "This all seems silly."

He waved back into her apartment at the ties piled on her dining room table.

She ducked her head, conceding his point. She looked up with her eyes narrowed. "Your mother betrothed you to a bear and you're balking. What if you like her?"

"I don't want to marry her," He barely kept himself from rolling his eyes at his ridiculous story.

"But you want to marry any other stranger." She frowned.

"I am not asking a stranger, I'm asking my best friend."

"Right, yeah. You know what I mean."

He cupped her cheek. "Just give it some thought. It would help me out of a bind."

She held his hand against her cheek and stared into his eyes, he assumed, trying to see through his bullshit. He kept his face straight, praying she'd not call him on his bluff. She nodded.

"Okay, I'll think about it."

The breath he'd been holding left his chest in a whoosh. "Thanks, Nay."

His phone buzzed in his pants and he sighed.

"You gotta go," she pushed out of his arms. "Go, I'll call you later.

He nodded, leaning down to steal one final kiss. Naomi lifted to her toes, slanting her head to deepen their kiss. Lord, he was going to bend her over the patio table if he wasn't careful. He backed away quickly and rushed from her apartment.

2...

Gabe had kissed her.

Naomi could still feel his lips on hers hours later. What in the hell had changed from the last time she'd seen him? Her power had reacted to him from the first moment she'd opened her door this afternoon, reaching out to him as though he'd called it. Her hands shook as she dabbed her paintbrush onto her palate. She stared at the canvas on her easel, the paint strokes and color just as chaotic as her thoughts. Gabe had been gone for hours and she had no answer for him and no painting in which to escape. She couldn't think. Or rather, she could, but all she could think about was Gabe. Marry him? Her heart raced and her face heated. What exactly would that entail, and why had all thoughts about it lead her to fucking Gabe.

God, he was betrothed to another woman. Would she lose him? She'd taken for granted that Gabe would always be there for her. The real possibility that she would have to share his time with another woman had never occurred to her. What would she do if his mother insisted he go through with the betrothal? More importantly, why did the thought of it make her nauseous?

She squelched her panic, feeling her power flare. If she wasn't careful, her feelings would trickle through the prowl link and agitate every panther in the building. It was her job as the Zeta to keep the panthers in their prowl calm, and stable. The current riotous feelings bouncing through her chest would not help that.

She could go along with the marriage, but was that selfish, keeping him for herself knowing she couldn't bond with a shifter? Although Gabe hadn't asked her to bond, he asked her for marriage, something totally different. The distinction low key offended her the more she thought about it. But, she'd told Gabe over and over, through the many years of their friendship that she'd never mate a shifter. So, she had no right to be offended. Still, the thought of him bonding with another woman had anger and jealousy fighting for a place within her tumultuous emotions.

Marriage...to Gabe. Could she do it?

She growled in aggravation at the chaotic canvas and pulled out her phone. He told her to think about it, but all she could think about was his kiss. He'd never kissed her before. Well, at least not on the lips. Kisses to her forehead and cheeks didn't count. They'd been friends for years. Best friends and he'd never gave her any indication that he wanted her.

Well, except for when he...

She shook her head, she would not be going back there, so she pushed that time out of her head. She dialed her sister.

"What's up?"

"Come over."

"KK." Charlotte hung up.

Her sister walked into her door moments later. "Give it up, what's going on?"

"I kissed him." She blurted out.

Charlotte's eyes widened. "Biiitttch," she dragged out.

Her sister took a look around her apartment. Naomi winced because she hadn't finished cleaning up.

"One kiss and he got you up in here tying ties?"

Naomi rolled her eyes. "That's not, no."

"Then what in the devil is all this?"

"I was tying the ties before he got here."

Charlotte blinked. "That makes it even stranger, you get that, right?"

"Charlie focus."

"Well, how was it?"

Naomi's body flushed and heat clenched her stomach.

Her sister inhaled and smiled. "Well then."

Naomi frowned. "Uh-uh, don't do that, don't do that shifter sniffing thing with me. Filtering through my emotions and shit."

Charlotte laughed. "Nay, you're a Zeta, with the way your emotions are, there are probably ten cats underneath you right now horny as hell."

Her stomach dropped to her toes. "That's not...that can't be true." Oh shit, was it true?

Charlotte walked around the sofa and sat, propping her legs on the coffee table. "Chill out, I'm just kidding. You know that's not how it works."

"Asshole." Naomi was new at the job, so she couldn't be one hundred percent sure that wasn't how it worked.

Her sister smiled, no hint of offense on her face. "He's a bear."

Naomi sat next to her older sister. "I'm aware."

Charlotte wrapped her arm around Naomi's shoulder. "Bears are slow, and assholes, sister, Gabe more than most."

Naomi sighed. "I want to say he's different, but I'd be lying."

"You would definitely be lying, he is no different."

Naomi leaned her head on her sister. "What am I going to do?"

"Try giving him some of the noni and see if that works. Maybe you can fuck him out of your system."

She snorted. "You give the worst advice."

"You love me anyway."

"He and I have been friends forever, Char. What if he's playing with me?"

Gabe was no stranger to women, though he was never serious about them. She couldn't think of a time when he'd called any of them his girlfriend now that she thought about it.

"Y'all have been friends forever," Charlotte parroted. "No way would he play you like that."

"What if he just wants sex?" Naomi worried her bottom lip with her teeth.

Faking a marriage seemed an elaborate way to go about getting sex from her, though. Especially considering after one kiss with him, she would have probably easily opened her legs for him.

"What if you only want sex? What if you have sex and it does nothing for you? No need in getting all wound up over some fucking." Charlotte said pragmatically.

She sighed, knowing that was impossible. The kiss they shared curled her toes. Sex with him would probably blow her head off.

"It feels different," she murmured.

"Between the two of you?"

Naomi nodded. She couldn't pinpoint what it was that had her seriously considering his proposal. It was not like she hadn't thought about Gabe in that way. She'd had a crush on him, no doubt. But, Gabe was everything textbook about a shifter. She couldn't handle a fox shifter, what made her think she could handle a rough ass bear shifter. There was nothing gentle about Gabe, except the way he treated her, if she were being honest. She'd long given up any hope of being with Gabe. Was she jealous of the many women he'd dated? Hell yeah, but she had no claim over him, despite his joking about them being mates. She sighed.

She debated telling her sister about the proposal and then decided against it. Charlotte would probably discourage it. It wasn't that Charlotte didn't like Gabe, they'd all grown up together. Her sister was used to being the center of attention, and Gabe paid her no mind. Charlotte didn't understand that Gabe ignored everyone equally.

"What are you going to do?" Charlotte asked.

"Cuddle with you on this couch and watch horrible horror movies?"

Her sister snorted, but pulled the blanket off the back of the couch and covered them. Naomi grabbed the remote and looked around for a movie to watch.

Sister time was interrupted when a couple of people from their prowl came into Naomi's apartment. She normally left her front door open. The panthers would come in and out, seeking comfort from the Zeta. Emotional healing was a part of her job, and she gave everyone that came into her home the utmost respect. Not that they required much of her. Most that came in would sprawl out on her sofa or floor in a pile of bodies seeking touch. Some came to talk to her one on one, in those cases she actively got to use her power, settling out their emotions. But so far that had been few and far in between. Usually just being near her was enough to relax them, according to her grandfather, that was the main benefit of having a Zeta. Her power was a passive one, its soothing energy natural with no interference needed.

When they came in, she normally painted or cooked and the cats would leave when they'd had enough. Three hours later, Naomi kicked the last straggler from her apartment and locked the door. Charlotte had left an hour ago once Naomi's living room had too many people crowding it. Her sister's parting advice had been to fuck Gabe until she was walking lopsided, which...Naomi sighed.

Jesus, Charlie gave ridiculous advice.

She'd come to a decision though. She picked up her cellphone and dialed before she could change her mind.

"Princess," he greeted.

"Are you sure you want a pretend marriage?"

"Had you taken me seriously years ago, we'd already be mated and none of this would be necessary."

Her heart jumped and her throat clogged. He'd asked her years ago to mate with him, but it was after she'd lost...she cleared her throat and hurriedly pushed that memory away.

"We're not going to talk about that." She whispered. "I'll do it."

His growl traveled across the line and directly to her sex. Was she using doing a favor for Gabe as a reason to have sex with him or as a way to keep him tethered to her? Maybe both.

"We need to discuss terms," she said breathily.

"Like a contract?" He didn't sound particularly happy about that.

"Not anything as serious as all that. But we need boundaries." She licked her lips.

"What type of boundaries?"

"I don't know, I didn't get that far. Maybe you can come up with some, and I come up with some and then we compare?"

He grunted his irritation but said nothing. She clutched the phone and wondered if he would back out.

"Okay."

She smiled and grabbed the counter to steady herself. That was the hard part out of the way. "I know you're busy, so I'll leave you to it. Just call me when you're ready to go over terms."

"I'll call you in a couple of days then," he promised.

Naomi hung up and pressed a hand to her chest ordering her heart to stop its galloping. She was going to marry her best friend. Did she panic now, or later?

3...

Gabe sighed as he got to Nay's door. The click-clack of a bullet being loaded into a Glock stopped his hand on the knob. He rolled his eyes at the sound. Would the bullet be silver? Probably. The panthers were nothing if not efficient at killing things. Rumors had it, that his family would have a hard time finding his body if that did happen. Whoever it was, was lucky he didn't startle easily like other bears. One swipe from his big ass paws would tear through skin, down to bones. The last thing he wanted to do was start a war with the panthers, so he kept his body still. He turned and stared into the green eyes of the panthers' head enforcer. Simon cursed then clicked the safety back on.

"Seriously, Hamilton?"

Taunting the cat was probably not a good idea. And yet..."Took you long enough to find out I was here."

He'd, of course, had to take a different route to sneak into the building than the last time, since they'd shored up security on that side. But lucky thing was, the new route hadn't taken him any longer.

Simon growled, the power in that sound raising the hair on Gabe's arms. "We clocked you coming over the fence, Beta told us to hold off to see where you were going. Is this going to be a regular thing?"

Gabe grunted a yes.

"I don't speak that bear shit." Was Simon's response.

Rude.

"She's my mate." Gabe spoke slowly, using words.

Simon shook his head and turned to leave. "God almighty."

Gabe should probably start using the front door of the building if the cats were going to get all huffy every time he snuck into their Prowl House. He knocked and waited, frowning when there was no answer or movement. He closed his eyes and pinched the bridge of his nose. He could take the door lock apart, but being threatened once today was enough for him, so he tried to remember her door code. He'd seen her type it in before, what was it? The doorknob turned easily in his hand, which meant it wasn't locked.

He needed to talk to her about that.

He let himself in and called out to her, looking around. Her place was empty, neat as it usually was. He should've called before he came over, but he knew she wouldn't mind. It was the first time he'd taken a Sunday off in a while, so he wanted to run some errands. He'd talked to her last night and she'd said she had a lot of things she needed to be done to catch up from the time she'd spent in New York. One of them was changing the oil in her car. He could easily take care of that for her. He and his bear agreed that she was theirs and they would do anything in their power to take care of her.

It had taken him a couple of days to get over the initial shock of her finally agreeing to marry him. He knew she wanted boundaries, but he only wanted her. He didn't care how and what it would take to get her. He called her name again and noticed the sliding door was open, which meant she was on the enclosed balcony painting.

He looked around for her car keys and didn't find them. He was reluctant to interrupt her while she worked, but he also had errands he needed to take care of while he was out. He walked over and leaned his shoulder on the door jamb and just watched her.

She was beautiful, the way the light caught her hair in its messy bun. Paint flecks dotted her face and neck, her nose scrunched in concentration as she painted. After a few minutes of watching her, he realized she hadn't heard him knock and enter.

"Nay."

She startled and looked up. Her eyes were hazy as she gazed at him. They cleared a moment later and her face softened and she looked happy to see him. She gave him a smile that set his heart on a ride. He walked to her and leaned down and sipped at her mouth.

"I didn't want to disturb you."

"Did we have plans? I'm sorry—"

He cut her off with a kiss. "No, I just stopped by. Where are your car keys?"

"Ummm," she looked around. "Maybe in my purse."

"Which is...?"

"Oh, on the table by my bed."

"Ok."

"What do you need my keys for?" She wiped a hand down the apron she wore.

"You said you needed the oil changed. I'm going to get it done,"

"Gabe, you don't have to."

He kissed her, wanting her used to his touch. It would make the conversation he'd planned for later easier.

"I'm leaving my keys on your kitchen counter in case you need to go out while I'm gone, don't drive my car crazy." He whispered against her lips.

She shook her head. "I'm not going anywhere. I want to finish this."

"Have you eaten today?"

She frowned. "I want to say yes, like maybe some kind of breakfast."

He sighed and gave her a final kiss.

"I take it to Keisha." She shouted out as he turned to leave.

"I know, love." He said as he walked out the door.

He took the elevator down to the underground parking structure. Simon stood on the other side of the elevator as it opened.

He passed Gabe a key card. "Quit fucking with our fences."

The panther walked away and Gabe snickered. Persnickety things, those cats. He slid the card into his pocket and walked over to Naomi's small pickup truck. He grunted and folded his large body into it.

Hours later, he came back, dragging the food out of the passenger seat along with his briefcase. He could work while she finished painting and then he'd make sure she ate. A full and content Naomi was key to their conversation going well.

***

Naomi looked up as Gabe came in. How long had he been gone? She glanced down at her smartwatch and winced. Four hours. He looked at the cats scattered across her living room, some in panther form. He growled but said nothing else. She walked into her apartment, meeting him halfway.

"What's going on?" He nodded his head towards the panthers.

"Zeta stuff," she accepted his kiss, closing her eyes at the feel of his lips on hers.

"You need me to leave?"

"Of course not." She grabbed the food from him and put it in the oven. "Sit. Work, I'm nearly done with the section I'm working on, and then we can eat."

He grunted in response and sat at her small kitchen table saying nothing. He took his laptop out of his briefcase and tuned out the rest of the chaos going on at her house. She breathed out a sigh of relief, happy that he wouldn't have an issue with this part of her life. She was new to the Prowl hierarchy and didn't want to do anything to mess up the job. It was one of the boundaries she wanted to go over with him. She went back to her painting, determined to finish at least this small section. She had a few commissions due in a few weeks to the gallery she'd worked with in New York and she didn't want to get behind.

She lost herself in her painting as she usually did, only looking up once she realized how quiet her apartment had gotten. Her stomach growled reminding her that it had been hours since she'd last eaten. She got up from her stool and stretched out her back, satisfied with the progress she'd made on the painting. She walked into her apartment, happy to find Gabe, typing away at his laptop. He hadn't left. But then, she shouldn't have been surprised. She and Gabe never had a problem sitting in silence together. She on one end painting, he on the other working. They'd spent many days that way over the years.

She went over and locked her front door since there were no other panthers left. The locked door would let them know that she was unavailable. She wanted privacy for her conversation with Gabe. She walked over and kissed the top of his head before starting the oven to reheat whatever he'd brought her for what should've been lunch. She peeked into the bag, happy it was from an Italian place she loved. It would also make it easy to reheat. She moved the food into an oven-safe dish and popped it inside. She walked back over to the table. He pulled her into his side before she could sit down.

"Tired?"

She rubbed the top of his head. "A little."

She felt so dainty engulfed against his big body. It was enough to make a plus-sized girl like herself swoon. Her five-ten looked tiny compared to his six-five.

"You wanted to talk about terms?" He released her and she sat on the stool next to him. He clasped their hands together on the table.

"Yeah, like I said we'll need some kind of boundaries," she licked her lips in nervousness.

He stared at her, running a finger across her knuckles in slow circles. Her cheeks heated, her body not too far behind. Why was her body going haywire around him? They'd been friends for years, she'd never had a problem with Gabe touching her.

"How will this work?" She steered her mind back to business.

"Just us being engaged will stall the betrothal for now." An uncomfortable look flitted across his face a moment before it disappeared.

"What will we say when your parents ask when the wedding is?"

He cleared his throat. "That we're not sure yet. Unless you want to take my bite? We can dispense with the wedding stuff altogether."

His eyes darkened and the tension between them thickened until she could hardly breathe. She swallowed and looked away to break the contact. She slid her hand out from under his and dropped it into her lap.

"I can't take your bite." No way would she risk trying another bonding.

"In order to convince my family, we'll need to do some kind of ceremony under the light of the full moon."

She crossed her arms over her chest. "You want to get married at night?"

He shrugged. "It's tradition."

She bit her lip. Her mother, Melody, would insist on a wedding. She wouldn't care if it was morning or night. She stood as the oven beeped, removing the food. She fixed them both a plate. Stalling, yes. She put his plate in front of him and sat back down.

"So, boundaries," she prodded.

"Let's get into it." He dug into his food.

They traded ideas as they ate. She had more than he had, his only stipulation that they not discuss an end date for the marriage. She didn't know what to say to that. Eventually, the ruse would end, so it seemed a weird place to put his foot down. He'd agreed to let her tell her family, and that she would keep her position in the prowl hierarchy, which was a big point for her.

She pushed her empty plate away and turned to face him. She took a deep breath, knowing this was where the negotiations would get sticky.

"So, with no end date in sight, does that mean sex is on the table?"

The corner of his mouth turned up in a smile that had the nerves in her stomach dancing. "I mean, could you go months without sex?" His eyes lit gold for a moment, and then he calmed himself. "Is sex with me something you would be interested in?"

4...

Gabe's bear froze, her answer of the utmost importance to him and his animal. Naomi's heartbeat fluttered and her arousal scented the air. It was likely he could convince his mate to bond with him without having sex with her, but there had been many nights when all he could think about was sex with Naomi. He'd fantasized about everything from the feel of her skin, to the way her inner muscles would clench around his dick. So yes, while he could probably make his plan work without sex, he hoped he didn't have to.

Naomi licked her lips and Gabe walked his fingers across her thigh. Her breath hitched and she lowered her eyes. He knew she wasn't modest, which meant, she was trying to hide her body's reaction to him. He reached over and dragged her stool closer to him until she was nestled between his legs, their thighs buffered together.

"Are you going to answer the question, princess," he whispered.

"I mean," she swallowed.

Gabe leaned over and rubbed his cheek against hers, the power of his animal brushing against her skin. She shuddered.

"We've never crossed that line."

"If you're uncomfortable, then I understand." He murmured against her skin.

She grabbed the back of his head, stretching her neck to the side. Gabe smiled, sticking out his tongue to taste her skin. Her body was trembling in his arms.

"Don't you want to see what we could be together?" He cajoled, slipping his hands under her t-shirt. Her skin was warm against his palms.

She gripped his head and brought him back up so she could look him in the eyes. "What if it doesn't work?"

Gabe grabbed her hand and guided it down to the erection straining his pants. "I don't think you understand how much I want you and for how long."

She squeezed his shaft and he groaned. If she said no, he'd absolutely honor that, but he was going to have to spend an inordinate amount of time in his shower when he got home.

"You don't think sex should be a boundary?"

"Princess, didn't you just spend the last hour negotiating this 'contract'? Don't add any unnecessary terms on at the end." He fussed, nipping her chin.

She rolled her eyes and stood, fitting herself closer to him. "Fine. I don't want to deny myself a taste of you."

Oh, he could get with that. He cradled the back of her head and brought her down to his level. "So that's a yes?"

"It's a yes."

She barely finished the sentence before he kissed her. Was it a little more aggressive than he'd planned? Probably, but need was riding roughshod over him. Gabe lifted her by the backs of her thighs sliding her onto the countertop, taking command of her mouth. Their tongues moved together frantically. Naomi propped her feet onto the top of his hips, opening her body to him. He slid his hand between them, moving her shorts and panties to the side. She was wet, heat radiating from her core.

"I don't want our first time to be on my kitchen counter," she panted, pulling back from their kiss.

He growled and lifted her, his hands gripping her curvy ass. He sucked on her neck as he carried her into her room, longing for the day when he could bite down and truly mark her. Naomi whimpered, grinding on his erection prodding her stomach. Lord, would they make it to the bedroom?

Naomi crawled down out of his arms the moment they crossed the threshold into her room. She dropped to her knees wanting so badly to taste him.

"Nay," he warned as she pushed his pants over his hips.

His dick sprang forward, flexing as she stared. She licked her lips, her hand circling his shaft. She licked across the head and moaned in anticipation. She sucked him into her mouth, her tongue lashing against the bottom. He braced one hand against her door jamb, the other fisting her hair, guiding her movements up and down his erection. He watched her with hooded eyes, his gaze riveted, covetous.

She teased with short, shallow strokes, until sucking him deep enough to reach the back of her throat. He growled and pulled her up, turning her into the wall.

"I'm going to fuck the shit out of you first, and then, I'm going to take you slowly." He rubbed his dick at the entrance of her sex, running it across her clit. "By the end of the night, I want you hoarse from screaming."

Lord have mercy.

"I'm on birth control, please tell me you're safe," she managed to pant. She wanted everything he promised and more.

"Absolutely," he assured her. "Last chance to change your mind, Nay."

She shook her head and wrapped her leg around his waist. "I want every inch."

The smile he gave her was savage, showing hints of the undomesticated beast he shared his body with. His first stroke stole her breath, her pussy fighting to accommodate the size of him. The second one was much better, and her body clenched around it. He did as he promised, powering into her, deep strokes that set her body on fire. His nails dug into her thighs as he held it up. Gabe was single-minded, his groin grazing her clit as he pounded into her.

Her body tightened, unable to take the unyielding pleasure. He kissed her, moaning into her mouth, his tongue coiling around hers. He bent his knee on every downstroke, gaining leverage for every up. She pulled from his kiss.

"Fuck," she rasped.

He chuckled, his teeth scraping down her chest. He bent over and sucked a nipple into his mouth and that was when she lost it. The orgasm bowled over her, stunning her with its intensity. Through it all, Gabe never stopped moving. His hips were driving into her, stretching her pleasure.

"You can give me another," he ordered.

There were many things in Gabe's life that he considered luxuries. Being in Naomi's body, feeling her clench around him, with her heat engulfing his dick had to be top three. Her every whimper and moan was a reward for every good thing he'd ever done in his life. He braced his hand against the wall next to her head, pushing in and out of her, determined to live up to his promise. Soon though, the pleasure became too much for him to handle. A heavy buzz of electricity started at the base of his spine.

He gripped her hips tighter, his strokes no longer controlled as he nearly reached his own orgasm. He slid his hand down between them, plucking at her clit until she exploded around him again, her scream sending him over the edge behind her. Her sex squeezed his shaft wringing out every ounce of pleasure. His legs weakened and he swung them around until the bottom of her bed hit his knees.

He fell onto the bed, bringing her down on top of him. His chest moved up and down and air seesawed in and out of his lungs. Naomi crawled up until her head was nuzzled between his shoulder and neck. She stretched her arms around him, holding him tight.

"Okay, you were right. I'm glad I left sex out of the contract."

He laughed, in between catching his breath, happy sex would not change their relationship.

5...

Naomi wasn't what anyone would call a prude, but, she felt a certain type of way standing in the elevator in Gabe's shirt on top of her torn dress, hickeys covering a good portion of her neck. She'd borrowed it when she'd snuck out of his house early this morning to get to her studio. The past week had passed in a haze of stolen moments and amazing sex and she'd enjoyed every second of it. She smiled awkwardly and moved to the side as a couple of panthers joined her in the elevator.

Pressing in her code for the top floor, she faced the doors, hoping they'd say nothing. It was silly, it wasn't as if they'd know she had spent a good portion of the night with Gabe sexing her on every piece of furniture in his condo. Her cheeks heated and she didn't regret a single second of it. They'd spent every spare minute he'd had together since they hashed out their engagement ruse.

Exploring the new part of the relationship was something she'd not been wholly prepared for. She hadn't realized the chemistry they'd have together.

"So, who's the bear?"

Giggling rose behind her. Naomi ignored them and clenched the portfolio in her hand.

"Word is, someone from the Hamilton clan has been back and forth to your apartment, all times in the night."

Naomi whirled on the female. "Excuse you all in my business."

"Well, cuz, is it true or isn't it?" The teenager smirked, the two girls with her giggling.

"Stay out of grown folks business," Naomi snapped at her young cousins and turned back to the door.

The three teenagers snickered as the door opened, moving past Naomi. It wouldn't be the last time someone asked her about Gabe. Hell, it was barely the first time. All week, she'd been fielding sly questions about the bear that had been sneaking onto their territory. She was tired of answering questions. It was the reason she'd gone to his place last night. She wanted to find out who was spreading her business to the prowl, but what she *needed* to do, was tell her family what was going on before they heard it through the grapevine.

Shit.

Now that song was stuck in her head.

She sighed. Jesus, what would her parents say? It would be foolish to go to them and say, 'oh by the way I'm going to marry Gabe as a favor, and just for play play'. For a pretend marriage, she was catching real feelings. Fast.

Damn.

The elevator opened to the penthouse on the top floor and there Naomi found her sister and her favorite cousin splayed out on the floor in front of the t.v. They smiled up at her.

"What's up Nay, taking a break from the sex?" Savi asked, a lascivious smile on her face.

"Nuh-uh, I didn't come to kiki with you heifers." She dropped her portfolio on an ottoman and stood over them, hands on her hips.

"Not heifers, chile," Savi and Charlie shared an amused look.

"I ran into some cousins just now who had an awful lot of questions for me about Gabe and they ain't the first. I would like to know which one of y'all is spreading my business across town."

"First of all, rude," Savi murmured into her glass.

"Second of all, you finally giving Gabe the noni is evident by your scent," Charlie said with a scrunch of her nose. "Ain't a section on you that boy ain't mark."

Savi cackled and fell back against the couch clutching her stomach. Naomi lifted the shirt and sniffed. Gabe didn't wear cologne, and with her dulled senses, she couldn't smell what her sister was talking about.

"Quit laughing," she grumbled to her cousin and plopped down on the floor next to her sister.

She winced at her sore muscles and sighed. Her sister was right. Gabe had thoroughly put his mark on her body. Savi stopped laughed and passed her the wine bottle they'd been sharing.

"I don't need to ask how it was," Savi said with wide eyes.

"Did you see her face when she sat down? Gabe put that thang on her," Charlie rolled her hips. "No wonder her ass showing up here late as hell. You were supposed to be here this morning for brunch."

"Shut up." Naomi mushed her sister's face. "I lost track of time at the studio. I have to ship a few of my pieces to New York."

Savi waved away her excuse. "He has a big dick, right?"

"Oh my God, will you two shut up." Naomi's face burned and she sipped out of the bottle, not bothering to get up for a cup.

"I knew it!" Savi laughed and high fived Charlotte.

"I hate you both," Naomi muttered.

They kept laughing and Naomi chugged more out of the bottle, shoring up her courage for what she had to tell them.

"So, what's going on? You look guilty," Charlie pointed a finger at her.

"Gabe asked me to marry him," she said quickly.

Savi sat up straight and clapped her hands. "Oh my God, Nay, that's fantastic!"

Charlotte narrowed her eyes. "What else?"

Naomi growled, mad her sister wouldn't take the news at face value. Charlotte knew her well.

"It's not a real marriage." She whispered.

"The hell does that mean?" Charlotte snatched the wine bottle from her.

Naomi sighed and crossed her legs under her. "He was supposed to be betrothed to another bear. He asked me to marry him to get out of that."

"Bullshit," Savi said, setting her glass down on the coffee table. "Gabriel Hamilton, wants you to fake a marriage with him? Child, please."

"I'm with Savi, sounds fishy," Charlotte was eyeing her sister.

"I can only tell you what he told me," Naomi shrugged.

"And you agreed?" Savi asked.

"You could fuck him without having to marry him, you now that right?" Charlotte shook her head. "Gabe is such a weirdo, I told you that."

"It's complicated."

"My ass." Savi sucked her teeth.

"Look, it's done. He asked; I said yes."

"Nay, you're going to catch feelings. How long is this fake shit supposed to last?" Savi asked softly.

"Just a couple of years, and then we'll reevaluate." Naomi avoided her sister's gaze. When no other protests came, she looked up. They both had shocked expressions. "He's my best friend, Gabe would never hurt me."

"Nay," Charlie sighed.

"We made a contract and everything." Sort of. They didn't need to know the exact details.

"Oh well, now, I have heard everything," Savannah stood and walked to the kitchen, pulling another wine bottle from the wine cooler.

"Like a 'friends with benefits' contract?" Charlie scoffed

"It'll be fine," Naomi assured them.

"Are you telling our parents that you're going to fake marry Gabe?" Charlotte closed her eyes and pinched the bridge of her nose. "Jesus. Mom will faint dead away."

"I'm not telling them anything except that I'm marrying Gabe. They won't be shocked, they love Gabe."

"That's true," Savi said, filling up her glass.

Charlie held out her own to be refilled. "So when is this fake marriage happening?"

Naomi shrugged. "We don't have the exact date, it just has to be under the full moon."

"Biiiiiitttch," Savi whispered, chugging from her glass.

"A full moon ceremony?" Charlie looked surprisingly calm. "Do you understand full moon ceremonies for bears?"

"He said his parents wouldn't accept it otherwise."

Charlie snorted. "Well, congratulations, sis." She held up her glass and tapped it to Savi's. "Better get your story straight before you go the grandparents because Rebecca sniffs out lies like a bloodhound."

"You ain't never lied" Savi responded.

"It'll be fine," Naomi said more to herself than them.

But would it though?

6...

Gabe wiped a hand down his face and forced his bear to relax. He was irritated and hungry, which had the animal agitated. Naomi had left his condo early in the morning, so instead of going back to sleep, he'd gotten dressed and came into the office. Now, it was a little after six in the evening and going on eleven hours straight in his office. His eyes were starting to cross. His desk phone rang and he squinted at the clock on his computer. His stomach was growling and he debated going home and ordering pizza or going to Naomi's. She'd cook for him, but he definitely wouldn't get any work done. His phone rang again and he picked it up.

"Yeah."

"Mom says you haven't been over. You should come to dinner." Brent, his brother sounded cheerful.

He always sounded cheerful. Brent was a strange bear as far as Gabe was concerned, especially for the next in line to be alpha. Most alpha bears were grouchy bastards. Not so his brother. He thought about the dinner offer. He could work there when he was done, talk over some of the stuff with his father.

"Fine." He hung up, not waiting for Brent to say anything else.

The timing of the call was perfect so he shut down his computer and gathered his things. He called Nay as soon as he got into the car. He wanted to hear her voice. He also wanted to gauge if she would be up for a late-night visit. He frowned as the phone went to voicemail. He texted her at a red light to see how she was doing. She didn't answer and he frowned, wondering what she was doing. It could be painting, she tended to be in another world when she was working, they were a lot alike in that. He didn't like not being able to get a hold of her, though.

Gabe marveled at the change in their relationship. Yes, he'd always felt possessive of her, but he'd never had a claim on her. Now that they were 'engaged', his bear was fiercer in its protection of her. He found himself wanting to know where she was at all times. Not that she'd put up with it. Naomi would do like she always did when he gave her order. Roll her eyes and ignore him.

He pulled into his parent's driveway, happy only Brent's sports car was there. He didn't feel like dealing with any of his sisters at the moment. Combined with his mother, the four of them would nag him about anything, from work to his love life. His mother opened the door before he even got out of the car. He sighed. It would be one of those type of nights. Catherine looked like she was in full meddling mode. He got out of the car, lugging his briefcase with him. She hugged him tight when he got to the front door and he returned his mother's hug. He loved the nosy, overbearing woman. He kissed her cheek and grunted in greeting.

"That's all?" She said.

He shrugged out of his suit jacket and dropped it and his briefcase on the chair in the living room. The dining room table was already set and it looked like he was just in time for dinner. Catherine grabbed his hand and walked him into the dining room.

"You've been working so hard, baby, have you been eating well?"

He shrugged. He could tell her that Nay made sure he was fed, even when he wasn't at her house. But then, he would have to discuss his mate with his mother, and he wasn't quite that desperate. As it was, he hoped no word of the fake engagement got back to Catherine. His mother would cuss him out, perhaps even slap the back of his head if she found out he was lying to his mate. Delaying telling their families was one of Nay's asks. He'd happily agreed because it gave him more time to stall. Brent bumped his fist as he got closer.

"Dad." He greeted and Julien nodded his head in greeting.

"I love having my boys over for dinner," Catherine gushed as she sat in her chair.

His mother said grace and they started eating.

"So what's new with you, Gabriel?"

"Working, mom." He said, fixing his plate.

She huffed. "You don't work twenty-four hours a day, Gabe."

"Pretty damn close," Brent murmured. "The Trips are slave drivers."

Gabe grunted in agreement. Their family law firm was run by their sisters since they were the oldest and Brent was right, his sisters were as serious about business as his mother was about the business of them mating.

"So, anyone new in your life?"

Speaking of.

Catherine had directed the question to his brother. Gabe shoved food in his mouth to keep from having to answer.

"Mom," Brent's warning tone floated over their mother's head.

"You're going to be the next Alpha, Brent, you can't do that without a mate; you know how the bears in this clan are." Catherine was not to be deterred.

His brother glared at him and he shrugged. No way was he pulling Catherine's attention to him.

"I heard the Tampa prowl's Felix complaining about bears in his building," Brent said off-handed.

This motherfucker. He kicked his brother's shin under the table, to which Brent only smiled.

His father stopped eating. "What kind of bears?"

"A very specific black bear, one who refuses to use the front entrance." Brent lifted his brows.

Julian rolled his eyes and continued to eat.

"You smelled like a cat when you came in here," Catherine remarked casually.

Gabe grunted that it was nothing and kept eating. His mother looked to his father and cleared her throat. His father grunted his intent to stay out of it and continued to eat.

"Lord have mercy, a house full of lawyers, and no one can use words." She snapped.

"Well, damn, mama." Brent laughed. "Don't get mad at us because your snooping isn't working."

She huffed and put her fork down scowling at her husband. "Our son is damn near mated and you can't be bothered to ask?" She groused.

His father blinked at him and grunted. Remarking on his changed scent. He sighed and shrugged, he hadn't yet given Naomi his bite, so his mother was jumping the gun a little.

"Well, there you go," Julian said.

His brother laughed. Catherine's mouth dropped open before closing with an angry snap.

"I can't," she muttered and left the table.

His father inclined his head towards the kitchen door and Gabe sighed again. He knew if he didn't answer his mother now, she'd 'investigate' and God help them all. He should have thought about his changed scent before he agreed to dinner, so it was definitely his fault. He could only blame it on distraction. A mate was on the horizon, Catherine would be dogged until she got information.

"Mama."

She turned around and growled. "You're so secretive, Gabriel." She accused.

"I'm not, mama."

He didn't care enough to be secretive, but there was no use in arguing semantics with his mother. She wanted to know about every moment of her children's lives and he didn't have the patience to indulge her.

"Well, you're sneaking into prowl houses and—"

"Not houses, mama, one prowl house." He interjected.

She growled. "Well, who is she, what does she look like, will I get grand cubs, how will a panther and a bear work, will I get grand cubs?"

He sighed. "It's Nay and yes, you'll get grand cubs." That was jumping the gun, but what else could he tell his mother.

Catherine frowned. "She's latent."

"But her family is full of alphas. Would you care if they were panther or bear?"

She held her hands up "No, I don't care. I just want more grandbabies."

They stood in awkward silence.

Catherine crossed her arms over her chest. "That's it?"

"Will it help if I invited her over?" He asked.

She clapped her hands, her face suddenly all business. "Are you free next Sunday? I've already put your sisters and their mates on notice. They know to be available so we can all meet her. It'll be great."

So she'd already known about Nay.

Fuck!

He shuffled out of the kitchen not saying a word and retook his place at the table.

"Fell into a trap, didn't you?" His father asked, scooping up more food.

He grunted and his brother snickered. He should've just eaten pizza tonight. He sighed and braced himself, avoiding his mother's smug gaze as she came back in and took her seat.

"I have to tell you all something." Gabe closed his eyes in dread.

Everyone stopped eating.

"This thing with Naomi..." he cleared his throat and his bear moved restlessly in his body. "Nay's latent, so she doesn't exactly understand that she's my mate."

"But she understands the concept of a mate?" Catherine's brows furrowed.

"Yeah, but she doesn't think she can bond with a shifter."

Julian grunted in sympathy, well acquainted with Gabe's dilemma since they'd had the conversation before.

"What can we do?" Brent asked.

He put his fork down. "I..." he sighed. "I had to finesse it a little to get her to agree to marry me."

"You're getting married, not mated?" Catherine was fully confused.

"Nay won't agree to my bear's bite."

"What?" Catherine puffed out her chest.

"But she'll marry you?" Brent frowned.

He nodded. "She agreed to marry me under a full moon. I kind of told her that if she didn't Mom and dad would make me marry the bear I was betrothed to."

Julian finally sat straight from his food. "Say what now?"

"I told her that if she married me, it would save me from a betrothal."

"You lied to your mate?" Catherine growled and stood at the end of the table, bracing her hands on the top.

"Mom, I couldn't think of another way."

"We paid your way through college and law school and you could think of no other way? Is that what you're telling us, Gabriel?"

"Mom." He sighed.

"And what exactly do you expect us to say when we run into her? Nay has known us for years, you want us to also lie to your mate?" Power infused Brent's tone, his bear riling.

"You don't have to say anything, just don't...you know, act surprised if she brings up the betrothal thing."

"Lord have mercy," Catherine said, leaving the table again.

Julian sighed and resumed eating. He grunted at his son and Gabe's ear burned in chagrin.

"Be careful of the game you're playing, Gabriel." His father reiterated using actual words.

"I know, dad."

"Fuck Gabe, the fallout if this doesn't work..." Brent's hushed tone was more baffled than judge-y.

"I know, B, but I'll do anything at this point to have her."

Julian sighed and put his fork down. "Dammit, now I have to go calm down your mother."

Julian stood to leave the table. He knew his father could feel his mother's aggravation and hurt through the mating bond. Gabe wanted that with Nay, desperately, and like he'd told his brother, he was at the point where he'd do anything to have her.

"I'm sorry." He said to his father's retreating form.

And he was, he'd known his mother would be mad. Appetite gone, Gabe started cleaning. Thirty minutes later, he was washing the dishes when his mother came into the kitchen.

"I'm not going to meddle, but I will say that I'm disappointed."

"I panicked, mama. It's my only excuse."

She sighed and touched his back. "Nothing good can come from lying, Gabriel."

"I know."

She picked up the dishtowel and started drying the dishes after patting his shoulder. That was all she would say on the subject which was honestly surprising to him. He leaned over and kissed the top of her head, his heart aching, though it did soothe his bear that his mother would forgive him. He hoped the same could be said for Naomi if she ever found out he lied.

7...

Naomi smoothed a hand down the side of her skirt and took a deep breath as she smiled at Gabe's assistant. She'd called the woman ahead of time and had Geri carve some time out of his schedule for her to bring Gabe lunch. According to Geri, Gabe had been in the office early and hadn't taken any breaks. It had only been a couple of days since she'd seen him, but her body acted as if it had been much longer. She smiled as she passed the woman, waving the takeout bag at her. She'd promised to be quick, but she'd still dressed for the occasion. The wrap skirt swished around her ankles, the long slit in the front separating with every other step, showing a long length of leg. He loved her thighs, he said it all the time.

Gabe's eyes lit when she walked into the room, which...she sighed. They'd been friends for some years, and now that she was looking, she realized he'd always looked at her that way. Her stomach dipped as she got a good look at him. His massive shoulders filled out the dress shirt he wore, clinging to his chest. He'd always been big, as bears tended to be, but now that she knew the weight of him on top of her, his size took on a whole new meaning. She shuddered in anticipation.

She smiled and closed the door behind her, locking it. She turned and shrugged so the oversized t-shirt she had tied in the back fell from her shoulder.

"Hi."

"To what do I owe the pleasure?"

"You said you were busy last night and tonight, I brought you lunch." She held up a bag from their favorite take out spot, crossing the lush carpet towards him.

"You are so good to me," he murmured as she rounded his desk.

She put the bag down on his desk and sat on his lap. "This chair is ginormous, I can't even straddle you."

He groaned. "Don't come in here starting shit, Naomi."

She smiled, loosening the tie at his throat. "What? I'm just saying."

He ran his hands up her legs, moving her skirt to the side. "Your skin is so soft," he murmured.

"Do you have time to eat?"

He plopped her on the desk in front of him and spread her legs. "I do". He murmured, his fingers trailing her thighs.

"I meant food." She closed her eyes and sighed in pleasure.

He grunted and positioned her hips at the edge of his desk. "Did you lock my door, princess?"

She nodded.

"Good girl," he whispered, pushing her skirt open wider. He hissed when he realized she wasn't wearing panties. "You came in here to start some shit," he accused.

She waggled her eyebrows. "I came for the dick, yes, if that's what you mean."

"Jesus Tyrone Christ, woman," he snarled and buried his head into her sex.

She arched her back as he gave one, long lick to her core, his eyes going dark. "I will never tire of your taste," he whispered.

He devoured her, his tongue wrapping around her clit tugging, his fingers driving up into her. He made her dizzy with pleasure. He alternated between slow, torturous licks, quick flicks of his tongue, and a sweet pulling, suckling that had her gripping the papers on his desk. She whimpered, biting her lips to trap her moans. Power rose in her, filling her chest until she thought her body would come apart. An orgasm shook her body, sending tingles up and down her skin. Gabe growled and stood, hurriedly unfastening his pants and shoving them down. He gripped his cock, his face a fierce, impassioned mask. He pushed into her while she was still coming, her sex clenching around his erection, deep pulls that clenched her womb.

"Damn, Nay," he snarled, his hips jerking.

She raised her hips, meeting his every thrust. He circled her back with his hands and lifted her, kissing her, swallowing her cries. She gripped his shoulders and wrapped her legs around his waist, purposely digging the heels of her shoes into his legs. He snarled, the pain speeding his rhythm.

"I'm not going to last, Nay," he whispered against her lips.

He went down to her throat, his teeth scraping against her skin,

"Come for me, Gabe."

She tugged on his ear lobe, using her nails to scratch the back of his neck. She couldn't break the skin, she knew that. She had no right to mark him, but the temptation was there all the same. He cursed, his strokes harder, his hips pressing against her clit with every push. Tingles started at her toes as her orgasm built.

"Oh God," she whispered, gripping him tighter, her legs tensing as it built higher, the tingles, full-body as he gripped her shoulder with his teeth. She wanted him to bite down so badly.

"Now, baby."

Her body followed his order, her climax crashing over her, heat bursting throughout her body. The orgasm was a searing heat that had flames dancing along her skin. She went limp, their harsh breathing the only sound in the office. Gabe's eyes were unfocused as he stared at her, the dark orbs tracing her face. He finally met her eyes and the depth of feeling in them brought a lump to her throat.

"What am I going to do with you, Naomi?" He whispered.

She cocked her head to the side and rubbed her hand over his prickly short hair. "You can do anything you want."

He groaned and wiggled his hips again. The phone at his desk rang. "Fuck!" He kissed her hard on the lips and picked up the phone. "What?"

"Just reminding you that you have a client in an hour." She heard Geri tell him.

"Fine." He hung up.

Naomi smiled and caressed his cheek.

Gabe stared down at his mate, wonder filling him. He leaned over her, wanting to wallow in her scent. She was beautiful and so damn sexy. He sighed. He wanted to take her home and spend the rest of the day making love with her. Instead, he was swamped with work.

"You need to eat before your client gets here, okay?" Naomi pushed at his hips, trying to dislodge him.

His bear growled, the sound rattling his chest.

She smiled and kissed his chin. "Calm down, grumpy."

She was the only person he knew who talked to his bear as if it were a separate person. Strangely enough, it worked. His bear settled, pulling back some of his power. He wondered if it was a part of her Zeta powers. She tapped his forehead and he realized he was just staring and hadn't spoken.

"I wish I had more time for you today."

"I got what I came for, Gabe. Now, get off me so I can clean up and leave with enough time for you to eat your lunch, Geri said you've been trapped in here for days, barely eating."

He grunted but did as she asked, gently sliding from her body. She pulled out a package of wipes from her purse along with a pair of panties. He growled and snatched the delicate lace from her, pocketing them. She rolled her eyes and handed him a few wipes to clean up. He pulled his pants back up, leaving them open. He lifted her from the desk and carried her to the small bathroom he had in his office. He'd moved into a bigger office since the last time she'd visited him at work.

"This is fancy," she commented as he carried her into the small space.

He grunted and propped her on the sink and found washcloths in the cabinet underneath. He took his time cleaning her off, his hands playing in the curls at her center. She made a soft sound that hardened his dick as though he hadn't just had her.

"Gabe," she sighed. "You don't have time."

Right, time. He should stop. He didn't though. He slid a finger between the folds of her sex, kissing along her shoulders. He wanted to tug down the strapless shirt and expose her breasts. He needed her naked underneath him as she took his dick. His chest rumbled with a growl of aggravation at the fact that he wouldn't have time to take Nay the way he wanted. She pulled his head up to her and kissed him, their tongues tangling in a lazy way that tugged on his emotions.

"I want you," he said against her lips.

"You just had me, and you're busy." She reminded him, hissing as he tugged on her clit.

"One more," he whispered.

"Gabe," she breathed out.

"One more, princess, to tide me over until I can see you again."

He loved this woman, even if she hadn't been his mate, he knew he would've loved her. He trailed kisses up her neck, scraping his claws against the skin of her back the way he knew she liked it. He was careful not to rip through her shirt.

"Say yes," he whispered, rubbing the head of his shaft against her entrance.

"Yes," she whispered.

He pulled her to the edge of the sink and slowly slid in. He closed his eyes as the heat of her sex wrapped around his erection. He kept his strokes slow, not wanting to relinquish the little bit of time they were stealing together. Her breath moved against his neck with her pants. She opened her mouth and gripped the skin and his bear jerked from his grip.

"Nay," he whispered desperately, his power filling the bathroom.

Answering power from her rose and melded with his, and he growled low, his strokes no longer slow and easy. She licked at his neck before biting down again and if she broke the skin, swear to God, all bets were off. He would mark her and claim her, damn everything else. He didn't know if she understood the gravity of her bites, but it was driving his bear insane. He pounded into her, dragging her head up to him so he could devour her mouth. She kept up with his rhythm, her hips canting into his. Her inner walls gripped him tightly as she came, her mouth opening in an O of surprise. He wasn't far behind her, his orgasm torn from him. He quivered, his legs going limp as he shuddered, releasing into her body. They sat there, embraced, neither of them making any moves. After a moment, when his heart stopped racing, Naomi lifted his chin and kissed him.

He pulled back and shook his head. "You're trouble woman."

She giggled. "Umm, if I recall, that last one was on you."

He pulled from her and cleaned her up again. He cleaned himself as well, tucking his still semi-erect shaft back into his pants. He cursed as he looked down at his watch, scrambling to tuck his shirt back in and right his clothes. She held her hands out. He slapped his palm down on hers and gave her five.

She snorted. "No, my undies."

"Psh, nope. I'm keeping them."

"Gabe!"

"What? You the one who brought your fine ass in here to start trouble."

She slapped his shoulder. "I did not."

"'I came for the dick.' Isn't that what you said?"

She reached around him, laughing. "Give me my panties."

"They're my panties now," he kissed her. "Now. Let's go, I'm gonna have to move my meeting to a conference room, no way will I let another male in here with the sweet smell of your sex filling this office."

She smiled and ducked her head. "You so damn nasty." She slid down from the sink. "Panties, Gabriel."

"No, Naomi."

She huffed and he smiled.

"Fine, I'll just walk past all the associates on this floor with no undies on."

He growled and whipped around to her, eyeing the skirt she wore. It had a gaping split in the middle, one he'd had no problem moving to the side to fuck her. The thought of that split opening every time she moved...*nah.*

"You play too much." He lifted her, gripped her ass, and nipped her bottom lip. *God damn she was thick!* He breathed deep fighting to calm down his bear.

"What?" She gave him an innocent face.

"You better be glad I don't have time to punish you for that."

"Hmm," she hummed and licked at his lips. "I like the sound of that."

"Nay." His bear rumbled in his chest, her words nearly sending him out of control.

He pulled the underwear out of his pocket and handed them over. The same jealousy that wouldn't allow another male to so much as smell his mate, would drive him crazy at the thought of her walking past another man with no underwear on. He snatched the phone on his desk and barked at his assistant to find an empty conference room for his meeting. Naomi took her time sliding her underwear up her legs. A growl rattled his chest as his bear fought to come out.

"Can I come over tonight?"

"I thought you had to work late," she peered up from beneath her lashes, the coy look sending blood right back to his dick.

He nodded, mentally trying to find ways to move around his case-load so he could see her tonight.

"Gabe," she prodded, pulling him from his thoughts.

"I do, but I want..." he paused. "I'm already addicted to you sleeping next to me."

Her eyes softened and every hint of playfulness was gone. She walked to him and fixed his clothes. "Okay. Come over, even if it's late." She whispered.

"Oh yeah, I almost forgot, my mother wants us over for dinner."

Her eyes widened. "You told her already?"

"Of course, I'm serious about marrying you, better she knows now."

Her nervousness scented the air. He cocked his head. It wasn't as though she'd never met his parents. She'd spent a lot of time at his house when they were growing up. He wrapped an arm around her waist.

"It'll be fine," he promised.

She raised on her toes, and kissed him. "Okay, just tell me when."

She stepped back from him and rushed to the door. He wanted to chase after her, hell, he wanted to follow her home like a stray animal and beg at her feet. He sighed. How did that woman wrap him around her fingers so tightly? How would he survive this fake engagement long enough to get his mate to agree to his bite? His desk phone rang.

"I know," he growled and grabbed the case files he needed to meet with his sister's client.

He thought longingly of the lunch Naomi had brought over. If he was lucky, he'd get to eat it before dinner time.

8...

Naomi walked through the lobby of the building that housed Gabe's law firm at a sedate pace. Even as panic skittered down her back and had her breaths coming out in choppy puffs. Once outside she pulled out her phone, her hands shaking. She made her way to the car as it rang, sliding into the driver's seat and locking the door. It connected with the Bluetooth in her truck as she cranked up, Savannah finally answering after a few rings.

"Yeah, Nay, what's up."

A tear crested her eye. "I just fucked Gabe in his office."

"Ugh, I didn't need an update."

"I...Vanna, I'm in love with him." Oh God, she was in love with Gabe.

"Nay," Savannah said softly. "What are you going to do?"

"I don't...what am I going to do when he meets his mate, you mean?" A sob choked out.

"Are you still downtown? Come home, I'll meet you at your apartment."

"No, I don't want to stop your day."

"I'm coming over, and I'll bring sugar and salt."

***

"What am I going to do, Savi?" Naomi asked as she opened the door to her apartment an hour later.

True to her word, Savannah held two grocery bags, one with chips and the other she knew would hold their favorite chocolate bars.

"Oh, Nay." Savannah gripped her in a tight hug and guided her over to her couch. She sat her down and pulled back, sitting the bags on the coffee table. "Are you sure he isn't yours? Y'all have been friends your whole life, why would you all of a sudden fall in love with him?"

Naomi hiccupped and hope had her chest aching. "Wait...You think?"

Savannah shrugged. "I mean, I was thinking of this the whole way over here. You get brought into the prowl, your powers unlock, and then all of a sudden you see Gabe in a new light? Doesn't it make sense that your new power lets you see clearly for the first time?"

Naomi blinked. "I don't..."

"Not to mention the midnight ceremony. That means a lot to bears. I don't imagine he'd propose that if he didn't mean it."

"How did you know when you met Carlos and Derrick?"

"I just knew. As soon as I saw them I knew they were mine."

"But that didn't happen with Gabe and me."

"Okay let's go through this rationally. How long after your powers unlocked did you see Gabe?"

She wiped her cheeks and looked away, going through the crazy schedule she'd had earlier this year. She'd spent a lot of time between New York and L.A. working on art shows. "Umm, end of summer, so, like August."

"And when you saw him, did you want to jump his bones?"

Her cheeks heated because she remembered seeing him differently. She'd only seen him from afar, but for the next few days after, she'd started thinking about her life and settling down. They didn't get a chance to see each other until the day he'd come over and asked her to marry him. It was the first time he'd ever kissed her. Her body heated in remembrance.

"Yes." Her heart thundered and the room spun. "What if it doesn't work?"

"I had those same fears, Nay, remember? You're already engaged, even though you claim it's fake. Why not give it a chance?"

She sighed. Savannah had had other worries about being latent and marrying the Felix, the main one being becoming Alpha female. Her worries seemed to pale in comparison. Could she do it?

"You can talk to Grandpa Harper. He always seems to know what to do," Savannah suggested.

She nodded. That was a great idea.

***

Gabe rolled his shoulders entering his office. There was something about his sister's current client that he didn't trust, and it was irking him. He took a deep breath as he sat in his chair, smiling as the scent of his mate still lingered. He loved the smell of Naomi's perfume. Most shifters didn't wear it due to their keen sense of smell, but she was latent and so always wore some kind of scented lotion and perfume. She claimed it was to cover the paint smell.

He dropped his files on the desk, his dick hardening with the thought of how he'd taken her on it hours ago. He made up his mind then and there that he was going to see her tonight.

"What was that?" His sister Tiffany burst into his office but stopped right across the threshold of the door. "Jesus, Gabe, I can smell her, whoever she is, all over this place."

"It's my office, feel free to leave."

"Who is she?"

"None of your business."

"Mmmhmm, mom clearly knows nothing about her because your brother is complaining about her badgering him into mating."

"What do you want, Tif?" No way was he telling his sister about Naomi. His mother was still perturbed with him, he could only imagine how his sisters would react.

Tiffany settled on the corner of his desk and drummed her nails against the top. "The meeting we just left. Why are you taking so long on those contracts? It's a simple real estate investment."

He scratched the back of his neck, his bear riling at the thought of the meeting. "It doesn't feel right, Tif."

"The deal?"

"Besides the fact that he wants to cut us more than our usual percentage, the rush on this feels suspicious. Not to mention one of his stipulations is us bringing in the panthers on the deal. Why should we even be involved in the investment part?" He passed the notes he'd been working on to his older sister.

She rifled through them, grunting now and then. "I went out to the property and didn't see anything wrong," she murmured, still flipping through the pages. "I talked to Trina about the stipulation, she's looking for a way out of it. Have you talked to their Felix?"

He gave her a look. "Not yet."

"Well, why not?" She looked irritated. "You're dragging this out, Gabe. Should we back away from this deal?"

He shrugged, "I don't know yet."

"Well, find out then. You know how Trina is. I don't want her in my office, so when she asks about the hold up on this deal, I'm sending her to you."

"Witcho scary ass," Gabe grumbled.

Tiffany snickered but kept going through the pages. She hummed, "Actually, let me take these, there is something..." she paused. "The numbers you have highlighted, don't look like the initial figures they sent over. I'll look into that, you talk to Felix Ayala."

He grimaced.

"What?"

"Nothing, I may be on their shit list a bit."

"What? Gabe, of all the cats to piss off, let it not be the Ayala prowl, please. Those women are vicious." His sister shuddered. "What did you do? Does it have anything to do with the cat smelling up this office?"

"I snuck in to see Nay a few times."

"Snuck in? You couldn't go through the front door?"

"It would've taken too long."

"Oh lord, make the appointment, Gabe. If you're scared, I can tell Daddy and let him handle it." She taunted.

"That's why I don't tell your ass nothing," he grumbled. "Why can't you or one of the Trips do it?"

"Because it's your hunch."

"It's your account," he reminded her.

"He says after he's been stalling me and not keeping me in the loop," she said dryly, rolling her eyes.

"Your contract is not the only one on my desk, you know."

Gabe rarely dealt with clients, he was a details man, so his sisters had him comb through their contracts before their clients signed anything. So, besides Tiffany's current client, he had others from his two other sisters and his brother.

She narrowed her eyes and took a deep breath. "Oh lord, it's Nay. You're finally fucking Naomi?"

He growled, "Watch how you talk about her, and it's not your business." He ducked his head and shuffled through some papers.

She put her hands flat on his desk. "That's why you don't want to go over there? You're sleeping with their Zeta."

"Naomi doesn't want anyone to know, yet."

"She's ashamed of you?" His sister put a hand on her hip and scowled, ready to come to his defense.

"No, that's not..." he sighed not wanting to tell his sister what he'd done. She'd tell the other two and then holy hell would fully rain down on him.

He eventually needed to tell his sisters about the engagement, but he stalled.

"She didn't say that, actually," he admitted.

"You're just assuming that?"

"Well, we've only...it's still new. I don't want to cause any trouble for her."

Tiffany hummed, studying him. "I knew you always had a thing for her."

"She's my mate," he admitted.

She gave him a genuine smile before it dropped. "She's latent, does she know?"

"She agreed to marry me." He kept out the fake part for now.

She narrowed her eyes. "The hell does that mean? Is that how latents do it?"

"Tif, just keep it to yourself for now, please."

She smiled and waggled her eyebrows. "I'll try, but you know nothing is tighter than a sister bond."

Fuck, she was going to tell the other Trips.

"You get on my nerves," he mumbled and she laughed, leaving his office.

"Make that appointment, Gabriel," she said on the way out.

He sent a text message to the firm he had performing a background check on the client and asked them to rush it. And then sighed. He had to tell Nay that he was meeting with her alpha.

It was a little after two a.m. by the time he used his keycard to go through the front entrance of Naomi's building. He waved at the panther guarding the lobby and entered the elevator. He was pushing his luck, especially since he needed to be up at six and into the office by seven. He'd arranged a meeting with Felix Ayala, but his sister wanted him in their office first to go over their pitch. He sighed as he got to Nay's door. He let himself in and took off his suit jacket and laid it across the back of her sofa.

He walked into the kitchen and debated eating. He'd finally got around to the lunch she'd brought for him a few hours ago. He fixed himself a glass of water and turned as his mate came out of her room. Her soft footsteps were nearly silent on the thick carpet, but his hearing picked it up anyway. She hugged against his back and sighed. He put the cup back, took a deep inhale of her scent, and stiffened. Something was different. He lifted her and she wrapped her legs around his waist.

He sipped at her lips. "You didn't have to get up, babe." He whispered.

She lay her head on his shoulder and said nothing, her deep breathing telling him she'd already gone back to sleep. He envied her that trick. The way his mind worked, it would be another hour before he could settle down and sleep. He cuddled her closer and walked her to her room. He lay her gently on the bed and hopped in her shower to wash off the day. He came out minutes later and just watched her from the bathroom door. She was so beautiful. He crawled into bed, not bothering with clothes, and pulled her into his chest. He breathed in her scent and his bear purred, the rumbling against her back made her sigh in her sleep. He knew what the change in her scent was and a deep sense of satisfaction traveled through him. She was his, and if what he was scenting was accurate, then she would stay that way. Their scent was melding, a perfect sign that their mating was on track. He kissed her neck and fell asleep.

9...

Naomi was a nervous wreck as she pulled her truck into her grand-parent's front driveway. She put her head down on the steering wheel and took a deep breath. Talking to her grandfather was no big deal, but...she needed to get through her grandmother first and Rebecca Watson was a sharp woman. Not much got past her. Shoring up her courage, she stepped out of the truck. Stalling at this point was just silly. She wanted answers and coming here was the best place to get them. She'd barely taken a step on the porch when the front door opened.

Her cousin stepped out, taking a deep breath. "You smell like a bear."

Naomi rolled her eyes. "Good morning to you, Brianne."

Brianne rubbed at the makeup on Naomi's neck as she got closer. "He ain't shy about it either I see."

Her cheeks heated. She'd tried covering up the hickeys Gabe took pleasure in leaving with makeup. Clearly, it was not working.

"Mind the business that pays you," Naomi grumbled, trying to step past her older cousin.

"I'm just saying." Brianne shrugged and let her by. "Allies ain't a bad thing," Brianne called out to her on her way into the living room to flop on the sofa.

Rebecca peeked from the kitchen. "Who talking about allies?"

Naomi suppressed a sigh. "Grandmother," she greeted the woman with a kiss on the cheek before rubbing their cheeks together.

Despite just being in the house, her grandmother was dressed to go out. Her trim figure was swathed in a colorful maxi dress. The greens

59

and blues went well with her pecan colored skin, the minimal wrinkles on Rebecca's face making her look much younger than her sixty-five years.

"Good morning, Nay. What brings you by?"

"I came to talk to Grandpa Harper, is he around?"

She was closest to her fastidious grandfather. His calm and quiet way always soothed her. He'd been guiding her through the process of her Zeta powers and she wanted to talk to him about Gabe.

"He's out with Jeremiah. They'll be back shortly."

Naomi sighed.

"Why do you smell like a bear?"

She stiffened. "Gabe."

"Hmm," was Rebecca's answer. "Have you eaten breakfast?"

"I have."

Rebecca studied her face and Naomi fought not to squirm. "Do you want some tea?"

"Yes, ma'am."

She sat down at the kitchen table and thought about what to say to her grandad. How would she ask him about mating without it being awkward? It helped that her grandfather had been her doctor for years. Up until he kicked her out years ago when she turned twenty-three, telling her to get an adult doctor. It was so unfair. She hadn't minded waiting in the waiting room with the other kids. Though the parents had given her strange looks.

"What did you want to talk to Harper about?" Her grandmother was pouring hot water into the coffee mugs.

It startled her out of her thoughts. "Umm..."

"Anything to do with that bear you smell like?"

"Grandmother, you know Gabe."

"I do," Rebecca smirked as she settled teabags into the mugs. "We've known the Hamiltons for years. Y'all finally decide to have sex?"

She choked. "Grandma."

Rebecca shrugged and inclined her head towards the living room. Naomi grabbed her mug from her grandmother and followed her into the comfortable room. They settled in opposite armchairs.

"So?"

Naomi sighed and eyed her cousin, not sure she wanted to talk with her in the room. Brianne was reading something on her Ipad, not making any motion to leave. Rebecca put down her coffee cup and picked up the knitting needles next to the chair. The needles were clacking in the silence as she debated talking to her grandmother. It wasn't that she didn't get along with her. Rebecca was a hard woman, and Naomi had always been a little scared of her.

Rebecca broke the silence. "Have you thought of how it would look, you mating a shifter, not panther? You haven't been in your position long."

"No one said anything about a mating," she denied, shooting a look at Brianne.

They would be getting married but there wasn't a mating. Not that her grandmother would care about the distinction. If anything, finding out it was fake would probably set the woman off. How in the hell were she and Gabe going to pull the whole thing off if she couldn't convince her family it was real? Brianne didn't look up from her tablet, but Naomi knew her cousin was listening. Which meant half the prowl would know before she left her grandparents' property.

"Mmhmm."

Naomi cleared her throat. "Gabe wants to marry me."

The needles stopped, the silence accusing. "Say what now?"

"I agreed to marry him since I can't mate."

"Nay, who said you aren't able to mate?" Rebecca set her knitting aside and narrowed her eyes. "Who told you that?"

"I tried before, remember? With Aaron?" She swallowed the lump forming in her throat, she didn't want to go down that path.

"Aaron? Is that the boy who got you pregnant?" Rebecca sucked her teeth. "Did it ever occur to you that that jackass was not your mate?

Never let it be said a Watson panther would mate with just any old thing that comes along."

Rebecca huffed and settled in her chair irritated with the thought.

"You didn't like Aaron?" She didn't know which part of her grandmother's statement shocked her most.

"Chile, nobody liked that boy." Her grandmother muttered.

Brianne snickered from the sofa, proof that she had been listening.

Naomi turned to her cousin, her eyebrows raised. "Brianne? You didn't like him either?"

"Little cuz, that fox was trash, ain't no way your panther would've accepted a mating with him." Brianne's eyes didn't stray from her tablet at her statement.

"I don't have a panther," Naomi muttered bitterly.

"Girl hush," Rebecca fussed. "You may not be able to shift, but your panther is there all the same."

"I love him," she admitted quietly, turning the conversation away from her 'panther'. She lived in her latent body, and she knew her grandmother would never understand what that felt like.

"Then that's that, love." Rebecca lowered her head back to her knitting.

"That's it, that's all you have to say?"

"Gabe is your mate, you love him enough to come in here and announce it, what else is there to be said on the matter?" Her grandmother shrugged and continued knitting.

Naomi's heart was racing from what she thought would be a confrontation and she didn't know what to do with the leftover adrenaline. What she wouldn't do, was correct her grandmother. If she thought Gabe was her mate, and Savi thought it was a possibility, then, couldn't she let it ride? Would that make it any truer than it was? Gabe had said it on more than one occasion in the past. Did he believe she was his actual mate? She'd snuck out of the bed this morning, still shaken from her conversation with Savannah. She wasn't quite ready to face him.

"Come here, Naomi," Rebecca said softly.

She sat at her grandmother's knee and put her head on her lap.

"What do you need me to say to make you feel better?"

Naomi sighed because she didn't know. She didn't know how to handle her feelings for Gabe. They'd been friends for years. He was the rock she'd come to depend on. What would happen if this fake marriage didn't work out? Would she lose him? Could she be with him and keep her position in the prowl? She'd just got her family back from her self-imposed isolation.

"Tell me I won't lose my family behind this."

Rebecca made a soothing murmur. "Baby, that's never going to happen."

"All that will happen is we'll have a bear in this house eating more than his share of food at Thanksgiving," Brianne teased.

Naomi let out a watery laugh and wiped her eyes. "He doesn't eat that much," she lied.

Brianne snorted.

"Was that what you were worried about? Why you needed to talk to Harper?" Rebecca asked.

She nodded. "I still have to tell Felix Carlos."

"You want me to come with you, Nay?" Brianna finally turned her gaze to them.

Naomi shook her head, "no, I can handle it."

"It will be fine, baby." Rebeca rubbed the top of her hair. "What else is bothering you about it?"

"I worry that I may not be able to bond with Gabe. My latency is so different from Savannah's."

Rebecca sighed. "Not so different love. The animal will get what it wants, regardless of how hard the human parts of us fight. It may have taken your cat a minute to wake up, but she's there at the core of you."

A tear escaped. It was exactly what she wanted, no needed to hear. Her phone beeped and she retrieved it from her back pocket. It was a single text from Gabe.

Meeting with your Felix today.

Her heart hammered and she scrambled from Rebecca's lap. "I gotta go."

***

Gabe sat next to his sister in the panther Felix's office anteroom, waiting. He stretched his legs out in the chair and leaned back, closing his eyes. He was tired as hell and Nay had been gone by the time he'd woken up, which meant no morning sex. It was no wonder his bear was pacing his body. He needed to go out and let his bear loose.

Tiffany punched his arm. "Wake the fuck up," she hissed.

"Damn, what is wrong with you?" He grumbled, rubbing his arm.

"You were late this morning, and now you're falling asleep."

"I was not falling asleep, I just closed my eyes for a second."

She opened her mouth to most likely cuss him out, but the door to the Felix's inner office opened, and the Ayala prowl's Beta stared down at him with a scowl.

"Did you use the front door today, Hamilton?" Derrick crossed his arms over his chest.

"Your security ain't as tight as you think. Ain't my fault," Gabe taunted, standing.

"Jesus Tyrone Christ," Tiffany murmured next to him as she stood. She held her hand out to the Beta to shake. "There are not a lot of ways to keep bears off your property when they're determined."

Gabe shrugged and followed them into the Alpha's office.

"Felix Ayala," Tiffany greeted, lowering her chin into a small dip of respect, not meeting his eyes.

"Please, call me Carlos," He waved them into the chairs in front of him.

They sat and Gabe took a look around the swanky office with its view of the Ybor channel. Carlos settled into his leather chair behind the huge desk and eyed them. Power surrounded the male, radiating alpha vibes demanded caution. Behind his human eyes, The Felix's panther lurked, curious, and watchful. Gabe's bear raised in alert in answer to the Alpha's presence.

"You're the bear sneaking onto our property," the alpha said offhanded, speculation in his eyes.

Tiffany groaned next to him.

Gabe shrugged, because, what could he say to that. "You guys should look into bear proofing."

His sister shot daggers at him from her eyes.

The corner of Carlos's lips tilted up. "I thought we had."

"And yet," Derrick said, shaking his head.

"And yet," Gabe tsked.

Tiffany gripped his arm, her sharpened claws a warning. Gabe fought to keep his face straight as the points of his sister's nails pierced his skin. His bear didn't bother reacting, used to his sisters' violent warnings. His lips twitched as he raised an eyebrow at her. She growled under her breath, her eyes glowing before she settled her bear. *Ol' grumpy ass.*

Tiffany pulled her claws from his arm and rushed to defuse the tension. "Thank you for taking the time to see us, we know how busy you must be."

But, the Felix hadn't finished interrogating him. "So, you're the contact my mate had with the high council. Your father helped get us out of trouble."

Gabe shrugged. "Vanna called me, I called my dad, it's not a big deal."

"My mate has your number?" Derrick asked.

He grunted.

Carlos sucked his teeth. "I don't speak bear."

What was with these cats saying that?

"We went to school together and I've been in love with Naomi my whole life, so yes, Nay's favorite cousin has my number." He explained.

Carlos grunted, and let it go. "So you say you've come on behalf of a client?"

Tiffany let out a relieved breath and pulled the paperwork from her briefcase. She slid them onto the alpha's desk. "Our client is interested in buying the building down from you."

"The one they're turning into retail spaces?" Carlos picked up the paperwork.

"Yes, they're in the investment phase and our client thought to extend the offer to you." Tiffany sat forward, ramping up to start their pitch.

The Beta cut her off with a hand up. "Why did he send his lawyers instead of contacting us himself?"

"I think he thought given our family's relationship that it would have some sway," Tiffany answered.

"And you would use that relationship as leverage?" Carlos asked, his steely eyes watching them.

"The Hamiltons don't do business that way," Gabe spoke up. "But, ethics dictate we bring the client's offer to you."

"And what do you think of the investment?" Carlos slid the papers back into the folder.

"I think you should pass." Gabe met the Felix's eyes.

Tiffany sucked in a sharp breath, but she kept her head forward and her face blank. She showed solidarity with him when in truth she'd told Gabe to keep his mouth shut during the meeting. His sisters hadn't wanted any hint of impropriety to touch their firm. She'd argued that his relationship with Nay would keep him from being impartial. She wasn't wrong. She should've left him at the office if she wanted him to be quiet.

Carlos took a deep breath, Gabe knew to filter through their scents for deceptions. Tiffany growled next to him, her irritation palpable, but he wouldn't apologize. He'd made it clear during their meeting that if asked, he'd express his doubts about the whole thing.

"We, of course, can't divulge any client information. Our personal ties make this all a little sticky, ethically," Tiffany added.

Gabe crossed his ankle over his leg and shrugged. The whole thing stunk and he wasn't dragging his mate's family into it.

Carlos nodded. "But you had to bring it to us."

"Right," Tiffany cleared her throat. "We're still in the beginning stages, and can't necessarily tell you what you should do. The final decision is, of course, up to you."

"I understand," Carlos said, pushing the folder back to her. "Then, we will respectfully decline."

Tiffany stuffed the file back into her briefcase. "Having completed our obligation on behalf of the client, that's that. We'll keep you posted if anything changes on our end."

"That will be fine, thank you." Carlos turned his gaze to Gabe. "Anything else we have to discuss?"

Gabe cocked his head, understanding what the Felix was hinting at. But, he'd promised Naomi that she could tell her family, so instead of saying anything, he shrugged. He'd sent her a text message, but she hadn't responded, so he'd leave it to her.

"So nothing about the late nights at Naomi's?" Derrick asked.

"I've been friends with Naomi for years and in all that time she's never had a problem speaking for herself," Gabe said.

Derrick and Carlos both growled, their power raising. Gabriel's bear rose, answering the challenge.

Tiffany stood abruptly, breaking into the stare-off. "We've taken up a lot of your time. Thank you so much for meeting with us, Felix Ayala."

"It's no problem. As you've said, your family and the Watsons have been friends for years. I certainly don't want to do anything to mess with that relationship." Carlos narrowed his eyes as he stood and shook her hand.

His sister dragged him from the office, his bear fighting the whole way. He'd wanted to answer the challenge the alpha had thrown down. Tiffany was steaming as they waited on the elevator. Gabe took deep breaths, calming his bear as the got into the lift, crossing his arms over his chest. His sister was silent up until they got into her coupe. She slapped his shoulder as he buckled his seat belt.

"Ow, damn. What is wrong with you, today?"

"I'm not trying to fight an alpha giving off that kind of power on his home turf." She snapped, hitting him again. "Why the fuck did you taunt them?"

He had to smile because she hadn't said she wouldn't fight, just that she didn't want to have to. His sisters were good like that. They'd have his back no matter what.

"It might have been fun though," he smirked. His bear did need to expend some energy.

Her lips twitched. "You know bears don't get down like that."

She was right, bears didn't do direct confrontation. His sisters were sneaky fighters, they waited until the other person wasn't expecting it. She sighed.

"I'm letting you tell Trina the panthers are out of the deal." She shot him a smug look.

Fuck. He'd almost rather fight the panthers on their home turf than to tell his oldest sister that their deal wouldn't go through.

10...

Naomi smiled at the Felix's assistant as she walked past her and into the Alpha's office. She'd been nervous the entire drive from her grandparents'. She trusted Gabe not to say anything, but still, she wondered why he met with Carlos. Her talk with Rebecca had made her feel way better, but she still worried at the prospect of what the Felix would say about her mating.

The alpha sat behind his massive desk, a scowl over his handsome face. His curly hair was falling around his forehead, nearly obscuring his eyes as he scribbled at his desk. Carlos's face cleared as he looked up and saw her. He smiled and came around the desk.

"Naomi, hi."

She rubbed her head under his chin in greeting and her nerves settled somewhat. He waited until she sat before he did.

"Savi said you needed to talk to me, what's on your mind?"

"I…" she cleared her throat. "I'm getting married."

He frowned. "Married, not mated?"

"It's a little complicated." She sighed.

He grunted, "Was it that smart-assed bear that just left my office not too long ago?"

Her heart thudded, but he didn't sound mad, more annoyed. "Yes, Gabe, he came here?"

Carlos nodded. "Is there a problem with you getting married, you need me to talk to his Alpha?" He adjusted in his chair and rubbed his hand over the top of his head. "I can sic Derrick on him if you want, he's been looking for a reason to box that bear around."

Her hands shook, relief making her mute. It didn't sound like the Felix had any issues with her being with Gabe.

Carlos frowned, "what's wrong, Naomi, is it serious?"

She shook her head. "I just thought…"

He stared and waited on her to finish. His golden eyes roved her face, his nostrils flaring as he took in her scent, trying to figure out what was wrong.

"I thought you'd make me give up my position."

"Because you have terrible taste in men?"

She snorted. "Gabe is awesome."

"To you, he's a typical asshole bear to everyone else," he muttered, "with an affinity for picking locks. I may have to hire him to test some of our systems."

She laughed and the pressure on her chest released. "So there won't be a problem?"

"Nay, as far as this prowl's concerned, having you as our Zeta is a miracle. Your position in the hierarchy is safe if that's what you're worried about. Marrying Gabe won't change that."

"Thank you," she stood and wiped her sweaty palms down her jeans. "I know you're busy, so I'll leave."

He nodded and waved her away as the phone on his desk rang. Naomi rushed from his office, her heart still racing. Outside of the initial confusion about them marrying vs getting married, none of her family had batted an eye. She wanted to see Gabe, but there was one more obstacle to overcome.

Her parents.

She groaned the whole elevator ride down to the parking lot.

***

Hours later, she let herself into Gabe's condo. The conversation with her parents had gone about how she thought. Except…they'd been almost relieved when she told them. *'Gabe is already a part of the family'* her dad had said. She scoffed and changed into the shorts and tank top she found in his drawers. She didn't even remember leaving it there. She would have gone back to her apartment, but honestly, with how confused her mind was, she'd be useless to anyone who stopped by. She certainly wouldn't be able to calm them. She was in the middle of making dinner when her phone rang.

She sighed at her mother's name. "Yes, mama."

"I was just thinking, I know you said you want it to be small, but honestly, babe." Melody gave a long-suffering sigh. "There are just too many family members for that to happen."

Naomi lowered her head and closed her eyes. "Mom, you promised, not even an hour ago."

"My God, Nay," Her mother chided. "How am I supposed to keep the list to twenty?"

She flinched at the hand she felt on her shoulder and relaxed into Gabe's embrace. She hadn't even heard him come in. She turned and shook the phone at him, her face apologetic. He shrugged and left her at the mercy of her mother.

"— and when you think about it, there's not much of a difference."

Naomi pinched the bridge of her nose. She'd missed half of what her mom said. "Can we talk about this later, mama?"

"Well, I'll just call Catherine. Don't you worry, love, it'll be put together, you just work on a date."

"Wait…shit, mom. Mom?" Naomi snatched the phone from her ear and cursed again.

Melody was calling Catherine, so the wedding was officially out of her hands. For a fake wedding, it was starting to stress her the hell out. Not to mention, she still needed to sort through her feelings about Gabe. She turned around and found him sitting at his sofa, his laptop out, working. She needed to talk to him. Later…yeah, much later.

He was pretty sure he'd read the sentence in front of him twice already. His concentration was shot, and the reason was parading around in front of him in tiny shorts, watering the plants his mother kept sneaking into his condo. He put his pen down and gave up the pretense. He watched her, more to say his bear watched her, hunger filling his chest. Her ass switched side to side as she carried a pitcher, humming a song he'd never heard. Did she even realize how much he desired her? He flexed his fingers, the urge to touch her skin making his palms itch.

He could sense her nervousness. She'd been on edge since he'd arrived at his apartment an hour ago. She'd been distant, in her head, which was unusual for her. He'd come home from work early so that they could talk, but she didn't seem entirely receptive. He wanted to bring up their ceremony, and the possibility of her taking his bite. But, in the past few weeks every time he'd brought it up, she'd dismissed it. He sighed. He'd have to roll with this fake marriage until he could get her tied down, then he would work on convincing her to take his bite, and hopefully, even with her latency, she'd be able to bond with him.

Tired of her watching her pace his living room, he put slid his laptop away from him.

"Nay."

"Hmm," she didn't look up from her task.

"Come here, princess." He put a little bit of power into his voice.

Her head popped up, her eyes widening. She licked her lips but stayed where she was. "Yes?"

"I'm not repeating myself."

Her arousal scented the air and he gripped the sofa cushion, careful of the claws sliding from his nails. She would come to him, and he would be patient. His bear growled and swiped at his chest. *We will be patient!* He barked at his animal. He and his mate were locked in a battle of wills, one he planned on winning.

Her heartbeat thundered, the sound of it filling the tense silence. She took a step towards him, the watering can clutched to her chest. He gave her heated eyes, his chest rumbling in hunger. She moved closer to him and he waited, timing her small steps until...

She gasped as he pulled her into his lap.

He nuzzled into her neck, retracting his claws as he traced her hips with his hands. "Do you know sometimes I can still feel you pulsing around my dick?"

Her arousal scented the air, and his bear rumbled in approval. He nibbled down the side of her neck. Slowly the tension left her body and she relaxed in his arms.

"What happened today?" He ventured.

She sighed and stood, not to leave, but to straddle his body. She laid her head on his shoulder. "I told my family about us."

"Good," He rubbed her back.

"They bought it, so by that, yes it was good." Her breath heated the skin of his neck.

"In what way could it be bad, princess?"

She lifted her head and stared in his eyes. "Are you serious? What if they find out this is all fake?"

His eyes traced her face and he lifted his hand to cup her cheek. She was so beautiful to him. Turmoil darkened her eyes, and she chewed on her bottom lip. A sure sign she was worried. He used his thumb to rescue her lip. He dropped a small kiss there.

"Nay, this can all be real. Just say the word." He watched her face for her reaction, his bear tensing.

She looked away, but not before he read the panic in her eyes. He let the silence between them sit, giving her space to make a decision. She turned back to him.

"Grandmother said that it was likely we could bond," she whispered.

"Our scents are already melding," He kept voice soft and squelched the aching hope from his face. But his heart beat with it, the thundering loud in his ears.

"It's just..." She sighed. "I couldn't with Aaron."

He swallowed his growl, only by a hairsbreadth. His bear thrashed in his body, power flooding him at the other male's name. It took him a moment to be calm enough to simply say, "I'm not Aaron."

"I know that, Gabe." She sighed and laid her head back on his shoulder. "Just give me some time."

"I can give you time," he promised.

And meant it...hopefully. He'd given her time before. That hadn't exactly worked for them. This time it could be different, but he was starting to lose faith that it would.

"You're not going to pressure me?"

"Nay," he whispered. "I'll take you any way I can get you, honestly."

"Because you don't want to marry the other bear?"

Guilt struck him for the lie. "Fuck the other bear. This is between us at the moment."

She rolled her eyes, "I'm saying, we're only doing this to get you out of the other thing, so I'm just..." She stopped.

He cupped her face and stared at her, absolutely enraptured with his mate. Everything about her was fascinating to him and beautiful and he couldn't understand how to get past her misgivings about mating.

"Gabe," she whispered, breaking him from his thoughts.

"Sorry, what were we talking about?"

"Bonding." She raised an eyebrow at his attempt to change the subject. "What if we bond?"

"Then it will everything I've ever wanted." He answered honestly.

Her eyes softened and he leaned over and nipped her bottom lip.

"You're not worried about—"

"Nay," he growled, tired of her finding excuses.

"Fine," she said, smoothing his chest. "Give me some time."

What could he say to that? At least she was finally considering it.

11...

Gabe stood at the railing of the porch at Naomi's grandparent's house watching the sun descend behind the fields surrounding the panther prowls territory. He was woolgathering, tinkering with the latest snake cube Nay had given him on the way over. It was half gift and half bribe. A gift to keep him from getting bored with her family, and a bribe for him to 'mind his mouth'. He snorted in amusement, she knew him well.

Despite the size of his fingers, he deftly moved around the small wooden pieces, his mind both on it, and the random wanderings that plagued him. Nothing new for him usually, especially outside of work. He never had issues concentrating on the minutia of the contracts that littered his desk, but anything else outside of that was never enough to keep his attention. It was once he left his office that he found his thoughts bouncing around. Except when it pertained to Naomi.

His conversation the other day with Nay filled his head, the 'what if' scenarios playing over and over. What if she was finally ready to take his bite? What if she didn't and would never be ready? Would he honestly settle with just being married to her?

Hell yeah, he would.

He and his bear were in complete agreement with that. He would be damned if he let her go this time around. She'd brought up Aaron and helpless fury flooded his body. That fucking fox. Gabe hadn't realized how serious Naomi had been about the bastard until she'd called him excited that she was pregnant. He'd said the right words to her and managed to get through her call, but his condo had told a different story. He'd trashed the place and then spent two days straight in his bear form.

By the time he'd come back to some semblance of sanity a week later, Nay had shown up at his condo, her face tear-streaked and her body battered from her miscarriage. Gabe squeezed the wooded cube in his hand, breaking the puzzle back into its small pieces. He wanted to roar all over again. That fucking fox had dropped her before she'd been able to check out of the hospital. The beating he'd given Aaron had caused the first fight Gabe had ever had with Naomi. She was pissed for weeks. What had she expected though? It was the first time he'd offered to mate with her. That was partially why she'd stopped talking to him. Naomi hadn't wanted what she'd seen as pity from him. He sighed and scrubbed his hand across his face.

The front door slammed as kids ran in and out of the house, their loud noise blending into the cacophony that seemed to surround the panthers. Not that the bears in his clan were any different. He just didn't have to socialize with them, and thus never really had to hear it. He took a sip of his beer and wondered how long Naomi would make him stay. They'd only spent a few hours with his parents this morning since the panthers had Thanksgiving closer to the evening. He'd have thought Catherine would be pissed, but she pat his cheek and sent him out with his favorite cheesecake and a smug smile. Him having a mate seemed to mellow the woman out.

He sighed thinking about the cheesecake he'd dropped off in his apartment. He wondered if the panthers would mind if he took a pie off the dessert table. He debated getting up to check on Naomi. She should be exhausted, he'd kept her up all night, but being in the midst of her family seemed to energize her. He'd gotten his share of stares when they'd first arrived, but after the third, *'Oh, it's just Gabe'* her cousins dropped the tittering and moved on to juicier gossip.

He withheld a growl when the panther Felix slid up to him on soundless footsteps. Carlos couldn't disguise his power, though, so silent or not, Gabe had felt him coming.

"Felix," he greeted, sliding the puzzle pieces into his pocket.

"Hamilton."

They stood next to each other in silence.

"Good looking out on steering us away from that investor," Carlos commented.

Gabe shrugged. "No problem."

"Did you and your sisters face any kickback for it?"

"The Trips dropped him long before the Feds came in." Gabe took another sip of his beer.

"The Trips?"

"My sisters, they're triplets."

Carlos grunted but said nothing more. They stood on the porch in companionable silence and Gabe could appreciate that. He hated making small talk. Savannah's son Jamie came over and stood in front of them.

"Want to come play with us?"

Gabe grunted a question at the kid he'd known since he was in diapers.

Jamie smiled, "well yes, we just want to wrestle a bear."

Carlos gaped at his step-son. "You understand that bear shit?"

Gabe and Jamie both snickered as he moved towards the front steps. The front door opened and the scent of his mate reached him.

"There you are, I was looking for you." Naomi had a plate with a large slice of pecan pie on it.

He dropped a kiss on her forehead, used the fork to cut a big piece, shoving it in his mouth. "Going to play with the cubs for a bit." He lifted Jamie and chucked him over his shoulder.

Jamie's peal of laughter brought attention to them. He ignored the stares of her family and walked down the front steps.

Naomi came scrambling behind him. "Gabriel Hamilton, you will not strip and shift in front of my family," she hissed.

He gave Naomi a warning look and grunted for her to watch her tone.

She growled, "that's not…ugh." She turned and walked back into the house much to the amusement of the gathered cubs.

He smiled at Jamie and walked the cub into the woods and put him down. Jamie took off running and Gabe made sure none of the kids were around when he stripped. He released his bear and his ears twitched as he followed the sounds of more than one cub crashing through the brush surrounding the house. He was more comfortable out here, in the wild, no expectations restraining him. He knew his mate would have words for him when he got back inside. He let out a snarl as the non-stealthy panther cubs surrounded him. He heard giggles from the smaller one who'd not yet got their cats one second before they charged him.

***

Naomi watched the door and pulled out her cellphone to check the clock. The jackass had been outside playing with the kids for going on an hour. Her heart skipped a beat when the door opened bringing a cool breeze. Gabriel stood there, his large body taking up so much of the doorway. Lord have mercy, that man was so sexy. The simple slacks and golf shirt he wore was nothing fancy, but the way he filled out his clothes. She tamped her reaction to him down, already seeing the sly looks from some of her female cousins. He saw her and all the rest of the room fell away. His focus was so intent on her, her body flushed. He was single-minded and it was a heady feeling. He lumbered over to her, his face relaxed, his eyes hungry as they raked over her body.

"Did you save me some pie?" His body was tight on her back, the words growled into her ear.

"Should I have? You'd rather play with the kids than socialize with my family," she grumbled.

"I'd much rather play with you," he whispered, his nails scraping at her back.

Her body shuddered and she cleared her throat. She would not rub against this man like a cat in heat in front of her family. She whipped around and glared at him.

"Behave."

"Or?" His eyes were alit with a challenge, his bear flashing in his gaze.

She swallowed, having no real answer to that. Especially not with the way her body had gone up in flames.

"Home." He ordered.

He didn't raise his voice, he certainly hadn't touched her, but the power of that order settled onto her shoulders and started a steady drumbeat in her clit. He stepped from her, releasing her from his trance and she shuddered from the loss of his body heat. Her eyes sought out her parents and she rushed to them and said their goodbyes. Her mother shoved two pies into her hands, kissed her cheek, and went back to gossiping with her sisters.

Gabe waited for her by the door, his attention wholly on her. Her power flared and rose to meet the energy dancing around him. She rushed through the front door before she embarrassed herself in front of all her cousins and aunts and uncles. Gabe was a silent wall behind her as they walked to the car. He helped her into the passenger side and walked over to his side without a word. She slid the pies into the backseat and hurriedly snapped her seatbelt. He drove down the dark road away from her grandparents' house and had only gone about a hundred yards when he pulled the car over.

"Here, now, Nay," he rumbled.

She couldn't unsnap her seatbelt fast enough. She rushed over to him, the radio blasting static as her butt hit the buttons. He turned it off before pushing his seat back as far as it could go as she tried to straddle him. Gabe had the dress she wore up around her hips, tearing her panties. He gripped her hair and slammed their lips together, eating at her mouth.

"Need you," his husky plea sent answering need spiraling through her.

Their tongues tangled as she fumbled to open his slacks. She winced as her elbow hit the horn, the sound loud in the otherwise quiet night. Gabe kissed any exposed skin he could reach, shifting in the seat in impatience. Finally freeing his erection, she lifted, fitting him right at the entrance of her sex. He pulled back to look down as she sank onto his dick. His eyes were lit with feral power as he nipped her chin, his hips rising to push himself in. Naomi moaned as he filled her, her body stretching to accommodate him. She rolled her hips, air leaving her body in a rush as he lifted her and pulled her back down onto his erection. Their power filled the car, melding, heating the air around them.

Gabe reached up and gripped her hair, using it to pull her head back. His teeth gripped her exposed neck as his hips lifted, stroking her and sending full-body chills down her spine. The car was shaking with the force of their movements. Lord have mercy, the strength of the orgasm already tightening her stomach. She used her elbows to boost up from his shoulders struggling to get a longer stroke in their limited space. His knee hit the emergency brake as his feet moved for better leverage.

She pulled his head up, feasting on his mouth, grinding her clit against the front of him to chase the climax coiled tight within her. Gabe growled, his bear flickering in and out of his eyes.

"Mine," he proclaimed, sucking on her bottom lip.

"Yes," she hissed as his shaft hit a spot inside her that had her seeing stars.

"Bond with me," he pleaded, his strokes picking up speed.

Her breath hitched, her stomach dancing in nervousness. *Did he mean it?*

"Now?" She stopped moving, her hands guiding his face to hers so she could see him better in the dark.

He stared at her, his eyes heated, hungry, and damn near savage. "Not now, under the full moon. Say yes, love."

He rolled his hips and her sex clenched. Naomi shut her eyes, willing her body under control. How crazy was it to make a decision of that magnitude with her body begging to be dicked down? He dragged his claws down the skin of her back and she whimpered and nodded.

"Yes?"

"Yes," Naomi whispered, wiggling to get him to restart his strokes.

The fierce smile he gave her sped her heart. He gripped her waist, lifting her and slamming her back down on his erection. He was relentless, his strokes as deep as he could get them in their current position. She used a free arm to push off the roof to keep her head from hitting against it, her waist working, and taking every stroke. The orgasm she'd stalled built back up, and she threw her head back, her sex gripping him tight as she came. Gabe cursed, coming right behind her. Their ragged breaths were overly loud in the silent car. Not even the bugs outside were humming as they panted for air in the now steaming car.

"Fuck, I love you, Nay," He murmured, his eyes closed, and head resting on the seat.

Naomi cuddled into his chest. "I love you too. We need to move, though, before someone comes up on us."

His chest shook with laughter. She joined him, her throat tight with emotion. She lifted, wincing as he pulled out. She slid into her seat and righted her clothes. Gabe looked over at her, his eyes soft. He shook his head and restarted the car.

Naomi bit her lip and looked out the passenger side window, realizing what she'd promised. What if she couldn't bond? How long before the next full moon?

12...

How long had it been since she and Gabe had started the ruse of their fake engagement? *Shit. How many weeks, months?* Panic slid down Naomi's body, her dinner from the night before coming back up. She hovered over the toilet and closed her eyes, praying Gabe didn't hear and come investigate. She looked over at the pregnancy stick taunting her from the sink.

How fucking long?

She took a deep breath and immediately regretted it, lowering to throw up for a third time that morning. The only thing she had going for her was the fact that she was at least at her house. Otherwise, how would she have taken the test sitting on the edge of her sink?

Only six months. Max.

They'd only been pretending to be engaged for six months. How was she already pregnant? What kind of super sperm was Gabe slinging around? She sat on the floor in front of the toilet and willed the tears burning her throat away. Bad enough she was throwing up, Gabe would know if she was crying. He was good like that.

Two lines. Pregnant.

Oh God, when had it happened? She thought about weeks ago when she'd went to Gabe's office. They hadn't used a condom, either of the times they'd had sex. She sighed and cursed her stupidity. She and Gabe had never used a condom if she were being honest with herself. Had she forgotten to take her birth control in the time that they'd been dating?

No way. Melody had drummed protecting themselves into her and her sister's head at the first sign of their periods.

So it was back to super sperm.

She was already stressed with the full moon coming up next week, why then would the universe throw a surprise pregnancy into the mix? She'd talked to her grandfather about bonding with Gabe and he didn't foresee a problem. It didn't stop her from worrying about it. She'd begged Gabe to keep it a secret from their mothers just in case it didn't work. He had been irritated because she was so negative about it, but he'd promised.

And now this.

Fear reared up. Should she tell him? The last time…she shook her head, she would be more positive this go around, surely…oh God. She couldn't go through the loss of another pregnancy. Just thinking about the frantic trip to the hospital, the poking and prodding, the intrusive questions. She couldn't do it. *God, please let this time be different.* She jumped as a knock sounded at the bathroom door.

"Hold on," she scrambled to hide the stick.

She wrapped it in tissue and shoved it under the sink. She was splashing water on her face when Gabe came into the bathroom as though she hadn't locked the door.

"How did you?"…she growled, "Never mind."

He cupped her face and stared. Just stared. She shook her head, knowing in his head he was either having the conversation by himself or going off on a tangent.

"Gabe," she said softly.

"Sorry, what's wrong? Are you feeling sick?"

"Yeah, just nausea."

"Do you want to cancel lunch at my mom's?"

"No, that's, oh God, I would feel terrible."

She'd survived the first dinner with his family easily. No one had brought up the marriage vs mating, and she'd had a good time. Now that Catherine and Melody were in constant contact for the wedding, there wasn't much Naomi had to do. Today's lunch was no special occasion, but, Naomi had been ducking calls from both women, guilt making it hard for her to be as excited about the wedding as their moms were. If she skipped lunch, there was no telling what his mother would think.

"If you're not feeling well, then it's okay, she'll understand."

"No, we'll go."

"Okay." He kissed her forehead.

He started the shower and without even asking her, pulled her nightgown from her body and lifted her into the shower. He washed her body thoroughly, carefully running the loofah across her skin. He skimmed the soft curves of her stomach and thighs, his gentle touch soothing her. She couldn't help the tears that fell. He could be so grumpy and prickly with others, but he took such good care of her. He washed her, toweled her off, and then left her to get dressed. All without saying a word. Did he sense her tension?

He had tea and toast sitting on the coffee table when she came out of her bedroom. She thanked him, tucking her feet under her on the couch.

"Lay down and rest." He ordered. "I'll work over here quietly until it's time to go."

Instead of watching T.V., she watched him work. His dark brows were furrowed in concentration. She reached for the sketchpad she kept in a drawer by the sofa. Turning it to a fresh page, she sketched, the lines flowing from her fingers effortlessly. He was a beautiful man, his cheekbones high, dark inset eyes, his heavy brows giving him a menacing look. His full lips were her favorite feature, so soft, and tender when he kissed her. They were currently pinched as he concentrated on whatever documents he had scattered across her table.

She sketched his wide shoulders, his bulk dwarfing the chair to her small dining table. She made a mental note to get bigger chairs. The panthers that came in and out of her apartment were huge men, but Gabe dwarfed them all. She looked up from her work and found him staring into space, that faraway look in his eyes. Her hands moved quickly as she fought to capture it. Love for him tightened her chest and panic about the pregnancy stole her breath. Gabe was a good man, she knew in her heart that she'd never have to worry about him leaving her if something happened. She put the pad down and walked over to him.

He pulled her into his lap. "You're not feeling well. Don't come over here starting shit," he whispered against her mouth.

"Not even a little?"

He growled and kissed her. She let out a surprised squeal as he stood, lifting her with him and heading into her bedroom.

***

Gabe glanced over at Naomi, his brows bunched in concern. She was unusually quiet. Out of the two of them, he was the quiet one. She usually kept up a stream of nonsense chatter, especially when she was in a good mood. His bear moved restlessly through his chest. She was nervous. To see his parents? She'd said she wasn't sick, but she'd been throwing up this morning. He should have insisted they stayed home. Although, if they did, he couldn't guarantee she'd rest. He had a hard time keeping his hands off her.

He rolled his eyes at all the cars on his mother's street as they pulled up. It meant his sisters were joining them for lunch. The women in his family were in full-blown wedding mode and he'd had more calls from them in the last month than he had in the twelve years since he'd left home. He parked and helped her out of the car keeping hold of her hand as he guided her up his mother's walkway.

Julian opened the door and grunted a greeting. Gabe answered back, pulling Naomi towards the door. His father took a long inhale, his eyes widening. His grunt was curious this time.

"I'm not standing on this stoop while you two grunt at each other," Naomi grumbled, tiptoeing to nuzzle against his father's chin in greeting.

"I'm sorry, my darling, come in, the girls are in the living room." Julian moved to the side, shooting Gabe a thumbs up.

Naomi waved to his sisters and brother as she came in. The lively conversation they walked into, ground to a halt. Gabe winced as all three of his sisters and Catherine took a deep inhale.

"Jesus Tyrone Christ," Brent whispered.

Catherine popped him on the back of the head before clasping her hands together, her eyes misting over. "Don't disrespect the Lord's name." She rushed to Naomi and pulled her into a hug. "Your cubs are going to be so beautiful."

Shock seemed to douse Naomi and she swayed as his mother released her. Her face went ashen and Gabe rushed to her side, catching her before her legs gave out. There was a flurry of activity as everyone rushed to make Naomi comfortable. Brent moved the pillows on the couch, making a nest for Gabe to settle her in. Tiana slid the ottoman close to her and Trina lifted Naomi's legs onto it. Catherine fluffed the pillows around her, her face alternating between worry and excitement.

Tiffany shooed the kids from the room and turned off the television. They all turned to him. Catherine smacked his arm. "Are you not taking care of your pregnant mate, Gabriel?"

"Mama, I bathed her this morning and fixed her tea and toast. I'm taking care of my mate and cubs."

Naomi groaned and planted her head in a pillow in embarrassment.

"TMI!" Brent held up his hand and left the room.

"Jesus, Gabe you take everything so literal," Tiana said in disgust, following Brent from the room.

Trina leaned closer and sniffed again, shooting him a smile. Tiana came back into the room with a mug of tea, handing the steaming liquid over to Naomi. What had he said wrong?

Naomi smiled in thanks. "How did you know I was pregnant?"

They all looked around confused. "What do you mean?" Tiffany asked.

"Latent," Julian answered in explanation.

"Oh," Trina nodded, "You probably can't smell the change in your hormones."

"A latent panther, I wonder what the cubs would be." His sisters debated as they left him alone with his mate.

Gabe kneeled next to her, "Are you okay, babe?"

"You knew?" Nay turned to him.

His eyebrows lowered. "Yes, of course, I knew."

"For how long?" She snapped.

He frowned. "You didn't know?"

Naomi growled. "Why didn't you tell me?"

"I thought we had..." he trailed off. Had they not had that conversation already? He could have sworn they'd talked about it.

"Gabe," she sighed. "You gotta get out of your head, love." She cupped his cheek with her free hand. "Are you okay with it?"

He put his hand on top of hers, turning to kiss her palm. "I couldn't be happier."

Her eyes studied him, as she bit her lip. "Will it affect the mating?"

He snorted. "If you think my bear is anything other than smug, then you're mistaken."

"Promise?"

"I love you, Nay."

She nodded and leaned over to kiss his lips. "Okay, then we just have to get through the bonding."

He growled and gripped her chin. "No negative thoughts, we talked about this. Your panther will bond with my bear."

He could see the doubt in her eyes. He hoped that doubt didn't affect their bonding. As far as he was concerned, the full moon couldn't get there fast enough. His bear was in complete agreement, and whether or not she was aware of it, her power constantly reacted to his bear, welcoming it. Maybe her latency kept her from feeling it. Could that be the source of her doubt? He scrubbed a hand down his face, frustrated that he couldn't help.

13...

"I have this if you need to work," Naomi smiled at Gabe's oldest sister.

Trina typed furiously on her phone. "You shouldn't even be on your feet, hon."

Naomi hand rinsed the plates in the sink, depositing them into the dishwasher. "I'll be fine."

Trina said nothing, simply sucked her teeth in aggravation at the messages on her phone. Naomi left her to it, filling the dishwasher and starting it. She was wiping down the counter her mind all over the place. The pregnancy, the upcoming bonding, she was stressed to the max. The whole lunch had been spent with Catherine and Gabe's sisters going over wedding plans and baby shower plans. In the six months, since she'd agreed to marry Gabe, her life had been one rollercoaster ride after the other.

What would he have done if she'd told him no? Would his family be making exciting wedding plans with the other bear's family? She stopped wiping and turned to Trina.

"What about the other bear?"

Trina frowned but kept her head down. "What other bear?"

"The one Gabe was betrothed to? What did her family say when they were told Gabe was off the market?" She propped her hips against the counter.

His sister looked up from her phone. "What betrothal? Bears don't do that shit."

Naomi stood straight. "What do you mean? Gabe told me he was betrothed."

Trina snorted, "If only it were that easy for our mother." She cocked her head to the side. "I thought you were his mate anyway."

"I'm latent." Panic clawed its way up her chest, her lunch lurching in her stomach.

"Shit, Trina, what are you doing?" Gabe rushed into the kitchen.

"You've been lying to me?" Naomi's gaze bounced between brother and sister.

"You lied to your mate?" Trina crossed her arms over her chest. "Are you serious?"

Her chest tightened, her breathing coming faster as Naomi realized what Gabe had done. She needed some air. She pulled her phone out of her back pocket and texted her sister to come to get her, pushing past Gabe. She grabbed her purse from the sofa and headed for the front door. She'd wait outside for Charlotte. Hopefully it wouldn't take her sister long to get there.

Gabe rushed behind her. "I'll grab my keys."

"Don't worry about it." She looked down as her phone beeped. "Charlie's on her way." She couldn't say goodbye to his family, she just…she had to get out of the house.

"Nay," Gabe came after her.

She stomped down his mother's front lawn, stopping at the sidewalk and cursing. Should she keep walking and wait for her sister to catch up? If she stayed in place, Gabe would want to talk, and right now, she couldn't deal with it.

"No, Gabe, you lied to me. To my fucking face, and now I'm pregnant and…now?" She growled, unsure how to articulate her fear.

Gabe caught up to her and used her arm to swing her around. "You are mine! And I won't let you leave until we talk about it."

"Don't touch me." She snatched her arm from his grasp. "Why Gabe? Why would you tie your animal to someone who can't reciprocate?"

Her throat was tight, her eyes scratchy and burning as tears built up. She was angry, hurt, and yeah, there were probably some hormones stuck in there. But, behind all that?

Fear.

Stark, ice cold fear.

Damn it, all she had to do was tell him what happened and he'd understand...and yet, a lump clogged her throat and shame kept the words lodged in her throat. Her hands shook as she swiped the tears from her cheeks. She thought she was passed being ashamed of her latency. She cursed the makeup on her fingers, swiping across her skirt to clean it off.

"It's not fair to your bear to bond him with someone who maybe can't..." she took a shuddering breath and walked off.

Shit. Everything was screwed.

She paced the sidewalk, keeping her head down. Nothing but bears lived on the street and already she could see the curious creatures peeking out their windows at the commotion. Why had she agreed to bond with Gabe? She had fooled herself into thinking that she could do it, that her magic would allow it this time. Pregnant no less. Just like last time. She rubbed her chest as the ache in her heart spread. Stupid. It was stupid.

She was stupid.

"Damn it, Nay, talk to me, please." He stomped after her.

She let out a shaky sigh of relief when she saw her sister's car coming around the corner. He was fucking up the entire fake marriage ruse. If she were being honest, she was to blame as well. She'd went and fell in love with him. They were supposed to go back to being friends, his family satisfied that he'd tried to mate once it was all over. Now she was pregnant and he would be stuck with her.

Oh, God.

"Why, Gabe?" she asked, but the question was rhetorical, the die cast.

"Nay, you wouldn't listen to me, wouldn't even give me a chance, I panicked. You were talking about dating and giving someone else a shot and I..."

Charlotte pulled up and Naomi rushed to the passenger side before her sister even stopped the car.

"Nay, please don't leave." He begged. His mind was spinning, and yet not a single coherent thought came to him. How would he get her to listen?

She opened the car door, but he held it before she could get it. She refused to look at him.

"I can't talk to you right now. I can't do this, Gabe." Naomi whispered.

"You are mine and I'm not letting you go." He had to reign in his bear because he was steps from ripping her sister's door from the car to prevent Naomi from leaving.

Tears were coming down her face, shredding him. His heart was breaking and his bear was damn near ripping his insides.

"And what happens when you meet your real mate?" She demanded.

He frowned, not understanding. "What do you mean? I'm not...there is no real mate. You're it for me, Nay."

After everything he'd told her, after all the promises from her to think about bonding with him, did she still not get it? She hiccupped and raised her face to look at him.

"What?" She dropped into the passenger seat of her sister's car, a stunned look on her face.

"Yes, I lied to you. I made up this whole marriage of convenience to get you to finally give me a chance." He stepped closer to her, "you're mine and I would do anything to have you. I love you, Nay." He whispered. "Is there no part of you that knows you're my mate?"

She sobbed. "I have to go, Gabe, I can't even think straight."

"Nay, baby, please." He refused to let her close the door.

Brent grabbed his arm, his face pained. "Let her go, Gabe, give her a little space."

No, he couldn't let her leave. "I need to..."

"Gabriel," his father said sternly behind him, the power of his father's bear washing over him.

"She's not ready, bro," Brent whispered, pulling their foreheads together.

"Fuck!" He roared and backed away from the comfort of his twin, watching as Charlie sped off.

He went back into the house. His sisters were arguing with their mother.

"Well, how the fuck was I supposed to know he was lying to his mate?" Trina demanded.

"We told your ass weeks ago!" Catherine snapped.

"Oh," Trina looked at him, her face chagrined. "I'm so sorry Gabe, I forgot."

"It's fine, Trina." He mumbled.

It wasn't fine, and he needed to get out of the house before his mother smothered him. Gabe read it all in her watery gaze. If he stayed, Catherine would wrap him in a blanket and coddle him to death. He grabbed his keys and turned to leave. His mother stopped him at the door.

She held up her hands. "I know it feels helpless right now, but she's pregnant and her mind and body are going through things you'll never understand. If she's asking for some time, give her that. But, you go home to your mate and let her know that you're still there when she's ready."

"Mom." Gabe shook his head. She hadn't seen the look on Nay's face.

"Don't badger her, don't even bring it up, just be there, son." Catherine cupped his cheek. "She'll come around."

He swallowed past the lump in his throat and nodded. His mother went up on her toes and he met her halfway, their foreheads meeting. The contact calmed his bear and he shuddered as the tears he fought broke through. He wiped his face and backed away. He would go in the woods and let his bear out and then do as his mother suggested. Instead of heading out the front door, he walked to the back. Brent was next to him, not saying a word, just shedding his clothes. They both released their bears, his brother's magic covering him, keeping his bear from charging in the direction Charlie's car had driven. Butting against his shoulder, Brent's bear guided him towards the woods in the middle of the clan's property. He roared at his brother, and Brent answered back, his power washing over Gabe, demanding obedience. His bear fought the order, and his brother's bear stared him down. Chuffing in irritation, Gabe's bear took off towards the woods.

***

Hours later he returned to Nay's apartment building, his body sore from tussling with his brother. Though they were equal in size, Brent was soon to be alpha and his brother's power in the end won. They'd talked after, Brent letting him vent his frustration. It helped clear his head, and he was thankful for it. He was stopped at the door, the panther growling as he met him.

"The fuck is your problem?" Gabe's bear was already on a hair-trigger. If the panther wanted to fight, he would give it to him.

The security guard flashed his fangs. "Our Zeta is in pain, I'm not letting you pass."

"She's my mate, try and stop me from seeing her." He dared the male.

"Let up, Turk," Simon called, coming up on them.

Gabe stared the male down until he moved at Simon's order. He'd only taken another step into the building before Simon stopped him with a hand on his chest.

"Fix whatever the fuck you did." Simon's panther flashed in his eyes, power saturating the lobby.

"Move out of my way," Gabe ordered.

Simon stared a moment more before he moved to the side. Gabe rushed upstairs, anxious to see Naomi. She was in her apartment, thank God, curled on the couch sleep. Charlotte was the kitchen cleaning.

"How is she?"

Charlotte gave him a stare that was full of her panther, the heat from her anger brushing against him. She sighed when he met her eyes.

"You made a mess." Charlie shuddered and looked over at her sister. "She's our fucking Zeta, Gabe. The pain she's pushing down the prowl link is..."

"What was I supposed to do, Charlie? She was tying ties and shit, talking 'bout giving some other shifter a chance at what's mine."

"Did it ever occur to you to just be honest?"

"I tried that before and she brushed it off. She wouldn't take me seriously." He wiped a frustrated hand down his face.

Charlotte shook her head. "Well, good luck getting her to believe anything you say now."

"I'll fix it."

"You better," Charlotte warned. She looked over to her sister, and sighed again, leaving.

He looked at his mate, curled up on the sofa. How the hell could he fix it? He lifted her and curled her into his chest, his bear finally settling. He carried her into their bedroom and lay down with her. He'd try his mother's advice. He'd wait until she was ready to talk about it, but show her that he wasn't going anywhere.

14...

Her head was pounding and Naomi could hardly swallow past her dry throat. She put her hand out, reaching for the cup of water she kept on her bedside table. She froze when she came into contact with Gabe's chest. When had he come in? She needed to leave, she wasn't ready to see him. She slid from under the blanket, happy to be in clothes, even if it was yesterday's. She tried tiptoeing from the room.

"You're not going to talk to me about it?" His voice was rough with sleep.

She took a deep breath and turned to him. He was propped against the headboard, his gaze boring into her.

"Gabe, I need—"

"Time." He cut in sharply, shoving the blankets from his legs and crawled to the end of the bed, sitting on the edge. "You're always asking me for time, Naomi. When do I get time? When do my needs and wants factor into your decisions?"

She sucked in a surprised breath. Gabe had never talked to her in the angry voice he was using.

"You want to end this because I lied. I'm so sorry I lied to you, Nay."

"But?" She whispered.

"No, buts, princess. I shouldn't have lied to you."

She clasped her hands together tightly. "Why did you lie?"

"I've loved you for half of my life, Naomi. I've wanted nothing but to be a part of yours, in any way you'd let me." He wiped a hand down his face. "You know what. No, I'm not begging." He stood and pulled his t-shirt from the chair next to her bed.

He slipped it over his head and turned to look at her. Panic had her stomach flipping at the defeated look in his eyes. He sighed and moved towards her. She braced herself for a pleading embrace, a kiss, anything he would use to convince her. But he moved past her, leaving her bedroom. She scrambled behind him, confused.

"Where are you going?"

"You either believe you're my mate, or you don't. Either way, I can't do this back and forth with you. My bear can't take it, Nay." His eyes searched her face.

She swallowed, her power raising. Would she lose him? Would she let her fear break them apart? Gabe sighed and shook his head. He turned and walked out of her front door. Fear seized her heart. Oh God, she couldn't lose Gabe. She raced down the hall and caught the elevator doors before they closed.

They stared at each other, tension building between them, the buzzer of the elevator the only sound in the hall.

"I'm scared to trust my instincts," she said softly.

"Hey, Naomi, are you okay?" a voice called over the elevator intercom.

She leaned into the elevator and pressed the button. "Yes, sorry." She turned to Gabe, "please don't leave."

He stepped from the elevator but stood in front of the closing doors. "I thought I could be sure enough for both of us."

She blinked away tears. "I tried to bond with Aaron and it didn't work." She confessed.

He hissed and stepped back, his eyes flickering back and forth between him and his bear. "You tried to give him what was mine?"

She swallowed her trepidation, knowing Gabe would never hurt her. She closed the distance between them. "I was ashamed to tell you."

"I knew he'd gotten you pregnant, but I never knew you tried to mate with that piece of shit." Gabe's expression tightened in anger. "I should've killed him."

"Gabe, no, that's…" She grabbed his arm. "Can we go to my apartment, please?"

He stared at her for what felt like forever before he gave her a brisk nod. She breathed out in relief and walked in front of him. He sat on a stool in her kitchen rather than going into the living room. Was he going to still leave? She took a deep cleansing breath and decided to lay it all on the table.

"When I found out I was pregnant, I assumed it meant Aaron was the one for me. I think we both assumed it. I…I don't have panther instincts, and I loved him." She leaned her back against the wall and slid down until she was sitting on the kitchen floor. "The night we tried to bond, he bit me. It didn't work, obviously, but worse, his power, and what I now know was my power clashed, reacted badly and it set off the miscarriage in my body."

"Oh God, Nay," he whispered, rushing over to her. He stooped to her level, running a finger across her cheek. "He was nothing, less than nothing, Nay. He didn't belong with you, no way he could've held on to you."

"Do you understand why I'm hesitant to go through with the bonding, especially now that I'm pregnant?"

He had to understand. She didn't know what she'd do if he didn't.

"Why didn't you tell me this?"

She shrugged. "As I said, I was ashamed. Being latent is always being on the outside looking in."

"Nay." He sat down and gathered her onto his lap. "You said you loved me, do you mean it?"

She nodded, unable to talk past the lump in her throat.

"I want all of you, the bond, everything, I don't want half of my mate."

Tears spilled across her cheek, knowing what was coming next. And what could she say? He deserved a mate that could give him everything.

"What if we waited until after the baby is born to try and bond?"

She stilled, holding her breath while her mind turned over his words. Did that mean… "What are you saying?"

"I'm not giving you up, Nay. If I have to wait a year to bond with you, I will. So long as you promise to try."

"I swear," she scrambled from his lap and got up to her knees. "I want more than anything to be able to bond with you, Gabe. I'll do whatever I need to."

He cupped her cheek, his eyes luminous. "Including marrying me first?"

She chuckled. "I don't think our mothers are letting us out of the wedding." She gripped his arms.

"Do you trust me, Nay? Do you trust that I would never do anything to hurt you?"

"I do."

"Then we'll enjoy your pregnancy, keep you calm and healthy," he murmured, dropping his head close to hers. "After that, you'll be mine, in every way." He whispered against her lips.

Naomi closed the distance between them, sealing their lips together. She pulled back.

"Do we need to do another contract?" she teased.

He growled and nipped her bottom lip. He sucked it into his mouth to soothe the bite, his tongue sliding inside her mouth, their tongues tangling. She would put all her doubts aside and trust in Gabe, in their relationship. She loved him and would have faith that it would all work out.

15...

Gabe rolled his shoulders, as he stepped into the elevator. He pressed the button for the top floor and frowned. A red light flashed saying he wasn't authorized. He sucked his teeth and worked the front panel of the elevator open. Naomi had called him at work and told him she'd be at Savannah's so that's where he was going. Damn all the unnecessary security measures the panthers had on every damn thing. He grunted in victory when the car started moving.

He walked into the Tribond's penthouse apartment a few minutes later. His bear moved in happiness when he spotted his mate on the sofa talking to her cousin.

"How the fuck did you get in here?" Derrick growled.

Panther cubs were wrestling in the middle of the floor but he only had eyes for his mate. She was beautiful, her whole aura glowing with her pregnancy. Her power flared to meet him, his bear answering in response. His chest expanded, his bear insanely happy. He crossed to her, bending down to kiss her. He'd missed her, though it had only been hours since he'd last seen her. They had another month before their wedding, and work had been crazy, but they had given up alternating apartments, with him just moving his clothes into hers. He'd talked to her Felix about moving her into a bigger place. They would need one for the cubs they were having. If it were up to him, he'd move her into a house on the bear clan's territory, but he understood that her position as Zeta was important. She needed to be in proximity to the panthers.

Naomi snapped her fingers and he focused on the room noticing everyone staring at him. "What?"

"Hamilton, how the fuck did you get up to the penthouse?" The Beta snapped

"You don't notice the cubs crawling all over you?" Savannah asked, snickering. "Bears are so damn big."

Naomi said nothing, just smiled, her eyes going soft.

He felt tiny claws along his legs and back, and he grunted and shook his body, dislodging the panther cubs. They darted back at him and he backed up and picked up one, recognizing his eyes.

"Small fry, you got your panther?"

The cub growled and nuzzled against his cheek. He leaned down and set Jamie gently on the floor. He picked up the other one, a little girl, "I don't believe we've met."

"That's my daughter, Ella." Savi supplied.

He stared into the little girl's serious eyes and nuzzled against her head. "I'm Gabe," he told her.

She nodded and he put her down and the cubs scurried away.

Derrick was standing, hands on his hips. "You didn't answer the question, bear."

He blinked. Naomi smothered a giggle.

"He's a bear babe, I haven't seen a lock that's ever stopped, Gabe," Savannah told her mate matter of factly.

"What?" Derrick said. "It's an electronic lock...on the whole fucking elevator, he shouldn't even be on this floor."

Gabe shrugged and decided against telling Derrick he'd dismantled the electronics. He'd fix it when he went back down. Gabe stalked back to Naomi, bracing his arms on either side of her on the plush sofa. He studied her, his mind on all the things he'd do to his mate once he got her into their apartment.

"Your sister called me an asshole," he grumbled to Nay as he leaned over her.

"You saw Charlotte?"

He grunted his assent.

"Did you do something to her?" She put her forehead against his.

He grunted again, and she laughed. His bear was smug at the fact that their mate understood his grunts.

"So you didn't speak." She teased him. "You know Charlotte doesn't like it when you ignore her. It's rude."

"As hell," Savi chimed in.

"Nickel in the jar," a small female voice said.

Gabe's eyes never left Naomi, instead, roving her body, lingering at her belly.

"We're fine," she whispered.

His heart turned over. Nay was finally showing, a rounded bump that made him way more emotional than he wanted to admit.

"You're taking it easy?"

"I am, swear." She cupped his cheek. "We're not alone, Gabe, you haven't even greeted my family." She chided softly.

He blinked in that slow way of his she loved, his attention again on the room. "I didn't?"

Savi snorted and pat his shoulder. "Oh, Gabe."

"Beta," he grunted in greeting, and Derrick cursed.

"I'm telling my enforcers to shoot you next time you come onto this territory."

"What? Why?"

He looked genuinely curious, not at all worried, which made Savannah burst out laughing.

Naomi sighed. "Babe quit breaking into places."

"Why? All that security, it takes too long."

Derrick just stared at him and growled. Naomi couldn't help but laugh. Gabe was a lot for people.

"Gabe!" Jamie rushed down the stairs, his shirt backward.

"Small fry," Gabe said, catching her little cousin as he jumped. "You got a panther, are you all grown up now?"

"Nearly," was Jamie's answer.

She got misty watching Gabe with him. Gabe was so good with kids, it was the adults he didn't much care for. She couldn't wait to see him with their children. She touched her baby bump, more fascinated every day that went by.

"Cousin Nay is having a baby, is it yours?" Jamie asked.

"Jamie!" Savannah admonished.

Gabe nodded. "What are you going to do if your cousins are bear cubs? They're going to be bigger than you."

Jamie put out his chest. "Bet they still can't beat me."

Gabe smiled and she blinked away tears.

"He's nice to kids," Derrick muttered next to her, perplexed.

She nodded.

Derrick sighed. "I guess we won't shoot him."

She slapped at the Beta's arms. "Don't shoot my mate." She fussed.

Gabe speared her with a look that had her heart speeding up. It was the first time she'd admitted out loud that he was her mate. And from Gabe's reaction, he'd been waiting to hear her say that.

"Goodbye, small fry." His voice was deep, his bear rising to the surface. He said goodbye to Ella, and lifted Naomi, swinging her into his arms.

"Bye, Gabe," Savi called as he punched the button for the elevator.

She gasped and burst out laughing when she saw the wires of the elevators everywhere. "Oh my God, Gabe, they're going to shoot you."

He nuzzled under her neck. "You won't let them shoot your mate."

She put both hands on his cheeks, kissing him lightly. "Yes, I will protect my mate."

"Your mate," he murmured against her lips.

"Mine." She kissed him. "You know, the full moon is tonight."

His eyes heated, longing filling them. "We said we'd wait."

Her power flared, all the confirmation she needed that their animals would bond. She'd talked to her grandpa Harper and according to him, she'd already started the mating process. He'd told her that she and Gabe's scents were already intertwined. It had never done that with Aaron, he'd said.

"I want it all. I'm not afraid anymore."

He set her down on her feet, pulling her into his chest. "Be sure, princess, absolutely sure, I don't want you hurt."

"I talked to a healer, we'll be okay, I swear." Though, nerves still danced around in her stomach.

He studied her face, gauging her sincerity. Finally, he seemed to believe her, closing his eyes and shuddering. When he opened them again, her breath caught at the longing heating his gaze.

"You need to fix the elevator first," she told him.

He laughed and turned back to the control panel to do just that.

***

Gabe's hands were shaking as he stepped from the shower. He pulled the towel down off the rack and dried his body, his bear restless, moving around in his body. He'd promised Nay he could wait to bond with her, but now that she'd proposed it, he found himself anxious, impatient. It was nearing midnight and hours ago, she'd gone to her sister's to 'prepare', whatever that meant. As far as his bear was concerned, there was only one requirement for their bonding and he'd done that before he even stepped into the shower. The windows of Naomi's bedroom were wide open, the curtains back, allowing the light of the moon to bath her room. He'd lit both lavender and rose-scented candles, praying the scents would soothe his mate, and keep her relaxed throughout the whole process.

He walked out of the bathroom and his breath caught. Naomi stood at the foot of the bed in a thin white satin gown, lace along the bottom, and in a vee deep enough that her breasts were just barely covered. The way the satin hugged the soft curves of her body made his mouth water. He swayed, hungry need filling him. His bear's power filled him to overflow, spilling out into the space between him and Naomi. Her power rose in answer and her eyes widened. He dropped the towel he'd been using to dry off, rushing naked to his mate.

"Did you feel that?" Her breathless question was full of surprised wonder.

"You're mine, did you not think our power would play well together?"

He skimmed his shaking hands down the curve of her hips, closing his eyes at the soft fabric. He hated that he would rip such a beautiful garment from his mate's body. He cupped her stomach, pride damn near bringing him to his knees. Naomi was his, and tonight, he'd bond them together.

"Are you sure about this, my love?" He waited for the answer, inhaling deep, sifting through the many scents of her emotions. Her nervousness was there, but there was no trace of fear in her scent.

He loosened his power, probing at the deep well of hers and it responded, flaring in answer to his. It had been like that since their scents had melded. It was reason Gabe was so sure their bonding would not hurt their cubs. He and his bear had never had any doubt, but for their mate, he'd been patient. And would continue to be if her fear kept her from their joining tonight.

"I want this," she tiptoed and licked his neck.

It was all the sign his bear was waiting for. With a growl, Gabe lifted her, laying her across the bed. He grew the claw on his pointer finger, using it to rip through the fabric of the gown. Naomi lifted her chest, gasping. He leaned down, kissing her exposed skin. She squirmed beneath him, her hands softly stroking his head. He nibbled the underside of her breast, rubbing his cheek along her soft skin. Their scents had melded weeks ago, but still, his bear was nothing if not thorough about leaving its mark. He nipped her skin, pausing to leave hickeys along the way. He lavished her nipple, raking his teeth across it.

Naomi hissed, holding his head in place. "Please, Gabe."

He released her nipple, kissing his way to her neck. His bear bucked, anxious to seal them together. He scraped his teeth across her skin, closing his eyes as her power rose to meet his. He nudged her chin down, their lips meeting in a fierce kiss. God he loved her.

"You ready, princess?"

She nodded and reached down to grip his shaft. He groaned, putting his hand on hers, helping her guide him inside. They both moaned as he entered, kissing deeply as he slid inch by inch into her on that first stroke. Her sex fluttered, gripping his dick, pulling him in further. Her body relaxed beneath him, her legs opening wider as he fit fully inside. Their foreheads met and he started to move his hips in an easy rhythm. His strokes were slow at first, careful, their soft sighs the only sound in the room. She ran her hands all over his shoulders and back, swaying her hips to meet him halfway. Moonlight bathed her skin, its pale light painting her curves. His bear pushed forward, a feral need gripping him. He sped his strokes, and Naomi's nails scraped his back urging him faster, harder.

His power started building, hers flaring to respond. It filled Naomi, reaching out and wrapping around Gabe. Her heartbeat was a runaway train in her chest. She pulled his head in close offering herself. Gabe whispered against the skin of her neck, telling her of his need, his love. How could she have denied him for so long? His teeth scraped against her shoulder, and for a moment panic threatened. But his bear's power encased her, calmed her.

"I have you love," He murmured, his voice a deep growl, full of his animal.

"Now, Gabe. Make me yours," she panted.

Gabe growled, his hips jerking, a deep stroke that brought a scream from her. His breath was hot on her skin, his tongue laving the spot on her shoulder before his teeth gripped her, sinking into the muscle. Her back arched, power entered her body and an orgasm slammed into her, stealing her breath. Gabe's hips flexed, rolled, deep strokes, fucking in and out of her, prolonging her climax. He sucked on his mating mark his tongue pushing his bear's hormones into her. Her power melded with his, their spirits swirling together until Naomi could barely tell where she ended and he began.

"Your turn, Nay," he pleaded, gripping the back of her neck with his hand, bringing her closer to him.

She didn't have the teeth he had, the animal he had, but instinct drove her and took over. She licked against his shoulder and bit down, wanting with everything in her soul to mark this man for her own. He cursed when her magic filled him, his hips powering into her, no longer a controlled stroke. Naomi tasted his blood as her teeth pierced his skin. It sent Gabe over the edge.

He stiffened on top of her, one last stroke before he was coming. He cradled her head, keeping her close to him, his body tense, jerking with aftershocks. Naomi licked across his skin, marveling at the fact that marks were closing, though still leaving tiny indentations of her teeth. Gabe sighed and rolled over, pulling her with him. He didn't pull out, instead, adjusting to keep his shaft inside. Naomi snuggled into his chest. Tears of joy were running down her cheeks. She felt Gabe's contentment, his incredible love for her as well as the remnants of his orgasm. Once their heartrates were under control, his worry easily transferred across their new bond. But then there was joy. A joy that matched the one filling her heart.

He lifted his head from the pillow, his face excited. "I can feel you and the cubs."

She swallowed her tears and smiled. "It worked."

"I told you it would," he traced the mark on her shoulder, smug.

"Oh my God, you're going to be annoying aren't you?" She couldn't believe how happy that made her.

He laughed and rubbed his hands down her back. "If you give me an hour, I'll make it worth your while."

She'd wondered how he was so sure about them, but her power rose, and wrapped the two of them in a calming bliss. Now that the veil of fear was gone, she realized that her power had always welcomed Gabe. Every time they were together it sought him out, threading with his. Now that they were fully bonded she understood that he had never felt foreign to neither her power nor her body.

She kissed him, incredibly satisfied, and just a bit smug herself. For a moment, the thought of what she would've lost had she let far take over flitted across her mind. But then her new mate, and soon to be husband flexed his hips and all thoughts of what-ifs flew from her head. They were bonded, mated, something she never thought her latency would allow. She would spend the rest of their lives making up the time they'd lost from her doubt.

Gabe rolled back over, his head dipping to kiss her, his shaft flexing inside of her. "Tell me you love me, mate."

"I love you," she whispered against his lips.

Epilogue

"Isn't it all so beautiful?"

Brent tensed as Catherine snuck up behind him. She was right, the ceremony had been beautiful. Watching his twin finally marry the love of his life was amazing. But, now that it was over, their mother had a new target. He adjusted the bow tie at his throat, loosening it for the conversation to come. He turned around and faced his mother. Her smile was serene. Anyone passing by would never know the sneakiness that lay under her saccharine expression.

She placed a hand on his arm. "My God Brent, you'd think I was about to walk you down the aisle in the next five minutes."

"You're up to something, mama, don't think I don't notice," he said softly.

Catherine sucked her teeth. "You're the next in line for alpha, Brent, I'm sure I don't have to keep reminding you of that."

"And yet," he murmured.

She pinched his arm. "Excuse your tone."

Brent took another sip of champagne to hide his smile. He looked around and spotted Gabe on the other side of the reception hall, a look on his brother's face he knew all too well.

"Excuse me, mom, I need to go rescue Gabe before he embarrasses us." He didn't wait on her response, instead, cutting through the crowd to get to his brother.

From the expression on Gabe's face, he was at the end of his socializing rope. Brent sidled up next to his twin, smiling at the bears surrounding him.

"If you'll excuse us," He said, putting a little power behind the request.

The group around them dispersed, leaving him alone with his brother.

"Thank God," Gabe grumbled. "There are too many damn people here."

Brent snickered, "That's what you get for mating with a panther. They take the biblical 'be fruitful and multiple' to heart."

Gabe groaned and wiped a hand down his face. Brent grabbed his brother's arm, pulling him out onto the balcony. The expensive hotel where they held the reception was downtown and had an amazing view of the city. The Florida humidity had him regretting leaving the comfort of the ballroom immediately, though.

"Where's Nay?"

Gabe gave a long-suffering sigh, "Changing. Apparently, there is a second reception look."

"Should've eloped," Brent murmured.

"Well if you wanted our mother's attention on you months ago, you should've said something." Gabe snapped.

Brent shuddered. "Lord, I didn't think about that. Good looking out, then."

"Time's up for you big brother."

Brent kept his face straight, though nerves danced around his skin, bringing his bear to the surface. He'd been putting off mating knowing that once he did, taking over as Alpha was the next step. He wasn't ready, but telling his father that would do him no good. So...instead, he'd used a technicality to skate. As his mother had told him on multiple occasions, the clan wouldn't accept an unmated Alpha.

"She already tried to corner me."

His brother laughed. "Might as well cancel dinners at the house. She's going to trot out every single bear in the area."

"Damn it." He chugged the remaining champagne in his cup and wished it was something stronger.

"You're headed to Cali, right. That should buy you, what, a month?"

He shrugged. He didn't know if it would take that long to close the deals for their client, but he would stretch that shit out. Never had he been so happy to be the only sibling who'd passed the California bar. So long as he was out of the state, Catherine would be limited in her meddling.

He changed the subject. "I'm happy for you, Gabe."

A smile transformed his brother's normally grumpy face. "I didn't think we'd get here if I'm being honest."

"And now you're mated with cubs on the way."

"My God," Gabe said in wonder. "I love that woman."

That was evident to anyone who saw the two of them together in a room. Brent knew the lengths Gabe had gone through to be in Naomi's life. He was glad it had worked out for them. Gabe moved to the door, and he followed behind him. Ignoring all the well-wishers, his brother made a beeline for his bride. Naomi smiled, and posed, the white off the shoulder jumpsuit showed off her ample curves, as well as the baby bump that had been hidden in her wedding gown. The crowd around them clapped and whistled as Gabe lifted her, sealing their lips together. The kiss was passionate, and borderline inappropriate, even for a wedding.

"You're next little brother," one of his sisters taunted at his side.

Brent cursed and looked around for one of the roving waiters. He needed a stronger drink if he was going to be dodging his mother's matchmaking attempts.

Tiana laughed. "Relax, she's dancing with dad."

"Not funny." He looked around, only relaxing when he saw his parents swaying together on the dance floor.

"Yes it is," she teased. "Besides, you're leaving tonight, she can't do too much in these few hours."

"We're talking about our mother." He gave Tiana a droll look.

"You right. Just make a break for it, I'll cover for you."

Brent whirled to face her fully. "Swear?"

"I mean...I'm gonna stir the pot, because that's what I does." She waggled her eyebrows. "But when she asks, I'll just tell her you headed out to prep for the trip."

"You're a lifesaver." He leaned over and pecked his sister's cheek.

"Well, I've never been called that," she laughed.

Brent caught his brother's eyes and pointed towards the door. Gabe gave him a thumbs up and turned back to his bride, as usual, completely devoted to her. He'd catch up with him when he got back from California. He knew running would only stall his mother but for so long. As far as Catherine was concerned, Brent was the last of her children standing, and she was going to find him a mate, no matter what it took.

The Alpha's Affair

1 ...

After three weeks away from home, Brent didn't know how he felt to be back. On the one hand, he was happy to sleep in his own bed, but on the other hand, everything he'd run from was waiting on him when he got back. Time was running out for him, and that business trip had been his last stalling tactic. For three weeks he'd avoided his father's prodding and his mother's loving meddling. As the oldest male, it was Brent's turn to take over as Alpha for his family's bear clan.

It wasn't as though he'd not known and prepared for the change his whole life. And if asked, he couldn't quite say what was bothering him about taking his place. Actually, that was wrong; he knew what was bothering him. Bears were old-fashioned. He couldn't take the alpha position without a mate. And he wasn't fond of being rushed into a relationship for the sake of taking the place that was rightfully his. He didn't like his actions being dictated by someone else's schedule. But, his father was ready to step down and only what Catherine called Brent's 'ridiculous stubbornness' kept Julian from retiring.

He'd taken every out of town client he could to avoid his mother's match-making, but she was getting impatient. His bear more so. He sighed in resignation, knowing Catherine would have something up her sleeve now that he was home.

Adjusting his tie, he moved through the lobby of the building that housed his family's law firm. Christmas decorations were going up, the building's maintenance team hanging more from the high ceilings. Both greenery and lights crisscrossed around the whole entry. He smiled at the silliness of it all. It wasn't even November. He loved this time of year, though, because it was the only time his animal relaxed. With the alpha position on the horizon, his bear was more aggressive than usual, pushing for him to take his place. It being winter was the only thing keeping him sane at the moment. Gabe, his brother, waved him down as he entered the second set of glass doors that separated his family's firm from the other businesses in the building.

"Hey, when did you get back?"

He shuffled his briefcase and dapped his brother's hand, pulling him into a half hug. Gabe grunted at the contact, and Brent hid his smile. His twin wasn't much for public displays of emotion.

"Just last night. Where you headed?"

Gabe smiled. "Doctor's appointment for Nay."

Brent smiled, happy for his brother and his sister-in-law. She was in the sixth month of her pregnancy and they were all excited. He opened his mouth to ask about Naomi when a scent reached him. His mouth closed with a snap, and his bear rose to attention. A warm tide moved through his body, flushing his skin. He furrowed his brows, loosened the tie at his neck and inhaled deeply. His eyes followed the path of the scent to the reception desk. He cocked his head to look and was floored. His bear bucked and a hungry rumble left his mouth.

Fuck, she was gorgeous.

Dark skin, long braids, oversized hoop earrings, and long fingernails were the only things he could see from where she was seated. She was talking to the security guard seated next to her. Her voice drifted to him, sultry and country as hell. Her nails were sparkling, the jewels on them shining as she moved her hands around excitedly as she spoke. The phone rang and she lifted her index finger to the guard. She answered the phone and he pursed his lips, impressed. The code switch was immaculate. Her country accent smoothed out into a sultry, lilting cadence of what passed as 'proper' as she spoke.

Lord have mercy.

He took a step towards her, not entirely of his own volition. Gabe gave him a strange look.

"Yo, you listening?"

"Sorry, who is that?"

Gabe followed his gaze. "Oh, Mercedes. She's the new office manager."

"What is she doing on reception?"

"Hell if I know. She runs this whole place, though, so there's probably a good reason."

Brent said her name softly, running the taste around in his mouth. His bear most definitely wanted a taste.

"The Trips will murder you in your sleep," Gabe warned.

He blinked, breaking the spell she had over him, and gave his brother his attention. "What?"

"The Trips, especially Trina, will tear a strip off your hide. They like her." Gabe said it as though that explained everything.

Brent's curiosity skyrocketed. His sisters barely liked anyone.

"They hired her out of a grocery store," Gabe explained.

"What?"

"Yeah, Tiana told Nay that she was a manager at the grocery store down the street. The Trips and mom were there and saw her at customer service. She helped them, and then Trina hired her on the spot."

His eyebrows winged high. "What?"

"The fuck is wrong with you?" Gabe frowned.

"What?"

"Say 'what' one more damn time and this conversation is over," Gabe growled.

"The Trips like her?" He studied her, wondering what it was about her that his sisters liked enough to hire her on the spot.

Office manager. Did they make up the job title? He didn't remember anyone having that position prior to him leaving. Not that he interfered with the way his sisters ran their family's firm. He'd been anxious to leave the office, so who knew what other changes his sisters had made.

"Wait, you said mom was with them?"

Damn it. If his mother was involved, it could be a setup. His eyes roved her face, taking in her large, heavily lashed eyes and thick pouty lips. He couldn't work up any alarm over the fact that Catherine was probably up to something.

"Yeah, they were all together. They told me explicitly not to run her off." Gabe rolled his eyes.

"How long has she been here?"

Gabe shrugged. "How long have you been gone?"

"A few weeks."

"Bout that, then," Gabe answered. Looking at his watch. "Look, I need to go."

"Yeah," he said absently, his attention entirely on Mercedes.

He approached the desk on feet that weren't taking any input from him.

Gabe grabbed the back of his suit jacket. "I'm telling you, Brent, leave this one alone."

"She's mine," Brent growled at his brother.

"Damn, not even home a whole day and mama got you." Gabe snickered.

"That's not…"

Fuck!

His brother was right, but his bear didn't care. But then, the damned animal was ready to take over as alpha; it was the man holding them back. It didn't matter. Brent had to have her.

Gabe sighed. "I'll leave that between you and Trina."

Gabe left, and Brent finished his jaunt over to the desk. She smiled up at him, and his mouth dried.

"Hi, you must be the other half of the twins." Her smile was beautiful, her face lighting.

She gave him her phone voice. He wanted that relaxed, country tone she'd been using with the security guard. He swallowed and tried to speak. He took a deep inhale; wood fire and herbs laced her scent. He and his bear both realized something at the same time.

She was human…a witch.

He frowned. That changed things. He stepped closer to the desk, brushing aside the possible problems her not being a shifter could pose for him. His bear didn't give a damn, and currently, the man in him was struck dumb by her presence.

He thought briefly of Gabe's warning, but his bear overrode it. What his sisters didn't know wouldn't hurt them. The silence was turning awkward.

She cocked her head to the side and gave him a rueful smile. "So, grumpy like Gabe, then? Can I help you with anything?" She asked in that professional voice.

His chest rumbled in irritation. He wanted her normal speaking voice.

"No." He growled, his bear rising, the animal pushing to control the situation.

She reared back in surprise, the security guard tensing next to her.

"I'm sorry." He wiped a hand down his face. "Shit, I mean, sorry for the language. I'm not grumpy like my brother. I mean..." he paused, and she laughed, the sound flowing over him and pushing out all good sense.

He closed his eyes. He'd never had a problem talking with a woman. Why then was he stumbling like a jackass in front of Mercedes? His skin tightened, and his bear stretched, demanding him to reach for her. He sighed; that would be one reason he was tripping over his words.

She held up a hand, the jewels on her nails sparkling. "It's not a problem."

"You're gorgeous," he blurted out, flustered. "Shit, I mean shoot, I shouldn't have said that here. Workplace harassment."

Her eyes were dancing with merriment, and he wanted the floor to open up and swallow him.

The security guard next to her coughed to cover his laugh. "Never thought I'd see the day, Hamilton," the older man said.

Brent scratched the back of his head, unsure how to proceed with his foot stuck in his mouth. His bear pushed against his skin again, confused as to why they weren't making a move on her.

"I'm Mercedes and you're Brent." She held out her hand. He gripped it and electricity traveled the length of his arm, his power flaring out of control. Her eyes widened, and she gasped. "Well then," she whispered.

***

Mercedes pulled her hand back and cleared her throat, reaching into the drawer on the right of her to buy herself some time. Her hands shook as she grabbed the stack of rubber band-bound mail with his name on it. The man was fine as hell. It wasn't as though she didn't know that. His twin looked identical to him, save the beard adorning his face. But, nothing about Gabe had grabbed her the way Brent did. His aura was a beautiful golden color that she wanted to wade in. Nothing was dark about this man other than his beautiful chestnut skin. His hair was trimmed close to his scalp, waves on top.

Broody. She'd thought the same of Gabe when she'd first met him. But somehow, on Brent, those dark eyes shadowed by thick eyebrows—though still broody— set off little pings of awareness throughout her body. Brother was fine and wore a suit like nobody's business. At over six feet tall, the red suit he wore should've been garish, loud, but draped over his massive body, it was the embodiment of power. Everything about him exuded it. His presence was a magnet, pulling everything near him into his orbit.

She cleared her throat and forced herself to act normal. She put on her office voice. "Here's your mail from while you were gone. Trina had me give her anything pertaining to clients, so there's nothing that needs your immediate attention."

He nodded, his face as perplexed as she felt. She wanted to hear his deep voice again. Mercedes was tempted to tease him, but she liked this job and for damn sure wasn't about to ruin it playing games with one of the partners. Although, every instinct she had was telling her this man was important to her. She was the breadwinner in her family, so she would do nothing to lose her good job.

"Thank you," he said and beat feet from her desk.

She didn't breathe until the elevator doors closed on him. She let out a breath and sat back. "Lord have mercy," She whispered.

Terrell next to her started chuckling. "Girl, I have never seen Brent so tongue-tied. That boy is usually smooth as hell, and every woman in this building knows it."

She could believe it. That man surely sucked the air out of any room he entered. "He's definitely potent."

Just then, Justine rushed through the door. "Thank you so much for covering for me, Mercedes."

"I got you, sis," she said, standing. "Been kicking it with Terrell, catching up on the mess."

Justine cackled. "Ain't he messy? All in these people business."

"It's my job as a security officer to see everything." Terrell defended.

"See, and say," Justine said, holding her hand up to Mercedes.

She laughed and gave the woman five. "I'm out. Let me know if anything comes up," she told the two.

She got into the elevator that Brent had entered earlier and inhaled. His woodsy cologne still wafted throughout it, the only sign of his presence. She wondered what her grandmothers would think about him. The thought of them sobered her. She was the only thing keeping the three of them from homelessness. Not that her grandmothers cared. They were happy to be in their small house out in the country, living off the money they made selling vegetables and flowers at the farmer's market. She was essentially paying for two households, though calling her tiny apartment a household was a stretch. She sighed; she needed to focus on work and not messing up the amazing job she still had no clue how she got. She had two years of community college under her belt and no experience whatsoever in running a law firm, but instincts had bid her to jump on the job offer immediately. It paid her twice what she had been making at the grocery store, and she wouldn't look a gift horse in the mouth. It was the only reason she'd been able to finally move into the city and maintain her grandmothers' house.

The elevator door opened on the executive level, and she took a deep breath and straightened her spine. Time to get back to work. Instead of going straight to her office, she weaved through the associates on the floor, keeping an eye out for tell-tale dark spikes in their auras.

It was her secret to keeping the office running so efficiently. She could head problems off before they spiraled out of control. Her grandmothers were happy to find out she was using her powers at work. Their worse fear when she'd moved out was that she'd lose sight of her roots. She snorted, as if they'd let her.

Her phone was ringing as she rounded the corner to her small office. She snatched it as she rushed around the desk.

"Sadie."

Speaking of grandmothers. "Hi Grams, what's up?"

"We keep getting letters from some developer. He's trying to buy our house." Lisa was never one to mince words.

"What?" She frowned and flopped into her desk chair.

"We're not moving."

"No one can make you move, Grams." What in the world?

"Doesn't sound like they plan to play nice about it. These letters sound threatening," Lisa murmured.

Mercedes's heartbeat picked up, and anxiety turned her stomach. "Do you want me to come by after work?"

"Well, are you coming out tomorrow?"

"Of course. I'm going to the grocery store, and then I will be there tomorrow afternoon. I talked to Nana and got your list."

Though, she kept her own supply list for the women. Her grandmothers weren't exactly absent-minded, but there were things she deemed important and necessary that they regularly rolled their eyes at.

"Do you need to add anything?"

"No, we're fine. It can wait until you get here tomorrow, then."

"Ok, well, I'll take a look at the letters when I get out there." She promised.

"I won't take up any more of your work time, then."

She smiled. "You're never a bother, Grams. I love you."

"I love you too, Sadie. See you tomorrow."

She frowned and wondered what kind of letters they were getting. She went back to her work and put it out of her mind.

2 ...

Brent let himself into his parent's house, calling out to them. His father called a greeting from his office towards the back of the first floor. He walked through his parent's immaculate house, rolling his shoulders. He'd considered waiting a while to visit his mother when he got back, but his sister-in-law Naomi had called and insisted he come over to a family brunch. It was probably a setup, but he could never tell the women in his family no. His bear was moving through his body restless, Mercedes a constant presence in his mind since yesterday. He'd spotted her as she moved around the office, doing whatever it was she did. He'd tried to ask his sisters, but they'd told him to mind his business and wouldn't answer his questions. Whatever it was Mercedes did, their firm was running better. The associates and paralegals under them seemed happier, and the work he sent out for research returned to his desk in record time.

"What you up to?" Brent asked Julian as he walked into the office and sat in the chair across from his father.

"Pro Bono stuff."

Julian had retired years ago from the firm, but he still took pro bono cases that interested him to keep him busy.

"Anything you need help with?"

His father cut him a scathing look which Brent laughed off. Julian grunted, asking about his trip.

Brent stretched his legs out and leaned back in the chair. "The trip was fine. I'm happy to be home."

Julian eyed him. "What's up with you?"

"What do you mean?" Brent asked, setting the legs of the chair down.

"Your bear is on edge." As current Alpha, of course, his father could easily read his moods.

Brent shrugged.

"Mmhmm," Julian hummed but let it go. "I talked to Trina. It's time for you to step into the Alpha position."

Brent straightened, his body tightening in anticipation. That didn't take long. "You're ready to step down?"

"Our bears are changing. It's time."

"You're not even sixty. You have time."

"But not patience," Julian grumbled.

Brent smiled at that. His father had never been blessed with patience.

"They're starting to come to you, so it's only a matter of time."

Brent nodded. Half the messages on his desk when he returned were from their bears. Though their clan spent a lot of time together, they usually only contacted the alpha when they needed something. So there weren't a lot of messages, but all the same, his father was right.

"You sure you're ready to step down?"

Julian shrugged. "Will you be ready for the challenges?"

"How many?"

"That I don't know yet. I hear rumblings, but nothing definite."

Brent sighed. He could name one off the top of his head. "The elders pushing for Abram to mate the way they're doing me?"

His father raised an eyebrow. "Despite Abram's arrogance, not many believe he's strong enough to take the position from you."

He grunted. "So that's a no."

"It's tradition for the alpha to be mated, Brent. We've talked about this. Your bear would be a lot easier to manage with a mate to tether you."

Brent swallowed a growl. He wasn't in the mood to hear the lecture from his father.

"It would be easier if your mother had grandkids to occupy her time with instead of me."

Brent snickered at the not-so-subtle warning. "Nay is giving you grandkids in a few months."

Julian grunted another warning.

"Yes, I'm aware she'll come after me next."

He crossed his arms over his chest and thought about Mercedes. Her scent had permeated the office, tempting him damn near all day. He saw the way she walked the floor, almost as if she was looking for problems. He found himself walking past her desk, hoping to get another glance of her. He looked up to find his father's dark eyes assessing him.

"It's like that then."

Brent shrugged, not admitting to anything.

Catherine breezed into his father's office. "My love," she said happily, leaning down and nuzzling the top of his head.

"Mom," Brent stood and grabbed her into an enormous bear hug. "I missed you while I was gone."

"I don't see how. You called her every damn day, twice a day," his father grumbled.

"Are you jealous, my heart? Should I spend extra time with you tomorrow?" Catherine asked.

Julian groaned, and Catherine and Brent laughed. His mother sauntered behind Julian's desk and kissed him deeply. His father growled and pulled her into his lap. Brent smiled and left them in privacy. He was coming down the hall when the front door opened. Naomi came in, her stomach large, his nieces or nephews slowing her gait. He walked to her and cupped her stomach, dropping a kiss to the top of her head. She nuzzled under his chin.

"How are you feeling?"

"Hands off my wife," his brother fussed, coming in behind his wife.

"Damn, I can't talk to my nephews?"

Naomi smacked his hand on her stomach. "You don't know what we're having."

"I have an instinct for these things," he joked with her, rubbing her belly.

He could tell her that his bear had already started the bonding process with her cubs, but he didn't think she'd appreciate it, so he kept quiet.

Brent also stayed quiet because it was a sign of his burgeoning alpha powers. Gabe would probably keep his secret, his twin was good like that, but all the same, he'd keep that tidbit to himself. Any hint of his expanding powers would have his mother on a mad dash to find him a mate.

His brother pushed him away from his wife with another growl. Lord bears got so possessive around their pregnant mates. Too bad for Gabe; it made Brent want to mess with him more.

Brent snickered. "You should be a fraction less grumpy now that you're getting sex on the regular."

"Brent," Catherine scolded, popping the back of his head. "Excuse you talking like that in my house."

"Was that not you in my father's lap getting freaky in his office?"

Catherine gasped and slapped his shoulder, swallowing her giggle. "I am your mother, Brent." she pushed him out of the way, her shoulders shaking with laughter.

The doorbell rang, and all eyes swiveled to him. He sighed, already knowing what was up.

"Mama."

His bear pushed against his control, perturbed. Whoever was on the other side of that door was of no interest to either of them.

Catherine shrugged. "I just...Eloise called and said her daughter was in town, and I thought to have her over for brunch."

Gabe snickered and guided his wife into the dining room, leaving him with their mother.

"I ain't been home but a minute, mama. Are you serious right now?" He worked to shove down his irritation and keep the bass of his bear from his voice.

"It's just brunch, Brent, my Lord." Catherine glared at him a moment before fixing her face into a pleasant smile, headed for the front door.

Brent debated leaving before he lost control of his bear and snapped at his family.

"Aht aht," Julian said, grabbing his elbow, his power settling over Brent. "You can survive brunch."

Damn it! Trapped.

***

Mercedes pulled her tiny SUV into her grandmother's yard, carefully backing close to the front door. She didn't want to have to lug the groceries far. Getting out, she gave a cursory knock to the front door as a heads up to her grandmothers. She called their names, looking around, lugging the box of cold items inside, and realized that they were in their garden. It took her three trips out to the car, but she wasn't in a rush. She glanced through the open back door and saw the two women bent over their plants. She smiled and put away the groceries, making a note of what they'd need for her next trip to the store. She finished and walked outside to their garden. It was flourishing, the fall season vegetables and herbs, ripe on their plants. She would have to come back and help them prep the harvest for the many products they made and sold at the farmer's market.

"Sadie, pumpkin pie," her grandmother Bea greeted.

Wearing her favorite pair of worn overalls and a straw hat, she was the picture of a farmer. Bea smiled at Mercedes, her beautiful face dark brown and her skin gently lined despite her age.

Mercedes rolled her eyes at her grandmother's usual greeting and joined the two women.

"You came out here in city clothes, I'm assuming you didn't come to help." Her grandmother, Lisa, commented.

Lisa's pecan-toned face was not hidden under a hat, and therefore was lined a little more than her best friend's. Her Gram wasn't much for appearances, though, and so couldn't care less. She wore a pair of khaki cargo shorts and a Hawaiian shirt faded with age.

Mercedes looked down at the simple jeans and blouse she wore. "I brought groceries."

"And thus her contribution," her grandmother, Bea, said with a cheerful smile.

Lisa rolled her eyes. "How was work this week?"

"Good," she said. "I like it there."

"I'm happy for you, though I am sad you've moved out," Bea said.

"She's allowed to grow up," Lisa told her best friend.

She'd lived with her grandparents her whole life. When her parents died, she had been barely a year old. The two widowed women moved in together, determined to each have a part in raising their only grandchild. Mercedes sat on the ground in front of them as they pulled weeds.

"Are you settling into your apartment?" Lisa asked.

"I am, Grams. It's small, but I like it."

"Well, this house is small, so you should feel right at home," Bea said.

Mercedes smiled. Her grandma could find the silver lining in anything. Bea's aura was lazily flaring, a deep green that let Mercedes know the homebody was particularly happy and content today. She took a deep breath and gazed at Lisa. The brown was swirling around her pragmatic grandmother, steady as well. She wondered how her own would look. Meeting Brent yesterday had shaken her up.

"What's going on with you, Sadie?" Lisa asked as she plucked away at her garden.

"Our Sadie has met a man," Bea said chipper, putting down her basket and beaming at her.

"Nana," she scolded quietly. "You've been reading me."

Bea shrugged. "Of course, you don't tell us anything. I have to check up on you."

"I don't lie to you guys."

"Omission is still a lie," Lisa fussed.

She looked around their garden, duly chastised. "Your cucumbers are droopy."

Lisa snapped upright and glared at Bea before glancing at the cucumbers. "I told you the moon was waning when we planted them."

"My God, must I continue to hear about that? I planted them on a whim." Bea grumbled.

Mercedes smiled, having successfully changed the subject. Or so she'd thought.

"So this man?" Bea put a hand on her hip and eyed her.

Mercedes sighed. "He works at the firm with me." Her mind went back to Brent, and her body flushed. "He has this beautiful golden aura."

"That sounds wonderful," Bea said, sighing.

Lisa scowled. "Workplace romances can be complicated."

Mercedes couldn't disagree. "He's a shifter."

"Really." Bea and Lisa shared a look.

"What?"

"Shifters aren't particularly fond of witches." Her nana worried her bottom lip.

"Not unless they're using us for our powers, you mean," Lisa grumbled.

"I don't think he's like that," Mercedes quickly interjected.

"Hmm," Lisa went back to weeding.

She knew witches and shifters didn't mix well, but there was nothing to her daydreaming about him. It wasn't like she was going to marry the man. But still…

"I don't have an animal to call. Do you think that would make a difference?"

Bea and Lisa shared another look. "You're pretty powerful even without that, so who can tell," Lisa answered gruffly.

"See if you can do something about my cucumbers," Bea ordered, changing the subject.

Mercedes narrowed her eyes but stood to do as instructed. She walked over to the cucumbers, reaching down to touch one of the leaves. She knew they didn't need her help, but her grandmothers wanted her rooted in tradition. They took every opportunity to make sure she was using her power.

"These are planted too shallow," She murmured.

Mercedes closed her eyes and took a few deep breaths to ground herself. She took off her shoes and dug her toes into the soil. Hovering her hand over the dirt, she slowly coaxed the roots of each plant deeper, giving them more space. She went down the row to each one, humming to herself and them as she worked. By the time she reached the end of the row and looked back, the plants looked better. Their stalks were standing upright. Bea smiled at her.

"Good job, pumpkin pie."

Feeling energized from the rush of power, she headed back into the cool of the kitchen to wash her hands. "Come, Grams, I want to get a look at those letters."

Lisa came in the door behind her, washing her hands at the sink. Her grandmothers kept their kitchen neat as a pin, so it was easy to find the letters they'd separated in their mail holder. She opened one and frowned at the legalese. She'd only been working at the firm for a month, so it was all gibberish to her. She bit her lip. It sounded ominous.

"I can get my bosses to have a look at this," she murmured, opening another.

"They asking the county to put a road right through where our house is," Lisa explained. "At least, that's what the pansy they sent over here told us. They're building a housing development back that way and need a road to reach it. Says if we don't sell the land to them, they'll get the county to take it using eminent domain."

Nerves started rioting in her belly. Could her grandmothers lose their land? They'd owned the house and land where it sat for decades, if not longer. The house had been in her grandfather's family long enough that the original records were scribbled on a single sheet of paper. Over the years, the family had legalized it, but her grandmother kept that aging IOU in a frame on the living room wall.

"I'll take these to work. I'll handle it, Grams." She kissed her grandmother's cheek.

"I know you'll take care of us, like you always do, Sadie." Lisa patted her cheek. "Now, are you staying for dinner?"

"Of course," Mercedes took a deep breath and pushed her worry to the back of her mind.

She would handle it when she went in to work on Monday.

3...

Mercedes fought not to fidget as she sat in the chair in front of her boss's desk. Trina was thumbing through the letters she'd taken from her grandmother, her eyes doing quick scans over the print. She'd thought long and hard about coming to the woman. She'd only been working for the firm for a month; perhaps asking for legal advice was out of line. But, Trina had invited her to sit and was seemingly unbothered by Mercedes's ask.

"The taxes and everything is paid on their property?"

"Absolutely, I handle all of that for my grandmothers." She hastened to answer.

"Hmm."

Quiet again, Mercedes clasped her hands in her lap. The silence stretched until Trina looked up.

"Gabe."

"Yeah?"

Mercedes jumped when he spoke up directly behind her. She hadn't heard him enter. For a bear his size, the man was stealthy. Distracted, she'd not felt the usual press of heat from his aura.

"I need info on eminent domain."

He sucked his teeth. "Don't you have paralegals for this shit?"

"Yes, but I want off the top of your head how successful they've been in the county." Trina shot him an exasperated glare.

Gabe frowned, and Mercedes could see the flare of his energy as he thought on it. He crossed his arms and cocked his head.

"Maybe thirty percent. What's the deal?"

"Mercedes' grandmothers are being forced off their land," Trina answered.

Gabe frowned and held out his hand. Trina put one of the letters in his hand.

"This is bullshit and easily won."

"What's going on?"

Though he'd been as equally stealthy as his brother, Brent's surprise entrance affected her differently. Her heart started racing, and heat climbed her skin from her toes up to the tip of her ears. All eyes swiveled to her. The smug smile Brent gave her made it worse. Her stomach gave a hard clench of desire. Not even her boss's raised brow could quell the temperature.

"Eminent domain case," Gabe said, dismissing her reaction and going back to the letters in his hand, effectively breaking the gathering tension.

"Dad could probably handle that in his sleep, you're wasting billable hours on it?" Brent didn't take his eyes off Mercedes.

Trina waved towards her, "It's for Mercedes—"

"I'll take care of it." Brent cut into whatever his sister was about to say.

Trina narrowed her eyes and grunted. Brent turned to Trina and gave her a guilty look, grunting back. Mercedes frowned, wondering if they were communicating. Gabe gave Brent the letter and walked out without another word to anyone. Trina and Brent were engaged in a stare-off.

She cleared her throat, and Trina growled, passing the papers off to her brother. Brent smiled in victory and shifted his attention back to her. His eyes turned smoky, lusty.

"Follow me to my office, Mercedes."

She followed his confident stride down the hall, her eyes devouring his ass in the subtle plaid suit that had to be custom made to fit such a big body. He held open the door to his office and waved her in. He left the door open, which she appreciated. Not that she'd jump him in his office, but it would be a damned close thing. She shivered as she passed him in the doorway. He'd leaned down and inhaled, letting out a low growl that sent a spiral of heat down her spine.

She settled in the chair in front of his desk, closing her eyes and taking a deep breath. Which...was a big mistake. His cologne, or whatever it was he wore, filled her senses, and now she wanted to see how it would smell right in the crook of his neck. She licked her lips and forced her eyes open. Brent was settling in his chair, his eyes devouring her. Mercedes cleared her throat and sat up straight. She needed to get her mind off the track where it was headed. She didn't breathe easy until his eyes dropped down to her grandmothers' letters.

"I went to Trina because I thought she handled real estate cases." She said after a moment.

He smiled but didn't look up. "She does."

She waited, but he didn't elaborate. "And you do corporate law."

"Mmhmm," he hummed.

She swallowed her irritation. She didn't want to seem ungrateful, but she also didn't entirely trust herself to be in this office alone with Brent for too long.

"So you can see my confusion..." she prodded.

Why was she pushing the point? Maybe she wanted to hear him say that he took the case so he could spend time with her. It would make her feel better to know that the molten heat taking over her body wasn't one-sided. He looked up then and smiled, and her stomach dipped as moisture gathered at the apex of her thighs. He sat forward, dropping his elbows to his desk, clasping his hands together. His eyes flashed golden a moment before they went back to their dark brown color.

"Do you have a problem with me helping you, Mercedes?"

And now she knew what Terrell was talking about. None of the awkwardness from their first meeting was there. In its place was control and self-assurance. It was intimidating and hot as hell. She took a shaky breath.

"I appreciate any help I can get," she said softly past the lust stealing her voice.

He smiled again, and she had to lower her eyes from the heat gathering between them.

"Who owns the property?" He asked after a tense moment of silence.

Brent leaned back in his chair and away from Mercedes' tempting scent. She was nervous. It was evident in the way she fidgeted in front of him, her hands alternating from playing in the braids draped across her breasts and flicking them over her shoulder. His eyes dropped to half-mast as he imagined gripping those braids and pulling her head back as she bucked against him. His dick swelled, tightening his pants.

"My grandmother Lisa owns it." Her soft reply broke off the fantasy that was just getting started in his head.

Right. He was at work.

He shuffled the letters on his desk and forced his mind back on the task at hand. Reading over the letter, the language in it was needlessly combative, but he wasn't surprised. Many of those companies tried to scare their elderly victims into giving up their property without a fight and at the lowest price possible.

"How long have they owned it?"

Mercedes licked her lips, and his bear snarled in hunger.

"I don't know exactly how long, but it's been in my grandfather's family for decades." She smiled, and Brent understood that he was fighting a losing battle with his bear.

"What condition is the property in?" He put his eyes on the letters and prayed he'd get through their meeting without pulling her across his desk.

"It's in great shape. My grandmothers still live there. I've lived there my whole life."

He looked up at that. "With your grandparents?"

"My parents died when I was young, so my grandmothers raised me together. My Nana moved in with Grams, and it's just been the three of us."

"Interesting," he smiled. "Is it a witch thing?"

She narrowed her eyes, studying him, deciding whether or not to get offended. Her face relaxed after a moment, and she shook her head.

"Not really, I think it's just a Grams and Nana thing. They both wanted to have a part in raising me." She stared at him and tilted her head. "You knew I was a witch?"

"Do my sisters not know?"

"They didn't ask." She crossed her arms over her chest.

"Well, it's laced all through your scent, so I assume they know and don't care," he waved it off.

His sister had tried to warn him about hurting Mercedes, which meant Trina held her in high regard. Having observed the way Mercedes ran the office, he could see why. Being a witch wouldn't change that.

She hummed. "It doesn't matter to you...to them?"

"I don't see why it would." It sure as hell didn't matter to him or his bear.

"I'm not ashamed. I just don't tell people unless asked." She explained.

"That's fair," he conceded. "So, as far as this case goes, these aren't from the county. For now, they're just threats. I will get someone out to their house to appraise it, though, to make sure they can't make a case for condemning it. We'll go from there."

"Just let me know when and I'll be there." She pulled a small planner out of her purse and made a note.

Brent nodded, his mouth watering as she leaned forward. The top of her white dress shirt gaped open, and he desperately wanted to open it wider.

He swallowed. "I'll email you when I get a date."

Her smile as she looked up tightened his chest. He had to have her. For how long was the debate he and his bear were currently waging. His bear wanted her for them on a more permanent basis. On the other hand, he didn't know how that would go over with the clan, so he would be content to have her for now...often. He adjusted in his seat at the thought.

"Thank you for your help, Brent," she stood and gathered her purse. "Of course, I'll let you know our next steps when I'm ready."

She nodded and departed, shooting him a smile over her shoulder. His bear wanted to chase her down, but he restrained them both. It would be easy to let his bear take over, but he had to remind himself of how much was at stake. As it was, his road to Alpha wouldn't be easy. His easy-going manner already had some of the bears doubting him. Bringing an alpha female in that wasn't a bear...he didn't know what kind of chaos that would sow.

4...

Mercedes straightened her skirt and looked around the small bistro. She'd put a little more effort into her outfit this morning. She'd been doing that ever since Brent had come back from his business trip. She unbuttoned the top two buttons of the linen shirt tucked into her pencil skirt. It was officially after work hours, so she could loosen up. She was regretting the heels, though. Though her grandmothers didn't have a big house, traipsing behind the appraiser as he went over every inch of it had her toes on fire. She walked over to the hostess's table and smiled.

"Hi, has Brent Hamilton checked in?"

The woman smiled and grabbed a menu. "He's here already; come, I'll take you to your table."

She followed the woman, looking around the swanky bistro. The high glass ceilings made the place seem cavernous. The hanging greenery and kitschy chandeliers worked to make the restaurant feel elegant. There were discreet and classy holiday decorations dotting the area. She spotted Brent, sitting alone at the far end of the plush bench lining the wall. There were multiple tables spread from one end of a bench to the other end's long length, chairs on the other side. It didn't seem like it would be private to her—having the tables so close together— but maybe that was a good thing. Surely she would be able to keep her hormones in check with all these people around. Although, there were at least two tables between Brent and another couple.

Her eyes took him in. He'd been out of the office all day, so she hadn't gotten her fix. Today his suit was navy blue, the jacket of it slung across the back of a chair next to him. It left him in a crisp white shirt that had to have been tailored to fit across his giant muscular arms. She wanted to snuggle into his broad chest and breathe him in. He was staring at some papers, but he looked up and smiled as she walked across the restaurant. His aura said he was tired, but it flared golden as she got nearer to him, showing his happiness at seeing her. It was hard not to be charmed by that. She hardly noticed the hostess leaving; her focus was solely on him. Brent stood as she neared.

He leaned over and gave her a small kiss on the cheek. He'd never greeted her that way, but she guessed that they could be a little less formal since they were out of the office.

"Thanks for agreeing to see me here instead of the office. I've had a crazy day."

She waved it off and sat in the chair across from him. "It's fine. Now I won't have to cook when I get home."

"Want to get business out of the way and then eat or the other way around?" He asked.

His stomach growled, and he lowered his head, a chagrined smile on his face.

"It sounds like we should eat first." She picked up the leather-bound menu in front of her.

"Like I said, crazy day." He waved a waitress over. "The restaurant is shifter run, so be careful what you order. The portions are pretty sizable."

She looked up from the menu, "thank you for the warning."

They ordered, and Mercedes' eyes widened at the amount of food he ordered. But then he was a bear shifter, so of course, he probably ate a lot. He ordered a bottle of wine for the table, and she was happy about it. She needed to unwind before she embarrassed herself in front of him. When the waitress left, silence fell between them.

"How was your day?" He asked.

She pushed her braids off her shoulder. "The appraiser said the house was in great condition. He's supposed to email you the report."

He grunted.

"How about you?"

He sighed and filled the water cup in front of him. "Meeting after meeting."

"The paralegals under you have been buzzing about the merger you're working on," she commented.

"Yeah, the negotiations are starting to get petty." He wiped a hand down his face.

They made small talk as they ate, the two of them falling into a comfortable rhythm. Was it a date? He said they'd discuss business, but every now and then, he'd touch her hand and give her longing looks that set her heart racing. Was she reading too much into it? She took another hasty sip of her wine. It was going to her head, making her giddy, and her body flushed with heat.

It was either the wine or him...

Either way, she was glad she was using rideshare to get home.

Brent stared at Mercedes, totally enthralled by her. She was beautiful, and now that they were working together, she had finally dropped the work voice, though she sometimes still used it. He asked her questions about her day just to hear that country twang. His bear was quiet, more reflective than content, biding its time. He wouldn't be completely content until he had Mercedes underneath him, taking every inch of him. That was one thing he and his bear agreed on. He adjusted in his seat, his eyes drinking in the sight of her. She smiled at him and picked up her wine glass.

"Are you gon' stare at me all night?"

He grunted, his muscles relaxing now that he'd eaten. One hunger down.

"You and your siblings are always gruntin', that's how y'all talk to each other?"

With every sip of her wine, consonants were dropping off the end of her words. His hands shook with the need to touch her. Brent wanted her whispering in his ear as he took her. It would be a miracle if he could keep his bear calm enough to be gentle with her.

At least for the first time. Let his bear tell it, she was their mate, made solely for him. That meant she would handle him, no matter how rough he got. Gods, he couldn't wait. She was staring at him, waiting on his answer.

He cleared his throat. "Yeah, it's one of the ways we communicate."

"That's interestin'," she murmured, swirling the liquid around in her glass.

She was a mix of elegant and country and so damn fascinating to him. He needed to think of something else before he moved the table from between them and pounced.

"How are your grandmothers?" It came out gruff as he struggled to get his body under control.

She smiled, her face lighting. "They fine. Fussin' about the construction and noise, but otherwise, not much bothers them."

They ordered dessert, and he kept the conversation on her grandmothers and the case they were working on together. Did it stop him from fantasizing about coaxing Mercedes into the bathroom here? He didn't think it was possible to keep the lecherous thoughts about her out of his mind. Mercedes checked the time on her phone and sighed.

"I ain't realize how long we been in here," she murmured.

"I'm sorry, I didn't mean to hold you up," he motioned for the check.

"It's fine. I enjoyed it." She lowered her eyes and typed on her phone.

The motion made him think of a submissive Mercedes, and that was dangerous. He gripped the handle of the coffee mug tight. Tension built between them until his bear was near bursting from his skin. He hastily scrawled his name across the receipt and stood.

Mercedes pulled her purse up on her shoulder. "My ride is here," she said softly.

He stepped closer to her, magic dancing between them. "I'll walk you out."

She turned, and he sighed in longing. He followed her to the front of the restaurant. The car she'd ordered was idling in the valet area. She leaned down to confirm the car was for her, and he growled at the valet attendant who was watching her. The man hastily took the ticket Brent held out, scrambling to get his car.

"This me," Mercedes stepped closer to him. "Thank you for dinner."

"It was my pleasure." He pulled her into a hug, lingering a little longer than usual. "Text me when you get home?"

She studied him a moment before nodding. "Good night."

He grunted, and she smiled.

"I'm going to figure out how to speak bear, just you wait."

He returned her smile, not doubting it, especially since it was but one of the many things he planned to teach her.

5...

Brent rubbed at his temples, glad that Friday had arrived. There were several reasons for him to be happy. One, it was the weekend, but two was sauntering over to his office, her hips swaying and hypnotizing him. She had an appointment with him. Or rather, her grandmothers did. He wanted to see the property for himself to gauge how far away the new development would be. He'd squeezed her grandmothers' case in between all the other work he had to do, stretching out the time he got to spend with Mercedes.

Once they were done at her grandmothers', he planned to ask her out to dinner. Ever since their dinner a week ago, she and Brent had been texting each other, and none of it business related. He was taking it slow with her, stalling the mating his bear wanted, and the more time that passed, his bear was growing restless, impatient. The animal was ready to claim both their mate and their position within the clan. Its aggression was starting to show in the more mundane parts of his life. Gabe and their father leaned heavily into their bear, and Brent still fought with the creature, loving the softer parts of himself. He sometimes wondered how life would've been with a different birth order.

Out of his four siblings, he was the only one warring with his nature. His father had warned him his whole life that it would take balance to control his alpha bear, and for years, Brent fought with the stubborn animal to maintain that balance. Now, with a mate on the horizon and the alpha position looming, his bear seemed to get stronger. That balance his father spoke of was getting more complicated every day to maintain. He'd upped his time outdoors with his bear, spending a lot of hours in his bear form to pacify the creature, but even that was starting to get harder.

He smiled as Mercedes stood at his door and shook away the morose thoughts. The skinny dress pants she wore clung to her shapely hips and long legs. He wanted her to take off the jacket she wore on top so he could feel the softness of the silky shirt she wore underneath. Today her braids were up in a high ponytail, and...he took a deep breath. The woman was walking temptation.

"Ready?"

"Yep. I'm ready." He shut down his computer and walked over to her.

She shivered as he put his hand to the small of her back. He didn't know if he should touch her...if he could trust himself to touch her. She leaned into his touch, and it satisfied his bear. They walked to the parking garage in comfortable silence. He opened the passenger side door for her, helping her get settled into his low sports car. He took a shaky breath as she squirmed to get comfortable in the seat.

Pure temptation that woman.

He tossed his briefcase into the backseat and removed his suit jacket, hanging it on the hanger he kept in the back. He cranked up and, using her directions, easily navigated to her grandmother's house. She was quiet, and the radio was playing rap. She looked at him and smiled.

He glanced at her quickly, "what?"

"Nothing, I didn't peg you for a trap music type of person."

"I'm from Tampa, ain't I?"

She smiled and turned back to the window, her head bobbing. He let the music's driving beat soothe some of the rough edges as his bear tried to assert itself. He sped up the car, the adrenaline helping. He pulled into her grandmothers' house half an hour later and cut the engine. The small brick house was painted white, and a colorful perfusion of flowers dotted the front lawn. He smiled because if ever he could imagine the home of witches, this house would be it. Two beautiful older black women came to the porch and greeted them.

"Sadie," one said.

Brent smiled at her over the top of the car. "Sadie?" She cut him a look. He laughed, "What? I like it."

"Pumpkin Pie," the woman said, coming down the stairs.

"Nana," she greeted, kissing the woman on the cheek.

The woman turned her happy gaze to him. His bear recognized her power, sitting up alert.

"You must be Brent."

"I am," he said, walking around the front of the car to meet her. He held out his hand.

The woman waved off his hand and grabbed him in for a small hug, her power wrapping around him. She hummed and stepped back.

"Well, aren't you a giant hunk of a man?" She said.

"Nana," Mercedes warned.

Brent swallowed his laugh.

The other woman called from the porch, "let them get in the house, Bea."

Mercedes looked back at him and came around the car to him. "Nana, Grams, this is Brent Hamilton. Brent, my grandmothers, Lisa and Bea."

Bea grabbed his hand, and he helped her back up the steps. She was spry for her age, definitely not needing the help of his arm. It was a small ranch-style house. The inside smelled fantastic, a mix of baked goods and herbs. It was bigger than it appeared from the outside, clean and neat as a pin. They guided him to the kitchen. The back door was open, a screen door keeping the bugs out while letting in a breeze. It was November and still not winter weather, but the wind was cool enough. He could see their garden and backyard. It was lush, extensive—almost two acres according to the appraisal he'd been emailed.

He noted the location as he drove up, passing a builder's sign announcing an upcoming neighborhood. Mercedes' grandmothers' house stood on the edge of the proposed community. He'd researched the builder, and according to Trina, they had a reputation of litigating their way into what they wanted.

Bea led him to sit down at the worn wooden kitchen table and offered him tea. He looked around, smiling at some of the school pictures he saw of a smiling Mercedes. He settled into his chair, his bear going quiet, a stillness that was both alert but relaxed. The two women had power, that much was evident, and his bear always respected power. He spent his life preparing to take over the alpha role, so he made it a point to be aware of it anytime it was around him.

But, he'd not met many witches in his life, so he kept his guard up. Bea set his teacup on the table, cupping his cheek.

"You're right, pumpkin pie. His aura is beautiful." Her eyes traced his face. "Warring with your nature can change that, though."

Brent felt the warning in her words, and his bear perked up in interest. He smiled to himself. Had she been talking about him to her grandmothers? That was a good sign. He was nearly as smug as his bear.

Mercedes ducked her head over her teacup. "Nana."

"Got a shit load of pent of aggression too, though. Gotta watch out for that," Lisa commented, sipping from her cup.

Mercedes just sighed.

Brent couldn't deny that, so he said nothing.

Brent smiled at her grandmother, and then her, and Mercedes' heart fluttered. He was absolutely charming, so handsome. He put his briefcase down on the table and loosened his suit jacket button, and crossed his leg over his knee, relaxing. She expected him to get right into business, but he didn't. He asked after her grandmothers, conversing with them as though he had all the time in the world. She sipped her black tea and watched him. His aura was tight around him, the golden color solid, which meant he was alert, despite his relaxed posture.

She spotted the places where his aura swirled with a deeper gold, noting the truth of her Gram's words. There was aggression there, but nothing toxic or outside of what she would find in any shifter, so she wasn't worried. Now and then, she'd see hints of that fierceness when he looked at her. She shuddered as she imagined how he'd release that pent-up aggression. Lord, she wanted to be under him when he did. She was brought out of her thoughts by his laugh.

He laughed again as her grandmothers regaled him with stories of her growing up, smiling and winking at Mercedes as they recounted her many childhood shenanigans.

She needed to be very careful around this man. Dinner with him the other night already had her halfway gone. Sexual energy sparked throughout his aura that entire dinner, and yet he hadn't pushed up on her. There were moments that she was sure he'd come across that table and demand she go home with him. Would she have said no? Her eyes traced his body. His dress shirt clung to his broad chest, and she longed to loosen the tie around his throat. How would his skin feel under her hands? She flexed her fingers.

Lisa stood, jerking her from the fantasy she was building in her head. Brent's heated gaze raked Mercedes' face, his chin lifting as he took a deep inhale. The smile he gave her made her squirm. There was a promise in that smile. It dared her to take what she wanted and promised to reward her if she did. She took a deep, shaky breath.

"I suppose you want to see the property," Lisa said, raising her eyebrow at Mercedes.

She swallowed, her cheeks heated at being caught with her nasty thoughts.

Brent chuckled and stood. "Yes, please."

They walked him outside, and again, Brent's pace was unrushed.

"They want to put a road straight through your property?"

Lisa nodded. "There's room enough to go around, but I guess our place don't match their aesthetic." Her Grams snarled.

"Look at that god-awful fence they've already erected," Bea grumbled.

"As far as I can ascertain, your taxes are paid, and there's nothing saying they have a right to your property. I've sent a cease and desist to keep them from contacting you. Everything should go through my office now."

Bea pat his hand. "Just like our Sadie, taking care of those around you."

Lisa sucked her teeth. "The boy is damn near taking up all the air with his alpha power; of course, he takes care of people he's claimed as his own."

Brent chuckled, not taking offense at her grandmother's words, which Mercedes appreciated. Not many of her boyfriends could get past the stern woman. She sucked in a breath. Why had she called him her boyfriend? They weren't that. Now, did she want to explore a relationship with him? She sighed. There was a lot she'd lose if a relationship between the two of them spiraled out of control. If she were smart, she'd leave it at that, but with every pass of his eyes over her, she was trying to figure out a way to have him and her cake, too.

"Have you taken over your clan yet?" Lisa asked.

"Not yet," he answered.

"You'll be a good alpha once you stop fighting your bear. What does that mean for our Sadie?" Lisa asked.

"Grams! Why is you in his business like that?" Her cheeks were burning.

"His business now involves you, which is our business." Lisa didn't back down.

Mercedes sighed. She knew Brent was attracted to her, but her grandmother was jumping the gun.

She turned to Bea. "Nana, please, we're here about the property."

"What you fussing at me for?" She growled. "Lisa is the one asking all the questions."

Mercedes rolled her eyes, because yes, her Grams was doing the interrogation, but she knew Bea had put her up to it.

"Julian stepping down from the high council as well?" Lisa asked despite Mercedes staring her down.

"Your father's a fair councilman. Hopefully, he's taught you well," Bea murmured.

Mercedes sucked her teeth. "Okay, that's enough, please."

Brent smirked at her. "I have some paperwork I want you to sign, officially retaining me as your lawyer and giving me permission to speak on your behalf."

Her grandmothers straightened, and they headed back into the kitchen. Hours later, Mercedes once again settled into his luxury car. Of course, her grandmothers had insisted on cooking for him. Gram pulled her aside as they were about to leave.

"He's an Alpha through and through, Sadie, you'll want to be careful."

Mercedes frowned. "Gram, we don't have any type of relationship, so I'll be fine."

Lisa scoffed. "Play all you want, Mercedes, but shifters play to keep. Don't bite off more than you can chew."

Mercedes watched Brent laughing with her Nana and nodded at Lisa's words. Brent was an easy-going person, and though she'd only seen limited glimpses of his bear, she was confident she could handle him. Right? She kissed Lisa on the cheek, her mind spinning. Waving as they drove off, her grandmother's warning was at the top of Sadie's thoughts.

"So, Sadie. Your grandmothers have a lot of power." He commented off-hand to break the silence.

"Does it bother you?"

He shook his head. "It's not my business one way or the other, just noting. Reminding myself not to piss them off."

She laughed. She liked Brent. And she liked how well he got along with her grandmothers. "So, all that stuff my grandmother brought up. I didn't tell them anything like what they were insinuating."

He smiled. "It's their place to look out for their Pumpkin Pie."

She groaned, and he laughed. "But for real, I'm not... I know we're not...We just had that one business dinner so—"

He put a hand on her leg. "Leave it, Sadie. Your grandmothers know what's what." He grabbed her hand and threaded their fingers together.

Her heart beat hard as his fingers lazily traced her knuckles. He kept his eyes on the road, seemingly content to just hold her hand. Did he just admit to being interested in her in that way? She wanted to ask, but then she didn't really. What if he said no, or worst, called her his friend...she sighed and dropped it. No need to get worked up about it.

6...

Clan time was something Brent had always enjoyed. Being amid the noisy, nosy bears soothed him, kept his bear grounded. Tonight was no different, although his mind wasn't in it like it should be. Usually, he used the time to catch up with cousins and make sure the bears were settled, happy. Tonight, his mind was where it had been for the past month.

On Mercedes.

He'd been spending time with her at work dealing with her grandmother's case, and if he were honest, simply finding reasons to talk to her. After work, they'd gone from texting to talking over the phone. Long conversations that kept him up well after they hung up. He checked his phone to see if she'd texted him back. Brent sighed at the three dots indicating she was typing. It was a simple question he'd asked. His bear was riled, waiting on her answer.

Sadie: *tomorrow?*

Brent smiled, anticipation brightening his mood significantly.

Brent: *The whole day?*

Sadie: *greedy*

He laughed because hell yeah, he would be...especially if he managed to talk her into coming back to his place.

His brother bumped his shoulder. "Where are you?"

He slipped his phone into his pocket and took a sip of his beer. He looked up at Gabe. "What's up?"

"You asked her out yet?"

He couldn't help the satisfied smile that tilted his lips. "Just now."

"About time, ol' scary ass," Gabe said.

"Man, what the fuck ever. I've been spending time with her."

"Working on a case that should have been over weeks ago," Gabe interjected.

"The case is over," he admitted. A few well-placed phone calls had put a stop to the letters and harrassment.

"Then what the hell are you meeting with Mercedes about in your office?"

He shrugged.

"Pathetic," his brother mumbled.

He couldn't even dispute it. "We went out to dinner again a couple of weeks ago."

"Did you tell her you wanted to smash?"

"What? No."

Gabe shrugged and took a swig out of his beer. "Then that doesn't count."

"I know you aren't talking. Didn't you trick your mate into marrying you?"

"After I told her we were mates and she didn't believe me. Completely different circumstances."

Brent grunted. "My bear insists that she's ours."

Gabe paused and lowered his beer bottle. "Is that right?"

"Shit, I don't know how I feel about it," Brent shook his head. He didn't want to scare her off. "Do you think the bears will accept her as Alpha female?"

"You shouldn't give a fuck what they think. You need to quit denying your bear's instincts. I've told you about that. "

Brent sighed. "You're not alpha, Gabe. It's a different struggle. You don't have to care how your actions affect everyone."

"And you care too much. Quit all that nice shit and get what you want. You are alpha. Worst they can do is challenge you." Gabe shrugged, uncaring about it one way or the other.

"So I'll spend my first few months as alpha battling with our clan?"

Gabe snorted. "Bust the first disrespectful one over the head, and then you won't have to worry about it."

Brent had to chuckle because his brother was ridiculous. "Thank the gods I'm taking over as Alpha and not you."

Gabe shrugged and dropped the subject, not the least bit offended. His brother looked around the bar, emptying his beer bottle. "Please tell me I won't have to keep doing this hanging with the alpha bullshit."

"Oh my God, Gabe, it's like two hours with your brother, you can't manage that?"

"I don't mind you." He waved around to all the other bears from their clan currently taking over the small bar where they were sitting. "It's all this shit."

"It's called socializing; it would do you some good. I'm sure Nay's happy to have you out from underneath her."

"I spend most of my time on top."

Brent snorted and ignored the innuendo. He did not want to hear about his brother's sex life.

"Nay's prowl socializes around a big bonfire outside. Can we do that instead?" Gabe said after a moment.

Brent pursed his lips and thought about it. "I don't see why we can't, except we have to do it outside of the city. Who has a big enough property that's not in the clan neighborhood?"

Gabe nodded over to one of their elder members.

"Bet," Brent said, standing. He walked over to the older bear. "Nate, how many acres you got out in the country?"

"'Bout eight," was the older man's answer.

"Gabe suggested a bonfire for our clan outing. You up for that?"

"That sounds amazing!" One of the younger female bears inputted.

"Yeah, we can all grab some liquor and food and meet at Nate's." The rest of the bears started murmuring, and soon the idea spread.

"Ok," Brent said. "Nate, we can all meet at your house, in what?"

"Give me an hour and a couple of the younger bears to gather wood."

A cheer went up around the bar. Brent looked over at his brother. Gabe lifted his drink.

"Let's roll, Hamilton Clan," Brent announced.

Brent met his brother at his truck and climbed into the passenger seat. "Satisfied?"

Gabe smiled at him. "I am, actually."

***

Hours and many red cups later, Brent convinced his brother to let him out at Mercedes' small apartment complex. He shuffled up the stairs to her place, tapping on the door. He tapped again after a few moments of her not answering, squinting as she snatched open the door.

"Why you bangin' on my door?" She demanded, her eyes narrowed. "The hell are you doing here? Do you know what time it is?"

Lord have mercy that accent. Brent closed his eyes and swayed. Bracing a hand on the door frame, he opened his eyes and watched Mercedes through lids that wouldn't entirely stay up. She put her hands on her hips, her breasts thrusting out with the motion.

"I wanted to see you." He pulled his phone out of his pocket and shook it at her.

She narrowed her eyes and sucked her teeth. "I thought we agreed on tomorrow."

His bear gave a hungry growl, his mouth watering as his gaze raked her figure. She wore thin, short shorts and a tank top that was clinging to her curvy body. Her nipples were poking out, and he closed his mouth to keep from drooling.

"Is it not technically tomorrow?" He gave her a lazy smile. "All I could think about all night was you."

She rolled her eyes and moved to the side. "Come in before you wake up the rest of the building."

He growled, lunging forward through the door. She closed and locked the front door, heading towards her bedroom. Brent followed, wobbling on his feet. He wasn't quite sloppy drunk but drunk enough for his bear to be more in charge than he. The damned animal was taking full advantage. His senses were cranked up to a thousand, his every breath taking in more of Mercedes's sleepy scent.

"Shoes off and wash your hands," she ordered, pointing him towards the sink.

He hastily did as she bid and followed her scent to the only bedroom in the place. She shook her head and flopped on her bed, stifling a yawn. She cocked her head to the side, her lips twitching as she fought a smile.

"So you came over here after a night out with your boys, drunk, wanting some pussy."

Her statement shocked him so much. And said in that sultry country tone, his dick danced in his pants. He growled, tugging on her legs, dragging her to the end of the bed. She squealed and giggled.

"I most definitely did." He dropped to his knees at the foot of her bed and buried his head between her legs, taking a deep breath.

Her scent wrapped around him, enticing yet comforting the shit out of him. Fuck, this woman was everything. The more time he spent with Mercedes, the more he and his bear were getting on the same page regarding her. She was his mate, and it could be the influence of the hooch he'd drunk, but all the reasons to resist her were seeming petty the longer he kneeled between her thighs. He shook his head and fought to push the animal back. Between his bear taking control and the alcohol, there was a slight haze over his mind.

"Boundaries," he managed to get out past his animal. "Am I going past your boundaries?"

His voice was gruff, his power raising, the cloying scent of the change permeating the room as his bear rushed forward to re-take control.

Her eyes softened. "I'll stop you if you go too far."

His chest rumbled with a purr.

She rubbed the top of his head, laughing. "My bed ain't big enough to fit you, though."

He growled and nipped her thigh. She hissed, her body relaxing beneath his hold.

"It'll hold me," he said, his voice full of his bear's magic.

Mercedes closed her eyes and fought the lust heating her skin. The fact that he thought he could come over to her house, all type of hours in the night, should've been a turn-off for her. But, she'd wanted him for weeks now, and between the calls and text messages, she'd worked up a fantasy that would make anyone blush. He'd been a perfect gentleman throughout the whole process, never rushing or pressuring her, despite the lust she could see in his eyes when they were together. To see him now, drunk with all his walls down, did something to her.

Brent slid her shorts to the side, his fingers expertly teasing against the folds of her sex. Lord, did he know what to do with his fingers.

"You're so fucking warm and wet," he said, his voice sending goosebumps down her skin. "I want a taste so bad, Mercedes."

"Brent," she whispered, her heart thundering at the need in his voice.

She was debating if he was too drunk for her to ride him. He dropped a chaste kiss to her pussy, his fingers playing in the folds. She whimpered, shivered. He was making it hard to behave. Brent's breath was hot against the skin of her thighs as he dragged open-mouthed kisses down her legs and back up to her sex. The coarse hair of his beard sent shivers down her back as it sensitized her skin further.

He looked up, and his eyes were flashing between molten gold and deep dark black, his bear peeking through his heated gaze. He was battling his bear, a war he was obviously losing. He was gone, his animal damn near in complete control. It spoke to Brent's strength that he wasn't sprouting fur nor claws with his animal so close to the surface. She'd witnessed firsthand the way shifters got when they were out of control in both manager positions she'd had. She sighed and decided to be the calm head in this situation. If he were sober, perhaps she would've taken him up on his offer. But, not while he was drunk. She didn't want any reason for him to regret what they did together.

She lifted his head by his chin. "You're drunk." She used her other hand to move his fingers from her sex before his petting had her changing her mind.

"Want you," he pleaded, nuzzling his head between her breasts.

"I know, baby," she whispered, pulling up his head and softly kissing his lips. "Trust me when I tell you I definitely want what you're offering, but I want you to know what you're doing for our first time."

He growled and leaned forward, giving her a deep possessive kiss. "Mine," he murmured.

"We'll see, won't we," she whispered against his lips.

He was making a lot of claims. Where was all this when he was sober, and they were alone?

"Now, come on, no outside clothes on in my bed."

The growl he released sent tingles down her spine. He stood, stumbling just a bit before standing, his denim-clad erection directly in front of her. His shaft was thick in his boxer briefs, the outline making her mouth water as she dragged his pants down over it. It pulsed, and she looked up, that golden stare sending heat throughout her stomach. His growl was all feral animal as he stared down at her. She licked her lips and debated getting just a taste. She wrapped her hand around it, reveling in the heat and steel feeling of his erection. It flexed in her hand, and Brent held the back of her head and grabbed her bonnet. He snatched it off and tossed it across the room, running his hands through her braids, tugging on them.

"Brent," she warned, moisture flooding her pussy as he tightened his grip on her hair. Lord, this man would be dominant as hell, and damn if it didn't push all her buttons.

"A taste, Sadie," he pleaded as he shucked his collared shirt, leaving his chest bare.

Her stomach clenched, and she licked her lips, fighting the temptation to suck on all that glorious skin he exposed. She kissed him through his underwear and stood, her hand lingering.

"No drunk sex for you," she said hoarsely, more to remind herself. She kissed his cheek.

"You teasing me," he whined, pulling her into his broad chest.

"Bed, Mr. Hamilton." She spun them around and pushed his forehead, and he fell back, dragging her with him. "We both can't fit in this bed, Brent."

He hummed and pulled her leg over his, burrowing his head into her neck. "I'll buy you a new one tomorrow. One that's bear-sized."

She chuckled as he licked across her neck, dropping kisses. "You can't fit a bear-sized bed in this apartment."

She'd had a hell of a time helping the delivery people get her queen-sized bed in. No way was he getting anything over a king-size through her door. He hummed in answer. Mercedes ran her hand down his thick arms, never daring to touch him like this before. He was massive, his body taking up the majority of her bed. She felt dainty, safe resting atop his chest. Brent nipped the skin under her jaw, the hair of his beard tickling her.

"Stop kissing me and go to sleep. The sooner you sleep, the sooner we can fuck when you wake up."

His growl against her skin sent electric pulses straight to her clit. He pulled their hips together, grinding his dick into her center.

"Bet," he whispered.

He gripped her chin, holding her still as he expertly claimed her mouth. She tasted the liquor he'd consumed and a taste that had her skin tight, her body needy.

"Good night," he whispered, pulling back. He buried his head back into her neck. "My mate," he sighed and whispered, sleep in seconds.

She reared back and stared at him in shock at his words. Were they drunken ramblings, or was he serious? She traced his strong jaw and full lips, her favorite feature. He would probably forget it all once he woke in the morning. She sighed.

Meanwhile, she was left horny and very much awake. She wiggled to get comfortable. Finding a spot, finally, she closed her eyes. She'd worry about it in the morning.

7 ...

Brent sighed as his bear pushed against his skin, waking him. What the persistent animal wanted was a mystery to him at the present moment. As it was, he barely remembered going out with his clan last night. He registered the weight on top of him a scant second later, and his morning erection twitched in reaction. He slid his hands up the warm skin of Sadie's legs and breathed in deep, pulling in her scent.

All at once, all of last night came rushing back to him. His bear had nearly gotten them into something they weren't ready for. He was in Mercedes' bed, his ankles hanging off the edge. If he moved one tiny inch, he was likely to tumble off of it. He needed to fix that. No way would he be spending nights in her tiny ass bed. He ran his hands down her back and over the curve of her ass, resisting the urge to squeeze. The shorts were already short and were now bunch high on her thighs, exposing her cheeks.

He rubbed his hand across her soft skin. She was gorgeous and surrounded by her scent, here in her room, he closed his eyes in bliss. She gave a sleepy sigh and nuzzled into his chest. He looked down, and his gaze traced her face, memorizing every single feature. She looked up at him and smiled.

"Hey, are you hungover?" She murmured, her sleepy tone making him crave the days when she would be in his bed permanently.

"I don't get hangovers." He shuffled her forward until she straddled him. "Your bed is too small," he complained.

She smiled and cupped his cheek. "I told your ass that last night."

"Sorry, I came in drunk."

"You took a lot of liberties, alpha."

He growled, his bear rising. "Why is there no deference when you use my title," he asked, nipping at Mercedes's collarbone.

She smiled impishly, and damn if he didn't fall in love just a little.

"Is that what you want in a woman, deference?"

He carefully turned until she was underneath him. "I'll take a little bit of it in my woman," he murmured, kissing her shoulders.

"Excuse you, one night in my bed does not make me your woman."

He grunted, using his leg to separate her thighs. He sucked on the skin of her neck. "I seem to remember a promise of sex this morning."

She laughed, "Oh, we remembered last night?"

He looked down in satisfaction at the hickey he'd left on her neck. His bear wanted to leave a lot more marks than that. "We most definitely remember last night. I behaved and went to sleep, and I was promised fucking this morning," he whispered against her skin.

"Let me up to brush my teeth, and we'll see about all that." She whispered.

She climbed from beneath him, and his gaze followed her to her narrow bathroom. He got up behind her, and she smiled, handing him a toothbrush still in the package. They brushed their teeth together, and he leaned against the wall, feeling the intimacy in the act. He could easily see them falling into the rhythm of life together. They finished, and she pushed him out so she could use the restroom. He walked back over to her bed, finding his pants and retrieving the condom he'd put in his back pocket before he'd come over. Palming it, he flopped down onto her bed. He cursed as it hit the floor. She rushed out of the bathroom, a towel in hand.

"Not you broke my damn bed," she snickered.

He winced. "I'll buy you another one."

She tossed the towel at him. "Tuh-day."

He sat forward and pulled on her t-shirt until she fell on top of him. "Today," he promised, kissing her, spearing his tongue in her mouth.

She moaned and wrapped her arms around his neck. Her legs went around his waist, and his hips jerked.

"Need you," he murmured against her lips. "Say yes, Sadie."

"Yes," she whispered.

He grew out his claw and tore through her shorts and panties, retracting it to cup her sex. Damn, she was wet. His bear rolled through his body and pushed power outward, anticipation making his hands shake. To say he wanted Mercedes was an understatement. From the first moment he saw her, he wanted her. Now, the most pressing question was whether or not his bear would play nice about it.

As it was, power flooded his body, amping up his need for her. He slid a finger into her pussy, and hissed as she clenched around him, moisture sliding between her thighs. Hunger and impatience nearly took over, but he pushed it down. He wanted to savor every bit of her.

"You promised to spend the whole day with me," he murmured against her skin as he kissed a path down her chest.

She grabbed his head, smoothing across his hair and arching her back. "I don't remember that."

He growled and bit down on her nipple through her shirt. She moaned and gripped his head tight. He released her nipple, nuzzling into her stomach, breathing in her scent. Impatient to taste her, he licked her skin, dragging his teeth across her hipbone. Mercedes arched her body the moment his mouth covered her pussy. Brent licked across the folds of her sex, savoring her taste. He feasted on her, sucking her clit into his mouth. Her every whimper spurred him on. He inserted a finger, hooking into her. Her answering moan was music to his ears.

He ate her with a hunger that had been weeks building. Mercedes was chanting his name with every flick of his tongue. Her legs tightened, and she screamed as she came. His chest rumbled in satisfaction as he gripped his dick. He slid the condom on, hissing as it snapped against his skin. His hands shook as he pulled Mercedes's legs open. He leaned forward, fitting their hips together.

"Look at me, Mercedes," he demanded.

Her eyes lifted to half-mast, lust darkening them. She bit her lip and lifted her arms to grip her headboard. "You gon' show me what you working with?"

"Taunting me?" He slid his dick against her wet folds. "You better take every inch."

He pushed in, working through her clenching channel. Mercedes sucked in a surprised breath as he kept going. She whimpered, closing her eyes tight. He leaned forward, resting his weight on her, nuzzling her neck as her body tensed the deeper he pushed.

"You can take me," he coaxed, dragging open mouth kisses over her skin.

He bit down slightly, careful not to go too far, despite his bear's urging. He hissed, closing his eyes once he was fully seated. She was hot and wet, squeezing around his dick. Her arms came around his neck, her nails scraping his skin. He gave her a moment to get used to his size. Her body gradually relaxed beneath him.

He inhaled against her skin, licking a path up to her ear. "You ready for me?"

She nodded, canting her hips. Brent gripped her waist and started moving. He fucked into her slowly, reveling in the feel of her. The feeling of their skin sliding together, the scent of her, he savored it all. He scraped his teeth against her neck, sucking on her skin, leaving marks that Brent knew he hadn't earned, but he couldn't stop himself.

"More, Brent," Mercedes whispered.

He sped his strokes, pushing harder, deeper. Mercedes took all of him, arching her back, her hips meeting his every thrust. He kissed her, swallowing her moans, their tongues slowly dancing. He'd known sex with her would be incredible, and yet he still hadn't been prepared for the way his body ignited.

"Fuck, you feel amazing, Sadie," he panted, pulling from their kiss.

Her magic danced across his skin, and he damn near lost it. His bear reared forward, his power electrifying the air between them.

"Oh God, Brent!" she hissed, her legs tightening around him.

Her pussy gripped him tight, and he cursed and went wild, holding her down as he fucked into her, chasing the orgasm that was barreling down on them both.

"That's it, nearly there," he panted. He closed his eyes tightly, trying to hold on for her. But she was clenching around him, her wet heat quivering on his dick. "Give it to me, Sadie." He ordered.

She obeyed his order, her nails digging into his arms as she screamed and came. Thank fuck, because he was right behind her. He drove in one last time before shouting her name. If he thought he was enamored with her before, it was a wrap now. He would hold on to Mercedes no matter what it took.

8...

Mercedes's body was still buzzing, her muscles languid and relaxed as she spread jam over the last piece of bread she had in the house. Brent was sitting at the small café table she had, squirming in the little chair, sipping at the black tea she'd fixed him.

She plopped a saucer down in front of him. "Don't break my chair with all that wiggling."

He gripped her waist and dragged her to him. "Don't do me like that," he growled.

She laughed, and cupped his cheek. "When I'm done feeding you, we're headed to the store."

"I love your smile," he murmured instead of answering.

Her heart tripped, and she cleared her throat. Brent still hadn't mentioned anything about her being his mate, and with the haze of lust gone and the clear light of day streaming through her sheer curtains, good sense was slowly returning. She couldn't get involved with someone who was technically her boss. What if something went wrong and she was fired? It was a significant risk.

"Brent, this morning was amazing..." she bit her lip.

"But," he prodded, his hands caressing her back.

"I don't think a relationship between us is a good idea."

"Hmm," he murmured, inhaling against her skin.

"That's all you have to say?" She pulled back so she could look into his eyes.

"Sadie, you can call this between us whatever you want, so long as it means I still get to see you and spend time with you." He stared into her eyes, his face serious.

She lowered her gaze when she couldn't keep eye contact. "I just don't think it would look good, me dating my boss."

He narrowed his eyes, and she could nearly see the calculation going on in his head. "So, your issue is people knowing we're dating."

Was it just that? "Partly. I mean, I need this job; I can't afford to get fired if it doesn't work between us."

He studied her before nodding. "So let's negotiate."

"Negotiate?"

"I don't want this between us to end. How can I reassure you?"

She bit her lip and backed away. She needed space to think. "My friend mated a cougar. It didn't go well. That, plus the possibility of ending this affair unemployed, has me nervous."

"Fine, anything that happens between us will stay between us. Plus, I'll guarantee it won't affect your job."

She scoffed, "You can't just say that."

"You want it written?"

His face was serious. Nerves fluttered in Mercedes's stomach, and she felt silly, childish even. But, she brought the bulk of income into her grandmothers' household. So...she nodded.

He stood and walked over to the small desk she kept in her living room and picked up a pen and notepad.

"Okay, your job is secure. What else?" His tone was neither mocking nor condescending.

She relaxed marginally. "You don't have to write this down, but for now, until we decide whether or not this will go anywhere, I don't think we should go public."

His body tensed. "You want to hide me."

"Not you, not...I just mean, like no dates in public, yet. Tampa's not that big, it could get back to your sisters, or heaven forbid, your clan. How would they feel to know you're dating a witch?"

He sighed but didn't argue the point, which meant there would be a problem with the bears if they dated.

"Promise you'll keep an open mind about us being maybe more," He demanded softly.

Her heartbeat stuttered, and she sucked in a surprised breath. So last night had not been a fluke.

"Brent, you're talking reckless," she whispered.

He started writing, ignoring her words. He looked up. "Anything else you want to add?"

She shook her head, wondering what he meant by 'maybe more.' He'd mentioned mating last night. Was that what he meant?

Brent scribbled his signature before sliding the notebook over to her. "Sign it, then."

Mercedes peered down at the page, swallowing the lump in her throat. "Renegotiate after six months?"

"At least."

"How did you come up with that number?"

He licked his lips, and his eyes flashed with his animal. "I can do a lot in that time frame."

She took the pen from him with shaking hands and signed next to his name.

His smile was pleased, just short of smug. "We have an accord." He scribbled 'Mercedes lil affair idea' at the top of the page and moved the notebook to the side.

"I can't believe us. Your sisters can pick apart that contract in minutes," she warned him, rolling her eyes at the title.

"Seconds," he admitted, pulling her back into his arms. "But do you feel more secure?"

She took a second to assess how she felt before nodding.

"Then it's worth it."

She hummed and picked up his empty teacup and peered inside. She needed to change the subject before she talked herself out of the whole thing.

"Reading my tea leaves?" He asked, pulling her into his lap.

"As a matter of fact, I am," she grinned at him and peered again. "Ooh, taking over the clan soon."

He rested his chin on her shoulder. "I am. How do you feel about that?"

"What does it have to do with me?" she stalled, seeing the answer for herself in his cup.

"So, you can see me becoming alpha but can't see yourself with me in the bottom of that cup?" He sucked at her neck.

"You're leaving all types of marks all over my skin," she scolded. "That's as good as a public declaration." Her body tingled, though, thinking of some of the areas he'd managed to leave marks.

"Mmhmm, too many liberties?" he teased, seeing through her deflection. "I'll keep it below the neck. What else do you see?" he asked quietly, nibbling on her shoulder.

"You're moving soon."

"I don't mind finally moving onto the clan property," he murmured against her skin. "My dad had houses built for each of my siblings when the clan bought the property. Now that I have you, it makes sense to use it finally."

She smiled and shook her head at his optimism.

"A lot of your leaves are concentrated near the handle, so a lot happening around your home and family."

He grunted.

She put down the cup and glanced at him. "This doesn't bother you?"

"What?"

"This! Me being a witch."

"Nope." He rubbed her back.

"I thought shifters and witches didn't get along."

"I get along with everyone," was his answer as he kissed her.

She could only smile at that truth she'd seen firsthand. Observing him at work was becoming a habit of hers. There wasn't a single person in the office who had a bad thing to say about Brent. She stood as the doorbell rang.

"That's probably the food."

"Thank God, I'm starving."

"He says having eaten all the bread and cereal in my house," she muttered.

He smiled, moving past her to answer the door.

9...

"I can't believe I talked myself out of you taking me on dates," she told him as they entered the furniture store.

He pulled her back into his chest, walking her through the aisles towards the bedding section. He nibbled on her neck. "Breakfast didn't count?"

She snorted and pushed out of his arms. "It absolutely does not."

"Hmm," he pulled her back and kissed her. "I'll have to find low-key ways for us to go out. We can always leave town for a weekend."

Ooh, she liked the thought of that. A baecation. Still, she stepped out of his arms. Making out in a furniture store was not a good idea.

He clasped their hands together, pulled her closer, and walked her to the store's bedroom section. She winced as she saw the prices on some of the furniture. He'd brought her to a shifter run store, so considering the varying sizes of shifters, she could imagine they wanted a pretty mint for the sturdy furniture. She would never have spent money in this store, but he was replacing her bed since he broke it. She stopped at a queen-size bed. It wasn't that much bigger than her full-sized one, but the textured wooden headboard and cinnamon-colored linen sheets looked like a dream. It was bohemian, and her breath caught at its beauty. Dare she look at the price?

"That the one you want?"

She nodded.

"That's too small," he grumbled, even as he waved down an employee.

"Everything is small compared to a bear," she reminded him.

"That's true." He wrapped his arms around her waist and nuzzled into her neck. "Since we're done here, let's go to my condo. We can spend the rest of the weekend there in a bed big enough for us to roll around in."

Her stomach dipped, her sex clenching. She slapped at his arms. "Public, Mr. Hamilton. But, that sounds tempting," she admitted. "I have to go visit my grandmothers, so I can't spend all day with you."

He growled but stepped back, coming around to stand beside her. "Aht-aht, you said all day. I can go with you."

"I wasn't inviting you, Alpha. And I did not agree to all day. You need to reread your text messages."

He growled and leaned down, his teeth nipping her shoulder. "There you go, using my title all flippant like."

She laughed, hissing as he gripped her hair tightly, applying just enough pressure to make her wet. She shuddered in need at the thought of all that power he'd unleashed on her this morning.

"I love these braids," he murmured, using them to pull her head back, exposing her neck.

The store employee cleared their throat, and Brent released her. Lord, they were already half-failing their rules.

"We'll take this whole set up. Is the bedding sold here as well?" Brent asked.

"It is," he answered.

"Okay. That too then."

She gasped at the expense. "Brent, you don't—"

"Did you need anything else?" He raised a brow, his face telling her that he wasn't taking no for an answer.

She shook her head, stunned and excited at the thought of her new bed. She was already rearranging the bedroom and thinking about the curtains she'd get to match it. She couldn't wait to get to a thrift store. She followed him to the register. He handled the whole thing, shaking his head as the guy started to read the total. He handed over his card and filled out her address for it all to be delivered.

"Are we leaving straight from here to go to your grandmothers', or do you have time to take the delivery?"

She licked her lips. "I normally help them in the garden, so I like to get over there before it gets too hot."

He turned back to the counter but then seemed to pause. He smiled and faced Mercedes, moving into her space. "You can spend the night with me after and then take the delivery tomorrow." He murmured into her ear.

She bit her lip and considered it. Brent's eyes glowed gold before releasing a low growl against the side of her neck. She swallowed a moan and assented.

"Okay."

The satisfied smile he gave before turning back to the register sent her stomach flipping in nervousness. Now, instead of going to see her grandmothers, she wanted to go back to his apartment. Brent grabbed her hand once he completed his purchase.

"I need to go home and change if I'm going to be gardening."

She eyed him as he unlocked the car. "You're seriously going to come over?"

"Think I can talk your Nana into cooking?"

"Oh my God," she chuckled and slid into his car.

***

Bea's face was beaming as Brent pulled into her grandmother's driveway. Brent chuckled as Mercedes sucked her teeth next to him. It was clear the witch was happy to see them both together. He knew Catherine would be the same if it had been him bringing Mercedes home. His mother would immediately start planning out their wedding. He reached over and grabbed Mercedes' hand.

"Your grandmother seems happy to see me," he teased.

She sucked her teeth again and rolled her eyes. "So anyway."

He laughed as she snatched her hand from his and opened the car door. He followed her out and went to his trunk, gathering the items they'd picked up at the grocery store. Brent was a family man, so he really admired how Mercedes cared for her grandmothers. He spent most of his off time at his family's homes, whether it be his parents or his siblings, so he could appreciate the way she put them first. He leaned over and bussed a kiss across her Nana's cheek.

"It's good to see you again, Ms. Bea."

She cupped his cheek. "So polite. Come on in."

Mercedes was already in the kitchen greeting her other grandmother. He dropped the bags on the counter and held out his hand for her no-nonsense grandmother.

"Ms. Lisa," he greeted.

She gave him a small smile and shook his hand. "Alpha."

He snorted. She had about as much respect as Mercedes had when she used his soon-to-be title.

"Not quite yet," he told her.

She stared at him, her eyes probing until she gave another small smile and nodded.

"I'm glad you're here. You can help me haul this soil around." Lisa said, patting his cheek.

Mercedes snickered from the refrigerator where she was stocking it. He followed her grandmother outside and, for a few hours, did as she ordered. Hauling dirt one way, along with any hoeing and digging she deemed necessary. The sun hit the back of his neck, and he was happy to be outside. His bear, ever-present and looming large, always enjoyed being outdoors. The physical labor was keeping the persistent animal under some semblance of control. At one point, her grandmothers had them both in the garden. He was fascinated watching the three of them using their magic to tend to the various plants.

Their power seemed effortless, dancing around the three women as they dug their hands into the dirt. He'd stood transfixed with Mercedes, her face flushed with effort as her grandmothers guided her. In their conversations over the phone, she'd told him that the learning never stopped. The older women were always helping her expand her power and hone it. Bea was a very traditional witch, wanting Mercedes well-versed in their family history, while Lisa, the more curious of the two of them, pushed Mercedes to work past her limits.

Seeing her with them, using her magic, was another side of Mercedes. One he liked, and his bear admired. Life with her wouldn't be boring, that was for sure. Nearly two hours ago, Bea had guided an exhausted Mercedes into the house and left him alone with her taciturn grandmother. Sadie would peek out of the door to check on him every now and then, shooting Lisa a warning look before heading back inside.

"So this dance you're doing with Sadie?"

Brent swung around, startled as Lisa walked up on him. Fur slid out of his arms, a growl rattling his chest. He gripped the shovel in his hand, pulling his claws from the wood. Lisa's face was calm as she waited for his answer.

"Ms. Lisa, it's not a good idea to startle bears," he said once he wrestled his bear down.

She shrugged and put her hands up to her trim hips. "Noted."

He took a deep breath. "Sadie and I are seeing how it goes, to answer your question. Whatever that means for us is between her and me."

She studied him with her head tilted. "Fair enough. We'll lose the light here soon, so I guess we've done enough."

He smiled at her gruff tone.

She still stared at him, her eyes out of focus. She sucked in a sharp breath. "The battle's getting harder with your bear, then? Part of Sadie's power is getting to the root of conflicts. She doesn't fight her nature, so I imagine her magic will start working on you sooner or later. She can't help it. Will you resent her for it?"

For helping him with his bear? His heart raced, and he closed his eyes, taking a deep, calming breath. "There are some finer points my bear, and I don't agree on, but I would never take it out on Mercedes." He admitted.

"I've asked around about you. They call you the 'Placid Alpha'. I take it you don't show a lot of people the power hiding underneath that affable demeanor."

Brent had to smile at that. He moved differently than his father and brother, and he saw no need to change that just because he would become alpha.

"Sadie says your aura is bright, not my area of expertise, so I can't confirm. I've taught her well enough to believe her word. What that means is whatever you're afraid of with your bear is not this big, dark thing you're making it out to be."

He sucked in a breath at how close she came to his fear. His bear rose, the animal pushing against his skin, alpha power flaring. He pushed it down along with his aggravation, knowing it stemmed from defensiveness. He smiled, putting on the camouflage he used so often to get out of uncomfortable situations.

Lisa held up her hand. "Aht-aht, no need for charm, I'll mind my business. Just warning you that my granddaughter won't let you fight your nature for long."

She walked away and left him standing there shook. How the woman got to the core of him after only knowing him mere days was disconcerting. It wasn't that he denied his bear or their power, but he didn't give the aggressive animal the leeway most shifters did. The closer he came to claiming the alpha position, the more he and his bear fought, but so far, he was managing the balance. Hell, if he gave in to his nature as she said, he'd have had Sadie tied to his bed very thoroughly marked and mated. He put the tools they'd been using away and went to retrieve Sadie, pushing the whole thing from his head.

He stopped at the screen door, his ears perking up when he heard Bea ask Sadie nearly the same question Lisa had asked him. He paused, wanting to listen to her answer.

"I like him, Sadie," Bea said plainly.

"Me too, Gram. He says I'm his mate." Mercedes pushed her braids over her shoulder.

"Explains the ties I see already."

"Ties between us?" Mercedes sat straighter.

Bea snorted, "Don't act like you don't feel them."

"I just..."

"Mmhmm, deny all you want, my love. My only worry is how his clan will take the relationship, have the two of you talked about it?"

Mercedes sighed. "Not yet. For now, I asked him to keep this thing between us under wraps."

"Oh, Pumpkin Pie, a secret affair? We'll see how long his bear agrees to that. You can answer that for yourself, Brent, if you're done eavesdropping," Bea said dryly.

His cheeks heated, and he walked into their kitchen. "It was an accident."

"The question about your clan?"

He looked to Mercedes, but she shrugged.

"We haven't gotten that far yet," he admitted.

Bea hummed but said nothing.

Mercedes stood. "You're ready to head out?" Her voice was overly loud, her discomfort with the subject easy to read.

He nodded, rushing to the sink to wash his hands. Brent was happy that they were heading back to his place. It would give them a chance to talk.

10...

Brent sniffed at the plastic container Lisa put in his hand as she walked them to the front door. The scent of cinnamon and honey had him smiling in anticipation. It was her thank you for the help she'd told him. Mercedes kissed her grandmothers' cheeks and headed down the stairs. Brent caught her in the driveway and spun her around, pulling her into his chest. She smiled and tiptoed, kissing his cheek. It had been a good day, and while she'd not been surprised—Brent seemed to get along with anyone—she appreciated that he'd spent so many hours helping out her grandmothers, and not one complaint had crossed his lips.

"Thank you for today," she murmured.

"It was no problem, and I got cinnamon rolls out of the deal." He wiggled the container.

She snorted as he walked her to the car, their hands clasped together. He released her and opened the door for her. He waited until she was seated and buckled in, and instead of closing the door, he leaned down and put his hand on the leather seat between her legs. She shivered, and her lids lowered. Lord, the man, was potent. He smelled sweaty, and his shirt was dirty, yet, it was the most attractive she'd ever found him. Her body softened, her heart more so as he crowded her space.

"You look tired. Let me take you home and cook for you," Brent said softly.

She nodded, a smile tilting up her lips. She'd already packed her bag, intending to spend the night with him, but he still hadn't taken it for granted. She liked that. He leaned down and kissed her. It started innocently enough, but he licked at her lips, and once she opened her mouth, all bets were off. He dipped in his tongue, twining it with hers for a long, sensuous kiss that heated her blood, making her crave him.

She pulled back. "Let's save the making out for someplace other than my grandmothers' driveway."

"There's no one else out here in these woods." He chuffed against the skin of her neck, his bear asserting its place. Still, he pulled back, walking around the front of the car.

She smiled and snuggled deeper into his seat. They were quiet on the drive to his condo, but it was a comfortable silence. She was tired and couldn't wait to get into the shower. Her grandmothers had worked her, both in the garden and then afterward, drilling her on hoodoo and minor spells. She was good at reading and working auras and cards, but spells were her weak point, and Bea was determined to make her better. Especially protection spells. Working with people's energies left her vulnerable; she knew that, so she worked hard at them. It was just something she hadn't quite had a knack for.

Mercedes would be happy to get into her pajamas. They agreed once they reached his place that separate showers were the way to go and she didn't argue, just dragged herself down the hall to his guest bathroom. She washed the dirt from her grandmothers' garden and took her time, letting the hot water relax her muscles.

He was already in the kitchen by the time she finished, standing over the stove in just a pair of jogging pants and no shirt, cooking. She watched him, her body relaxed beneath the robe she wore. He was at home in the kitchen, and she liked seeing him so serene. She pulled the scarf she'd tied around her edges off, keeping her braids up high in a bun. He put whatever he'd made into the oven and set the oven timer. He turned back to the island behind him and started cutting vegetables.

She paused. Brent's pants were hanging just on his waist, his shaft's heavy weight showing through the soft material. Her breath

caught…maybe they should skip dinner. He smiled, his chopping con-
tinuing, but he shook his head.

"Aht-Aht, don't even."

She laughed. "What?"

"I can smell you from over here, Sadie, behave."

She put a little sway into her walk and moved closer to him, wrapping her arms around his waist, leaning her head against his back. She
slid her hands up and down his stomach and chest.

"I ain't even do nothing yet."

She peered around his back, smirking as his dick filled, rising in his
pants. She gripped it, and he hissed, setting down the knife.

"Sadie, you better stop before you end up laid out across this countertop."

She shivered at the deep timbre of his voice and tightened her grip
on his erection. He growled and spun around in her arms, quick as hell.
He lifted her and swung her until her back met the pantry door. She
wrapped her legs tight around his waist.

"I may not be alpha just yet, but I have this thing about orders, dar-
lin'."

Oh yeah, she'd riled his bear.

She hid a smile and scooched down until she could feel the steel
of his shaft at her core. She lowered one leg to get that perfect angle,
throwing her head back at how good it felt.

"I don't know if I can do orders," she murmured, leaning in to nuzzle
against his chest.

She scraped her teeth down his skin, and his hips jerked, pushing his
hardness against her. Her magic rose and coiled around them, teasing
his bear's power. He ripped open her robe with one hand, releasing a
dark chuckle when he found her nude.

"It's like that, then?" His eyes flashed gold a moment, but he tamped
it down.

Now, that wouldn't do.

"Most definitely." She pushed his pants down, moaning when it
caught on the tent pole that was his dick.

She hastily shoved the fabric down and gripped him, guiding his dick to where she most wanted it. She used her magic to coax the walls down around his animal. Brent grabbed the back of her head and tilted her chin up. He slammed his lips down on her. First sliding his tongue across her lips before he thrust inside, his tongue filling her mouth much in the way his dick filled her. She moaned and sucked on his tongue, tilting up her hips to take him deeper.

Brent was slow, methodical, licking the top of her mouth, his tongue dancing with hers as he fucked into her with deep strokes that took her breath away. He had one hand at her waist, moving the other to grip her thigh, holding her in place for his pleasure. She clawed at his back, whimpering, as he seemed to take over her whole body. Brent filled her in ways she'd never felt before, and all she could do was hold on for the ride. He'd been slow to make his move, but damn if he wasn't making up time for it now.

She pulled back from their kiss, sucking in air as electricity danced across their skin. His power slid into the minuscule space between them, heating her from the inside out.

"Please, Brent," she begged.

The orgasm building in her center had her stomach and thighs clenching and her pussy flexing around him in greedy grips. She rolled her hips, screaming out as her clit rubbed against the coarse hair on his groin.

"Please, what, Sadie? Tell me what you want." It was an order, a dare, all that careful pent-up power wild and loose.

"I want to come," she panted as he hit deep. "Fuuuuck," she dragged out.

"Should I let you come, even after the flippant way you talk to me?"

He lifted his hand from her waist and gripped the front of her neck. Not tight, just enough for a warning. It sent her body into a meltdown. Her heart fluttered in her chest, and her channel spasmed around him. He chuckled, his strokes still slow, deliberate. His hot breath bathed her ear as he gripped the lobe in his teeth. She whimpered.

"I like that sound, Sadie."

He pumped into her, and she moaned. She clamped around his dick, heat filling her core.

"You ready to come?"

"Yes, please, oh please."

His grip tightened on her neck, and his strokes sped. She was lost. She threw back her head and shouted, grinding her hips against his as her orgasm barreled over her. Brent released her neck, both hands at her waist, lifting her up and down on his shaft. It dragged out her orgasm until she was shaking. He sucked on her neck, giving one loud groan before he tensed up. He whispered her name as he came, hugging her tightly against him. She didn't know how long they stood like that. Her body was jelly, so she had no plans to move. She stroked the top of his head as his body jerked again.

"Fuck, woman," he whispered against her neck.

She smiled, a lazy, satisfied tilt of her lips. She was ready to go to bed. The oven timer beeped, and he sighed, carefully sliding out of her. He grabbed paper towels from his counter, handing her a handful, before wrapping his shaft and tucking it back into his pants.

"You make me forget what I'm doing," he grumbled, heading to the stove.

She laughed on her way to the bathroom to clean up.

***

Brent grunted as his phone vibrated across his bedside table. He growled and snatched it up, squinting at the display. It was his brother.

"Yo, Gabe, what the fuck," he grumbled.

"Nay's in labor."

He shot up straight in bed, his heart thundering. "Now? I thought you had a few more weeks."

"Her water broke, and we're on the way to the hospital now," his brother's voice was panicked, so unlike him.

"Don't worry. I got you. On my way now." Brent promised his twin.

Brent slid from beneath the sheets and rushed to his closet. Mercedes was up, the sheet clutched against her naked chest.

"What's wrong?"

"My sister-in-law is in labor," he shoved his legs in some jeans.

"Gabe's wife?"

He nodded, rooting through his dresser for a t-shirt.

"Go, I'll get dressed and leave with you," she murmured, sliding off the bed.

"We've barely slept; I don't mind you staying."

She paused with a shirt on her arms, "Are you sure?"

"Positive. I don't know how long these things take, so I'll text you."

She nodded and crawled back between the sheets.

He kissed her quickly and rushed down to his car. He sped out of his parking garage and headed towards Davis Island, to the shifter-run hospital where his sister would be giving birth. By the time he found parking and rushed through to the maternity center, the rest of his family was crowding the waiting area. They were all in various states of dress, and though worry covered their faces, excitement was there as well. He hugged his sisters and their mates.

"Mom, anything?" He asked.

Catherine took a deep inhale, and her eyes widened. "Not yet. We all arrived right before you."

"I guess my grandbabies have decided that 3 a.m. is a perfectly reasonable time to be born," his father mumbled, Julian's gaze never leaving the double doors leading to the maternity suites.

"She'll be fine, dad." Brent tapped his forehead against his fathers, their bears reaching up as their power brushed against each other.

Catherine cleared her throat and raised her eyebrows. "So...any news from you?"

Brent turned back and saw the smiles his sisters were hiding. "Nope, nothing over here."

Catherine stepped forward and sniffed, annoyed with his answer. "You smell like a witch. My God, Brent, you're too old to be playing games."

"Catherine," Julian murmured.

Catherine shoved her elbow into her mate's side. "You need to get serious about finding a mate, son. Is this witch someone we know?"

The smiles dropped from his sisters' faces, and they all stared. He sighed. Lord have mercy, his mother was messy.

"How many witches do you know?" He asked instead of answering.

"I know one," Trina said with a raised eyebrow.

"Gabe is about to become a father, and y'all worried about me?"

The smile his mother gave him raised his hackles. "I, personally, have the time to worry about both."

He knew once the excitement with the babies was over, Catherine would be in full meddling mode. He looked to his sisters for help. From their expressions, there would be none offered. Tiana grabbed his arm and marched him from the waiting room and out into the hallway.

His sister's bear was shining from her eyes. His bear responded, pushing out power.

"What the fuck are you thinking?" Tiana snapped.

"What?"

"Trina told me that she specifically told you when you took Mercedes's case not to fuck around with her, and here you are, smelling like her at three in the damn morning."

Brent worked to keep the smug smile off his face.

Tiana saw it anyway and punched him in the arm. "Break it off, Brent."

The smile dropped from his face. "Hell no."

"I'm finna kick your ass," she growled.

"Please, try," Brent answered back.

Tiffany rounded the corner and marched up to them. "Cut it the fuck out, you two." She snapped.

"Your brother is a jackass," Tiana said.

Brent narrowed his eyes at his sister. "It is what it is, Ti."

"Brent, she's a witch. You can't bring her into the clan. They'll riot." Tiffany hissed.

"You don't think I know that? I'm being as discreet as I can about this shit."

Tiana crossed her arms over her chest. "You would've washed your ass before you came over here if you were trying to be discreet."

Brent sighed and paced the hallway. His fling with Mercedes was less than 24hrs old and already causing problems. His bear filled his chest, the hair on his arms standing up. The animal had no intentions of letting her go, and though Brent fought him over the finer points of that, he agreed. His sisters were staring at him, their anger easy to read.

"Look—"

Tiffany held up her hand and cut him off. "I don't want to hear it, Brent."

"Mercedes is amazing, and if she quits behind this, I swear to God I'll make your life miserable." Tiana cut in.

"We got it under control," he muttered.

Tiana snorted.

"Until someone outside of this family finds out," Tiffany warned him.

His bear growled, and Brent took deep breaths to tamp down the irritated animal. "We both agreed to keep this a secret between us."

Tiffany sucked her teeth. "God damned ridiculous."

His bear wanted to lash out at his sisters, but as usual, the man knew that charm would carry them a lot further than meeting their anger head-on. He smiled and stepped closer to them, kissing Tiffany and then Tiana on the top of their head.

"I swear, I have it under control. We even have a contract." He waggled his eyebrows. Infusing a levity, he didn't quite feel.

"Oh Lord, you're so weird, Brent," Tiana's lips twitched as she fought a smile.

"A contract?" Tiffany rolled her eyes.

"It worked for Gabe," he cajoled.

Tiana snickered. "Lord have mercy, a whole dumbass."

Brent laughed and pulled his sister into a hug. "Come on. You're about to be aunts, you can't be mad at me all morning."

"Bet I can," Tiana grumbled, wrapping her arms around him.

He kissed her hair. "I promise, I'm on my best behavior with Mercedes."

Tiffany wiped a hand across her face. "This could backfire, Brent, big time."

"I know, sis, I'll be careful," he said hastily, happy he'd got over at least this one hurdle.

All of their fears were warranted. It would be hard to integrate Mercedes into the clan...if it got that far.

His bear swiped at him, a growl rumbling his chest. Brent closed his eyes and lowered his head as the animal pushed against his skin in protest. He understood his bear's contention, but it wasn't up to them at the end of the day. Mercedes had all the power in this case.

The energy around them spiked as Naomi's family rushed down the corridor. His bear reared forward, his sisters stiffening. Their animals all reacted, various waves of dominance filling the space. He shivered under the power of his bear as it tested the limits of his human skin. Brent pushed the problem of his relationship to the back burner for now, concentrating on getting through his nephews' birth without a full-blown dominance fight breaking out in the waiting room.

He greeted the panther's Alpha, his bear anxious to test against the strong male.

It was going to be a long morning.

11...

For the second time that morning, Mercedes was woken by the phone buzzing. This time it was her own. She frowned as it vibrated against her cheek again. She'd fallen asleep with it on her pillow, awaiting a text from Brent. She sat up and groaned at her stiff neck. She'd left Brent's condo hours ago and was now spread out on her bedroom floor. She'd tossed the bed and mattress yesterday in anticipation of her new one being delivered today. She squinted at her phone; she had text messages from both Brent and her friends.

She swiped through them as she went through her morning ritual, rolling her eyes at her friends' threats to come over if she didn't answer their texts. She smiled as the phone rang in her hand.

"How did it go?"

"Two boys," Brent breathed out, his excitement palpable.

"Aww, how's your sister-in-law?" She put the phone on speaker and picked up the pallet she'd made on the floor.

"She's good, tired, but healthy." He paused. "They were beautiful, Sadie. I was in law school when my sister had her kids, so this was the first time I got to hold a brand new baby."

"That's awesome, Brent."

"I should've asked, do you want children?"

She paused, folding a sheet, startled by the question. "I..." She scrambled for an answer. "I mean, I guess, eventually."

He breathed a sigh of relief. "Ok, that's good. Eventually. I can work with eventually."

An awkward laugh bubbled out of her mouth. "We've been sleeping together barely a day, Brent Hamilton. I know you ain't asking about kids."

Suddenly she could picture a little boy with Brent's easy-going manner following her around. Her heart clenched. She was delirious from the lack of sleep, right? Is that why her mind was making the leaps and bounds over dating and straight into children with him? She needed more rest.

Brent's laugh cut into her thoughts. "You're right, of course. I just...I'm so giddy from holding them."

"I can understand that." She should've stayed at his place. She would've loved to share that moment with him.

She frowned at the knock on her door.

"Who's that?" He asked.

"Maybe the bed?" She bit her lip and walked towards her front door. She snorted as she looked through the peephole. "Scratch that, it's my crazy friends. I gotta go. I'll call you later?"

"Works for me. I want to see you later."

Her heart fluttered. "Get some rest, and we'll see." She opened the door and shook her head at her three scowling best friends, ending her phone call. "I was going to answer your texts."

Porsha pushed past her, toting a cup holder filled with steaming beverages and a brown bag. "Yeah, right, heiffa."

"She too busy being cute on the phone. Who that was?" April asked, hands on hips.

Mercedes smiled and ignored the question, moving to the side to allow her friends entrance.

"Word on the street is, you got a new man," Tasha said slyly, settling on Mercedes' small sofa.

Mercedes swung around to face them, panic speeding her heartbeat.

"And by street, she means, Ms. Bea," April said, snickering. She grabbed the brown bag and took a seat next to Tasha.

"Mmhmm, and by the look of panic on your face, it's true." Porsha pulled drinks out of the carrier.

"I don't know what y'all are talking about," she lied.

"Well, we went for mentoring yesterday evening and apparently just missed you...and your new man." Tasha waggled her eyebrows.

Mercedes let out a breath and sucked her teeth. "Fine, but y'all gotta keep it between us."

"Who we gon' tell?" Tasha pretended to be offended.

"Says a bitch who finna leave here and tell her husband." April rolled her eyes, passing the bag to Tasha.

"Couples share. You would know that if you could keep a man," Tasha shot back, reaching in and grabbing a muffin.

Mercedes and Porsha both cackled.

"Anyways!" April mushed Tasha's face. "Tell us about this 'big hunk of a man' Ms. Bea's exact words."

Resigned, Mercedes pulled a chair out from her table and pulled it into the living area. The four of them had been friends their whole lives, so it wasn't like she hadn't intended on telling them. She just didn't know where to start.

"So, his name is Brent. He's a bear shifter. And before you ask, it's not like that," she hastily added.

"What's it like, then?" Porsha passed around the drinks. "Y'all are just fuck buddies?" She frowned as she sat cross-legged on the fluffy rug on the other side of Mercedes.

"I mean, not entirely. Brent says he wants me to stay open to a serious relationship with him."

"Then what's the problem?" Tasha asked.

Mercedes turned to her friend, her mouth open in shock. "So you just forgot all about the shit you went through with the cougars during your mating?"

Tasha frowned and took a deep gulp of her coffee. "You right. Shifters don't like any type of magic they can't control."

"Are bears the same?" April asked. "Maybe you won't get as much push back?"

"We could do what we did to the cougars. That's always an option," Porsha shrugged.

"The hell you say. I'm not fighting them sturdy bitches. You know how big bears are?" April sputtered.

Tasha snickered. "For real, for real, I'll do it, but I don't want to have to fight no big ass bears."

"And now you see what I'm saying. Plus, if it doesn't work out, I'm not trying to lose my job behind it."

"That's fair." Porsha pursed her lips. "We can try spells this time. I'm sure after a few of them lose their hair, they'll back off."

April burst out laughing. "I'm telling Ms. Lisa you said that."

"Snitch," Tasha threw some chips at her.

"Aht-aht, don't come up in here messing up my spot." Mercedes laughed

"So, you two are going to creep around until you're what…just tired of each other? How is the sex?" April asked, narrowing her eyes.

Mercedes eyes widened, and she brought up her coffee cup.

"Like that, then?" Tasha smiled.

"Girl," was all Mercedes said.

"Shiiiit, guess we need to get ready to fight then," Porsha said, holding up her coffee cup.

April tapped it and laughed.

"Let's not get ahead of ourselves. It could still not work out." Mercedes cautioned.

Tasha snorted. "You keep telling yourself that. Shifters don't just back down from their matings. He ain't going nowhere."

Mercedes sighed. "He didn't say anything about a mating when we were negotiating." After his drunken confession, a very sober Brent had not once brought up the mating.

"I don't see a shifter talking about anything past a one-night stand if mating wasn't involved," Tasha reassured her. "Honey, it's inevitable."

"I still don't think we should go public yet, though. What if his sisters have a problem with it? Okay, yes, we can probably fight them, but then I'll lose my job and be broke as hell, then what?"

Her three friends winced and shared a look.

"This is the best job I've had since having to drop out of college. It could take me years to find another. And he's not just a bear; Brent's going to be the next alpha."

"Yikes," Tasha murmured.

"Exactly." Mercedes sighed, "it's one thing to accept a witch into the clan, it's a whole 'nother to accept a witch as the alpha female."

They were all quiet and having said it all out loud, Mercedes was doubly happy that she'd chosen to keep their relationship under wraps. Tasha had had a hard time getting Damian, her mate's, family to accept their mating, the women going so far as to jump Tasha to get her to back off from him. Unlucky for the cougars, they caught Tasha when she was with them, so they had paid for their audacity via a beat down. She and her friends had never been opposed to fighting, but was that how she wanted to live the rest of her life, fighting off bears because they didn't like that a human was Alpha female?

"Okay, so secret lovers. To the question I'm sure we're all thinking..." April waggled her eyebrows, "Is his dick big?"

They all busted out laughing, and Mercedes was happy like always to have these women as her friends.

12...

Brent swallowed a sigh and smiled as his mother told another friend, yet again, that she was getting ready to go. Catherine had been doing this dance for the last thirty minutes, and they'd barely made it to the back pew of the church. He knew what he signed up for, but his stomach was grumbling in hunger, and he was sliding quickly into hangry. His sister Tiffany had no qualms about complaining, sighing loudly and clearing her throat. Brent hid his laugh at the look his mother shot them both.

It had been three weeks since they'd last been to church. They'd all taken turns helping Gabe and Naomi out with the twins, and Catherine was making up for lost time with her friends, bragging about her newest grandchildren, whipping out pictures on her phone, and cooing with the other women. His mother was in her element. He pulled his phone out of his pocket, intending to send Sadie a message. He'd not seen her outside of the office in a week, and he missed her. They talked every day at work and every night, but still, he wanted to see her.

He debated inviting her over to his mother's house for Sunday dinner but thought better of it. He hadn't yet had the talk with Mercedes about their mating, and he knew if he brought her over, his mother would immediately start in on alpha female duties. He wasn't quite ready to throw that in Mercedes' lap. His phone vibrated just as Catherine turned towards the front door, giving them another narrowed-eyed look as Tiff cleared her throat, yet again. He sent up a quiet thank God and followed them out of the church.

Of course, someone stopped them on the front step. Brent pulled his phone out as his mother hugged her friend and pulled up pictures of his nephews. He squinted at the text he'd received from Mercedes.

Sadie: *Im drunf cone get me plsssss*

He snorted at the emojis.

Brent: *Where are you?*

He lifted his head and turned to his sister. "Tiff, I gotta go get Mercedes, you got mom?"

His sister sucked her teeth. "I'm 'bout to leave her," she muttered.

"You ain't that crazy," Catherine said, pinching Tiffany's arm and waving goodbye to her friend.

"Ow, sorry, mama."

"Where are you headed, Brent?" Catherine asked.

He held up his phone. "I need to go pick up a friend."

Catherine's eyes lit. "What kind of friend? Maybe you can bring them to Sunday dinner."

"Next time, mama." He leaned down and kissed her cheek.

No way was he bringing a drunk Mercedes to his parents' house or onto bear territory, for that matter. Who knew what kind of trouble she'd find. He jogged to his car and called her as soon as he got in.

"Breeeennnt, are you coming to get me?" An overly happy Mercedes asked.

He chuckled. "Where you at, love? You never answered my text."

"I did." There was silence, and then, "oh, no, I didn't. Hold on."

He started the car. "You can just tell—"

"Sent it!" She slurred.

He snorted. Lord, she was dizzy when she was drunk. He pulled up the text, recognizing the Westshore restaurant.

"I'm ten minutes away, be there in a second," he promised her.

"Yay! Drunk sex for me!"

The call disconnected as he choked, shocked by her declaration.

He pulled up to the valet station in the promised ten minutes and saw Mercedes and three other beautiful women laughing as a male worked to herd them towards his vehicle. He frowned and got out of the car, leaving it running. The scent of the cougar shifter drifted to him as he walked up. His bear sat forward, a warning growl rumbling his chest. Was the guy a rideshare driver?

"Brent!" Mercedes threw herself into his arms. It calmed his bear immediately, though he still eyed the cougar. "Meet my friends." She waved behind her. "April, Tasha, and Porsha." She looked around before leaning forward, whispering loudly, "This my man, y'all."

He snorted. "Subtle, babe, I'm sure no one heard that." He nodded to the women staring at him, hiding their own snickers.

His bear rolled through his chest as he got a good look at Mercedes. She was wearing a white suit jacket with gold buttons, but underneath that...oh, hell. His heart started racing, and for a moment, he could only stare down at her. She wore a pair of jean shorts that were short as hell and a silky top that was damn near see-through. So different than she looked at work or even on their dates. She was always put together, sexy and elegant. She radiated sex appeal. This...this was god damned fire.

"He big as hell," one of her friends whispered loudly, breaking through the daze Mercedes had him in.

"You right about his aura, Merc, that shit bright," another one said.

"Told ya'," Mercedes taunted, high fiving the women.

"Tash, babe, get into the car, please," the cougar pleaded.

"Hey, what's up, my man. I'm Brent," He held out his hand, his bear dismissing the male as competition, now that he noticed the ties between him and the other woman.

The shifter narrowed his eyes. "Hamilton?"

He grunted. "Yep."

"Your dad's cool people. I'm Damian." Damian shook his hand and turned back to the one named Tasha. "Come on, now. This the last time I'm playing DD for y'all asses."

"Booo," the women hissed.

Brent chuckled. "Want to split them up? It'll probably be easier."

"Bruh," Damian breathed out. "Thanks."

"They do this often?" He asked, biting the inside of his cheek as Mercedes started dancing against him.

"Nah, like once a month or so. I'll take my girl and April. Porsha lives right down the street from Merc." Damian guided Tasha and April towards his jeep.

Brent gripped Mercedes's hips as she started twerking. "Behave, hear."

She spun around and wrapped her arms around his neck. "I wanna dance."

"Get in the car, woman," he ordered, smacking her ass and turning her towards the passenger seat of his Jag. "Porsha, you need help getting in?"

"Nope, I got it," her friend slurred, opening the door and flopping into the back seat.

He closed the back door when she'd settled, turning around to buckle his mate into her seat since she was too busy fiddling with the radio to do so herself. Mercedes raked her nails down his back as he leaned over to snap her seat belt. His whole body clenched, his bear raising.

"Sadie," he growled, gripping the back of her neck. "You better keep that same energy when we get back to my house," he murmured before giving her a hard kiss.

Brent hurried his steps as he walked around to his seat and slid into the car. The two women were giggling when he got in. He didn't dare ask.

Brent glanced up into the mirror at her friend. "Where we going?" Mercedes opened her mouth, and he chuckled, putting a finger across her lips. "Not you."

She licked his finger, sucking it into the warm cavern of her mouth. His dick flexed in his pants, and he growled because he hadn't anticipated a horny Sadie, despite her parting words over the phone. He pulled his hand back and cleared his throat.

"I like this ride, Brent," Porsha commented.

"Thanks. I need the addy, though."

"Oh," the woman snickered, "I live down the road from Mercedes' apartment building. The townhouses."

He knew the ones she was talking about, so he pulled out of the valet area and headed there. Mercedes turned the music up, and she and Porsha danced and sang the whole way there. He kept one eye on the road, his gaze straying to the way Sadie drunkenly gyrated in the seat next to him. Lord have mercy! Porsha guided him through the rows of townhouses until they got to hers. She rapped along with the radio, sliding on her heels as they pulled behind the sedan in her driveway. Shaking his head in amusement, he got out and helped her to her front door.

She fumbled with her keys but finally got them into the front door. "Thanks for the ride, Brent, the Bear."

"Oh lord," he laughed.

"You better treat my girl right, or the four of us will put a root on you," she warned before stumbling through her front door.

He snickered, but he didn't doubt she was serious at all. He waited until he heard the lock engage before heading back to his car. Sadie smiled at him, and his bear growled in excitement.

"Behave," he warned her when he got in.

She leaned over and sucked on his neck. "I haven't seen you in a week; you can't possibly expect me to behave."

He pulled her braids back, smiling at her intake of breath. "You could've texted me at any time to come over if you needed something from me."

"You were helping your brother. I didn't want to interrupt that," she whispered, licking across his lips.

"I certainly appreciate that, but I'll always make time for you, Sadie, know that." He gripped her chin and kissed her deeply, their tongues twisting together.

He pulled back, his chest fluttering, and now his dick hard as hell. His bear was pushing against his skin, and he closed his eyes to fight its power. The animal was done waiting on him to claim Sadie. She promised him six months to consider a serious relationship, but he didn't think he'd last that long. His bear was pushing him to mate with her every time they were within five feet of each other. He gripped the steering wheel, fighting to keep from slamming his foot down on the gas as he drove them back to his condo.

Mercedes's hand was dancing along his thigh, making it that much harder to concentrate. He slid into his parking spot and unsnapped Mercedes's belt, pulling her over to his side of the car.

He slammed their mouths together, plunging his tongue inside. She whimpered, her hips grinding against his shaft. Brent cursed and pulled back, opening his door and letting her out. He scooped her up once he was out of the car, carrying her to the elevator, setting her down once they got inside.

"It's cameras in here?" She twerked back into him, her ass sliding against his erection.

"Sadie," he warned, gripping her hips to keep them still.

She laughed and did it again. He couldn't help but smile. Of all the ways he'd seen Mercedes in the weeks since they'd started their affair, this playful drunk person was new and endearing. He pushed his door code in, and before he could shut the front door, she was on him. Yeah, he liked Drunk Sadie.

13...

To be summarily summoned to his parent's house was new for Brent. One, because he already spent a lot of time at their home. And two, because out of his parent's five kids, he was the least likely to be in trouble. He wasn't alarmed...curious but not worried. He hadn't talked to his mother in a week on the phone, and it had been longer since he'd come to visit. More than likely, she wanted to badger him about his search for a mate.

He dropped his keys in a small tray that sat on her foyer table, his eyes searching out his mother. Instead of Catherine, he found his oldest sister, Trina, standing with her arms crossed in the living room.

"What's wrong?" He asked, frowning further as he fully entered the room.

His parents were across from him and his sister, their faces blank...careful. Julian sat in his leather armchair, Catherine poised at his side. His bear moved through him, wary of the whole thing.

"Someone saw you with Mercedes and told mom," Trina said between clenched teeth.

Shit.

He wiped a hand down his face and tried to figure out where he'd been for someone to see him. Brent had been sneaking Mercedes into his condo for the past two weeks—well after dark—and as far as he knew, there weren't any bears around to tell the tale. When was the last time they'd been out in public?

"You're serious about this witch?" Catherine snapped, bringing him out of his thoughts.

His bear rumbled, to which his father's bear sent out a flare of alpha power.

"Careful," Julian growled.

Brent tamped down his animal. "Her name is Mercedes."

"What do I care what her name is? You can't be serious about making a witch the Alpha female."

Trina sighed, and their mother quickly turned to her.

"And you, you knew about it?"

"He's a grown man, mom. What am I supposed to do about who he has sex with?" Trina grumbled.

"Brent, you're supposed to be taking over this clan. Why you insist on gallivanting across this damn town instead of settling down and choosing a mate is baffling to me. Are you not ready to take over the clan?"

"The position is mine," he growled, his bear besting his control.

"Then act like it," Catherine snapped. "Break it off with this witch and find a suitable mate."

His bear pushed forward, his claws expanding out, fur sliding out of his pores. "She is mine!"

His father stopped drumming his fingers on the arm of the chair and stood. "Watch.your.tone." Julian snapped.

Brent swayed for a moment under his father's power but kept his head straight. His bear's power rose, meeting and matching his father's.

"I'm not giving up Mercedes." Faced with his parent's disapproval, every instinct in him demanded he fight for his mate.

His father eyed him, a calculating gaze that was somehow less reassuring than the anger on his mother's face. "Is she powerful?"

"Dad," Brent sighed.

"Absolutely," Trina answered. "And you know what it could mean for the clan to have a witch as our alpha female."

Brent snapped his head towards his sister. "Trina."

Trina shrugged. "I hired her on the spot because I've never seen anyone control a room like her. I don't think the clan will have a problem once they meet her."

He was happy his sister was on his side, but at the same time, hearing her talk about his mate as though she were a boon to be used for their clan...

He sucked in a sharp breath as he realized how his actions looked to his family. Catherine was partially correct. He had been playing. The affair with Mercedes was something he thought would be light, fun until he was ready for more. His bear had always known different and had been fighting for Brent to take what he considered theirs. He'd wasted so much time fighting his instinct.

He needed to see her. He turned to leave.

"This conversation is not finished," Julian called out to him.

He stopped, wrestling his bear into compliance. His father was still Alpha for the moment, and respect was due. He turned back to face his parents.

"Do you even know if she has a familiar and what that animal is? What if it's a bear? You think we'll allow a witch who can control bears in our damn clan?" Catherine asked, exasperated.

Julian studied him, his gaze contemplative. "How do you propose to make this clan accept a witch?"

His answer was immediate. "By force if necessary."

His father growled in approval. Catherine sighed, and Trina slid him a low fist bump as he turned to leave. He would have his mate, whether he had to fight the whole clan to do it. His mother had a good point, though. There was so much about Mercedes that he didn't know. But, his bear didn't care, and Brent was on board with that.

***

"Lord have mercy," Mercedes mumbled and dragged herself out of her very comfortable bed.

She'd hoped for a nap after spending all morning at the beach with her friends. They were there with the sunrise, first meditating and then recharging their crystals. She loved the monthly ritual she held with them, but waking up early was catching up with her, especially after all the late nights with Brent. She sucked her teeth as the banging on her door sounded again. She knew who it was. Only one person knocked on her door like that. Was he drunk like last time?

She snatched the door open, her breath catching in her throat. It was Brent, but...not? He wore a black sweatsuit and a dope pair of sneakers and looked so unlike his usual self. The look he pinned her with was filled with his bear, his eyes glowing gold. His aura was spiked with adrenaline, and aggression and perhaps she should've been alarmed.

Instead, her belly did a slow roll, and her skin tightened in anticipation. Her magic instinctively reached out, massaging the spikes flaring widely around him. His eyes lit, and for a moment, his bear's power fought her magic. She stepped closer to him, beckoned by the fiery lust swirling in his eyes. She grabbed his chin and stared him in his eyes, meeting the bear's gaze. The animal's stare was primal, possessive.

Brent grabbed her waist and lifted her, kissing her, his tongue sweeping into her mouth. The kiss was hot, inflexible, and desperate. She rode out the storm of it, her legs wrapping around him. His power was raging out of his control, the fine point of his claws pressing against her legs. She pulled back, gulping in air. He growled and nuzzled into her neck, his teeth scraping against her skin. He bit down, not hard enough to break the skin, but for sure, there would be a mark.

Her pussy throbbed at the aggressive action, thumping against the ridge of his dick. He licked a trail across her cheek, sucking her bottom lip into his mouth. He devoured her mouth, licking and nipping before tangling his tongue with hers. Mercedes squirmed against him, one part confused two parts, ready to fuck him in the middle of her open doorway. The sound of a door closing down the hall brought her out of the sensual fog.

"That's enough," she whispered, cradling his head.

He growled low, the sound rumbling against her chest. He pushed his hips forward, his teeth lengthening. Mercedes gripped the back of his neck, her nails digging into his skin. She used her magic to dampen the spikes in Brent's aura.

"Enough," she said firmer, meeting his bear's gaze.

Her magic swept over him again, and Brent's body shuddered, the bear retreating to give him back some of his control.

"Fuck," he cursed, "I almost marked you. I'm sorry."

He released her legs, setting her down. He stepped back, his face chagrined. She closed her door, pulling him into the living room, and sat him on her sofa. She straddled his legs and waited on him to get his bearings.

"What's wrong?"

He brought his hand up to her neck, his thumb tracing over his bite mark. She called her magic forth, reading the confusion and insecurity all through his aura.

"What happened?"

He sighed. "My parents found out that you and I are seeing each other."

Her mind spun. If his parents knew, then that meant his sisters knew. What did that mean for her and her job? She stood from his lap and paced in front of him.

"We're doing a horrible job at this secret affair," she said. "What did your parents say?" She paused and stared, her heart hammering.

"They had some reservations about me dating a witch."

"Fuck," she hissed.

He sighed. "I realized some things today."

She narrowed her eyes. "What things?"

He smiled, that charming lift of his lips all Brent. "I don't know if you want to hear them, seeing as how this secret affair was your idea."

She scoffed, offended. "Hey, you were more than happy to be on board."

"You right." He grabbed the bottom of her shorts and pulled her back into his lap. "My bear, not so much."

"Your bear doesn't like me?" That was a surprise seeing as how he calmed under her touch.

He snorted, "My bear has more permanent plans for you."

"And the man?" She pushed against his forehead as he leaned over to nuzzle into her neck. She wanted to look him in his face.

"The man is very much on board with that."

They stared at each other, understanding that the affair had flipped on its head. Panic filled her for a moment, and she stood.

"Are you hungry?"

He chuckled. "You can try and run, Pumpkin Pie, but I plan to catch you."

Mercedes fixed herself a glass of ice water, her friend's words tumbling through her mind. Tasha had warned her that a shifter wouldn't carry on a casual affair. A little zing of nervous anticipation went through her, and she had to admit that she had no problem with mating Brent. She chugged the ice water she'd fixed for him and stared at the back of his head. If his parents knew, did that mean they didn't need to keep their secret any longer?

Brent turned on her sofa and watched her. She avoided his eyes, putting away the crystals she'd been drying on her kitchen table. She took her time, carefully storing them in the cloth bags individually. He chuckled at her stalling, and walked into the kitchen. He came behind her, wrapping his arms around her waist, rubbing his cheek against the back of her neck.

"What's going through your mind, Sadie?"

She wasn't ready to articulate it, couldn't— if she was honest. Everything about her and Brent seemed to move fast and out of her control. She didn't like it. Didn't like the dizziness that came with their whirlwind affair. It felt a lot like battling to keep the wind from snatching a kite from her clutches. But at the same time...it was all exhilarating. Hot.

She sighed. "So much."

He kissed her softly. "Oh, I did want to ask you, do you have an animal to call?"

Mercedes stiffened, her quartz dropping from her hand. Hadn't she just talked to her grandmothers about that same thing? She'd asked if it would make a difference, and now Brent was asking her about it. She turned to face him.

"I don't. Does that make a difference to your clan?" She whispered, scared of the answer.

"Shifters have always feared a witch coming into their clan or pack and controlling their animals. There's bad history. It's one of the main reasons shifters don't trust witches." Brent answered.

"Gram says that shifters would also use witches to expand their territories, overusing their power." She shot back.

Brent shrugged. "Like I said, bad history. It doesn't have to affect us, does it?"

She studied his gaze, knowing she'd trust Brent with her life. Hell, she'd trust him with her magic, which was scarier in the grand scheme of things. Mercedes nodded, feeling the shift in their relationship.

Brent cupped her cheek. "Are you still gonna sneak around with me?"

She laughed, releasing the pent-up tension that had gathered. "Yeah, we should definitely still sneak around. It's hot. Plus, there is a difference between your family knowing and the people at the office."

"Fair enough. I'll allow it...for now."

"You'll allow it?" She sucked her teeth and stepped out of his arms.

He laughed and pulled her back into his arms. "I am Alpha, woman."

"Whatever."

"No respect," he muttered, nipping at her lips.

14...

Mercedes shook her head as her phone beeped yet again with a text message. Porsha came into the bathroom and waved her phone.

"Girl, he is blowing you up."

She sighed, "I know. Brent thinks I'm going to chicken out."

"Well, no one would blame you. You're going to a party with his clan while fucking their next alpha, you bold, bold." Porsha smirked, smoothing down the gold strapless gown that fit her like second skin.

She snickered. "First of all, no one knows that." She frowned... "Well, okay, no one outside of his family."

"Didn't Tasha say they could smell each other? You don't think Brent left his scent all over you?"

She paused with her mascara wand halfway to her eyes. "You think so?"

Porsha shrugged. "When's the last time y'all were together?"

Mercedes' cheeks got hot, and Porsha snickered. She'd just snuck out of his condo this morning as she rushed to meet the party planner.

"Well, I don't know how many showers that will take."

Mercedes groaned. "Maybe I should chicken out."

Her phone beeped, and Porsha set it on the counter next to her. "I don't think he'll let you."

She picked up the phone and smiled at the sweet messages. Brent was eager to see her. Their not-so-secret affair had been on-going for nearly two months, and she still got butterflies in her stomach talking to him.

Brent: *You backing out?*

Brent*: hello?*

Sadie*: No, getting dressed, quit bothering me.*

Brent*: Just checking. What are you wearing?*

Sadie*: nunya.*

Brent*: mean.*

Sadie*: My friend says that the bears will be able to smell you on me. Will that be a problem?*

Brent: *I mean...*

Sadie groaned, her fingers moving fast over the phone keyboard.

Sadie: *Then maybe this isn't a good idea.*

Brent: *It's a company Christmas party, it'll be fine, promise.*

She groaned, putting down the phone and finished her makeup. It would look odd if she didn't show up after so many people had asked, and especially since she put so much effort into planning the damn thing.

She took a deep breath and did another once over in the mirror. The long, red, sequined mermaid dress she wore had a deep vee in the front and back, held up by thin crystal-encrusted straps. Her braids were twisted into a high bun, and Mercedes felt hot. She couldn't wait to see Brent's reaction.

"I got your back either way," Porsha said, passing her the small wristlet that held her ID and credit card.

"Let's hope there's no trouble."

It didn't take them long to get to the hotel where they were holding the party. The ballroom was decked out and beautiful. Mercedes ran her eyes over the details making sure everything was as she'd in-structed. She'd left the hotel only three hours ago, but still...

"Fancy, fancy," Porsha murmured.

She snickered to hide her nervousness.

"Girl, Brent shaved his beard?"

Mercedes looked up and spotted Gabe coming in their direction. "Nope, twin brother."

"Lord, have mercy, he taken?"

"Yep."

"Shame," she murmured

"Mercedes," Gabe said gruffly, grabbing her into a hug.

Shock had her stiff in his arms. He stepped back and cleared his throat.

"Sorry, Brent said I had to confuse your scent?"

Her cheeks heated, and she ducked her head. She looked up, "This is my—"

Gabe walked away before she could finish the introduction.

"Rude," Porsha said.

"He's like that with everyone." She smiled as her boss came closer. "Trina, hi, you look beautiful."

"You too, love this dress." Trina grabbed her into a tight hug, same as Gabe. What in the world?

"More scents," she said with an impish smile. She gave Porsha her attention, holding out her hand. "I'm Trina Hamilton."

"Porsha Scott."

"A pleasure to meet you. You did a great job with the party, Mercedes. Everything looks fantastic!"

"Thank you!" She took a relieved breath.

"I hope you both have fun tonight," Trina said and walked off.

"Affectionate bunch," Porsha whispered. "And April was right, them bitches big as hell. I'm not looking forward to fighting them."

Mercedes snickered. "We ain't fightin' nobody. Cut it out."

Her heart rate kicked up as she noticed Brent then.

The tuxedo he wore fit him perfectly, and she couldn't help the sigh that escaped her lips. He oozed sex appeal and power. Her body melted and warmed for him the same it always did when he was near.

He smiled at Porsha and grabbed her friend onto a hug. "Hi, Porsha."

"Brent," she greeted.

"Sadie," he whispered as he turned his attention to her and grabbed her into a tight hug, his head bending over the crook of her neck.

"You look amazing," he whispered with awe in his voice. His eyes skimmed her hotly, lust brightening them.

He stepped back, and the nerves that had been rioting through her stomach settled. The heat in his eyes did a lot for her ego.

"Took care of the scent problem," he gave her a rakish smile.

She couldn't help but return it. "I guess you did."

"Now, can we go in and have fun?"

"After you," she said, grabbing Porsha's hand.

Brent walked behind them, his eyes on Sadie's form as she walked further into the ballroom. She moved with an innate grace that had his stomach clenching in lust. He didn't know how Sadie thought hiding the fact that she was a witch would work. With her power wrapped tightly around her, she absolutely glowed. The heady scent of her magic called to his bear, unlike anything he'd ever experienced. How long would it take before he or his bear lost control and dragged her from the party? He waved down one of the waiters, passing champagne to both ladies before grabbing one himself. The waiter tried to leave, but Brent held up his hand to stop him, downing the small glass and trading it for another before he allowed the man to move on.

He would need something stronger if he wanted to get through the night without showing his ass.

Mercedes snickered and sipped from her glass, eyeing him over the top.

"Behave," he muttered.

She laughed and turned from him, greeting some of their coworkers.

"Think you'll be able to pull this off?" Porsha asked, her gaze raking him in curiosity, her magic skimming over him as well.

He sighed. "Not gonna lie, it'll be touch and go."

She snorted and patted his arm. "If it's any consolation, me and the others have already warned her that you're inevitable."

He smiled, liking the idea of her friend's approval. "How did she take it?"

"You know, Merc. She'll try to control it as much as she can." Porsha shrugged.

"Brent, there you are."

He stiffened as his mother snuck up behind him. He turned and kissed her proffered cheek. "Hi, mom, you look beautiful. Dad."

Julian grunted in curiosity.

"Oh, this is Porsha. She's friends with Mercedes," he introduced.

Catherine shook Porsha's hand with a polite but pointed smile to Brent. "And where's Mercedes?"

"Mercedes," he grabbed her arm and pulled her from the conversation she was having with their coworker. "My mom and dad."

Catherine took a deep inhale, her eyebrows bunching. Brent hid his smile as his mother looked between the three of them, probably trying to work out the dynamics.

"It's lovely to see you, dear," Catherine finally offered. "Trina told me you planned the party this year. Wonderful job!"

"Thank you so much." Mercedes smiled earnestly. She grabbed Porsha's hand. "I'm gonna go make the rounds; it was a pleasure seeing you again." Both women beat a hasty retreat.

"She's very beautiful, I see the appeal," Catherine said pointedly. "I wonder if she would be able to handle herself in the clan."

"Cut it out, love. Anyone with eyes can see that girl's power," Julian muttered, waving down a waiter.

His mother sucked her teeth at her mate. "I don't see any claiming marks on her."

Brent smiled but ignored her prodding. "I should also mingle." He kissed his mother's forehead and left before she started asking more pointed questions.

Yeah, the lack of visible marks on her bothered him too, but Mercedes wasn't ready to let anyone outside of his family know about their affair. And though it chaffed, he would keep his word to her.

15...

With every passing hour of the Christmas party, Brent was growing impatient. He walked around and greeted his coworkers, laughing and joking, but his eyes followed Mercedes, devouring her. His bear was becoming more agitated the longer she was away from him.

She flowed easily through the crowd of people, smiling and talking with them. His bear sat up with every male gaze that followed her around. Everything in him wanted to claim her publicly, put his mark for one and all to see. His bear was pushing for it. With every sip of the champagne in his hand, the idea sounded better and better. His brother might be right.

Who gave a fuck what the rest of the clan thought?

He was going to be alpha. Would he let the clan cow him from something he wanted? He watched her interact with them. She seemed just as comfortable with them as she was with the employees of their law firm. At the moment, she and Porsha were dancing, attracting a crowd, her beauty raising his possessiveness.

A growl built in his chest at every male who walked up to her. She waved them all off, her gaze catching his every so often. A heavy hand landed on his shoulder.

"I take it you're done hiding it?" Gabe asked.

He grunted.

Gabe chuckled. "I told your ass it wouldn't work."

"I'm trying to respect my mate's wishes," he muttered.

"Meanwhile, the bears hovering around her have no problem letting everyone know how much they want her."

Brent straightened, snarling as he watched one of his clan members push through the crowd around Mercedes.

"Is that Abram?"

Gabe growled. "I wish you'd let me slap him around."

"How many enemies would we have if I let you slap people around at your leisure?"

"He's an asshole and a bully."

"You're an asshole. Most bears are." Brent told him.

His brother shrugged. "You know he's going to challenge you for alpha."

His bear raised, thirsty for the fight. "And I can't wait."

Abram grabbed Mercedes's waist and pulled her closer to him.

"Oh hell no." Brent pushed through the crowd, his brother hot on his trail.

Sadie was pushing against Abram's chest, trying to get out of his grip. Brent didn't wait to see if Abram would release her. He gripped the male's wrist and twisted. Mercedes stumbled as Abram backed away with a hiss of pain.

"Keep your hands to yourself," Brent said between gritted teeth.

Sadie rushed to step between them. She raised an eyebrow. "We finna do this here, Brent?" She asked quietly.

But his bear was at the end of its leash, and he could barely talk around the possessiveness. He stared Abram down, the male holding his gaze. Brent smiled. His bear was anxious and excited to do battle, no matter that the setting was inappropriate.

Abram smirked. "Never say the Placid Alpha is getting hype over a witch."

"Watch your fucking mouth," Gabe growled.

Brent crossed his arms over his chest. "I'm not in the habit of repeating myself, Abram."

"I know you aren't seriously considering bringing a witch into our clan, so just let me know when you're done with her. Maybe I'll still want a turn after."

Brent's bear went still, the implication of Abram's words coalescing his and his bear's rage like ice. Lightning fast, Brent grabbed the back of Abram's head and pulled it down into his knee.

Mercedes gasped at the quick violence. Brent's face was calm, no trace of the anger that had tightened his eyes when he'd walked up to them. Abram was on the floor, holding his bleeding nose. Brent got down on one knee and gripped the back of the man's neck.

"I'm not repeating this lesson. Fuck with her again, and that's your ass."

The words were barely audible, but she heard them and her heart clenched. She looked around at the gaping crowd. Some of them eyed her, curiosity on their face. Shit, she'd spent the whole party avoiding him, and in seconds he'd wiped that away. They'd hid their relationship well enough that she'd not had any questions even as they worked together in his office. Now though, suspicion and speculation sent whispers through the room. They weren't even watching the violence in front of them; all eyes were on her.

Abram growled beneath Brent's hand, and he tightened his grip, claws sliding from his skin.

Brent gripped him tight enough to draw blood at the man's neck. "Am I clear or no?"

Abram growled again.

Mercedes's heart was hammering as she tried to pull Brent up. "Okay, big guy, let's walk it off."

Brent was unmovable until Abram nodded. Both men stood and still squared off. Abram opened his mouth to say something else, but fed up with the display, Mercedes pushed out her power, shoving both men further apart.

"Enough," she demanded.

The crowd murmuring was louder this time, excitement and a chorus of 'oooohh' going around. Abram was pissed, his eyes narrowing on her. Brent, on the other hand...his heated stare sent her stomach clenching in anticipation. His bear watched her through his eyes, the animal's intensity stealing her breath.

She steered him away from the crowd. His chest was still rumbling with quiet growls, but he allowed her to move him. Her hands shook as she took him into an empty hallway away from the ballroom. His eyes were glowing, and he was staring at her, breathing hard. What did she say? Their cover was as good as blown. She wanted to be mad, but why? He'd already said he wanted her to be his mate. From what Tasha told her, mates was a permanent type situation. Did that mean his sisters wouldn't fire her? Maybe not, but she trusted him enough to know he'd keep his word.

Still...

"Do you realize how that just looked?"

"I don't give a fuck." He growled.

Clearly, his bear was in charge because Brent would never talk to her like that.

"Brent," she sighed. "You just popped off in front of the whole damn law firm, not to mention there is a lot of your clan here. What do you think they're thinking right now? What happened to our 'secret affair'?"

"You're mine," he said.

"Excuse you. You can tone down the alpha now; I don't belong to anyone." She warned both him and his animal.

He stepped closer, his chest rumbling, and okay, yes, that made her wet, but the point stood, she was still her own woman.

"Brent," she whispered as he nuzzled into her neck.

His hand gripped her waist, and he pulled her into his chest. His coarse fur brushed against her skin as he fought with his animal.

"You need to calm down."

"It's not me, it's my bear," he said, sucking on the skin of her neck. "You have any idea how hot you are with your magic flowing through you? The bloodthirsty animal likes to see you asserting your power."

She shuddered as need slammed into her. "We're not doing this here."

His hands roamed her back, bared by the dress, and he gripped her ass. "You're right. I can get us a room upstairs."

Her pussy throbbed in response. She stepped back and took a deep breath. "No, we will go back to this party so we can pretend you had a momentary lapse of judgment. You don't want to put the alpha position in jeopardy."

"I'm not thinking about no position right now, Sadie." He stepped closer, "no scratch that, there are a couple of positions I'm thinking about."

She sucked in a sharp breath at the need in his eyes. He was potent, more so with his bear running just under his skin. Her phone buzzed against her breast where she'd tucked it into the bodice of her dress. She shivered because that added to the maelstrom of heat warming her body. She pulled it out. It was a text from Porsha.

Porsha: *You're my ride home, ma'am*

"Shit," she muttered. "I have to go. I'm Porsha's ride."

He didn't say anything, just stared, his lust-filled look pooling an answering need in her belly. His face cleared as he seemed to come to some kind of conclusion.

"Come, I'll ride home with you."

"That's...Brent," she sighed.

The corner of his mouth lifted in a smile that sent a flood of moisture down her leg. "Nah, my bear's not in the mood to talk about it, Sadie."

"Placid Alpha, my ass," she muttered.

He snorted and nodded his head towards the ballroom, indicating she walk in front of him. There would be no changing his mind. That power and turbulence he usually tucked away in his aura was on full display. This was a man who would be alpha. The end. Period.

She turned, resigned to their fate. Their relationship was out to the world for all intents and purposes, and perhaps when she took a moment to think about that, she'd panic. For now, though, seeing his body filled with his bear's power was a major turn-on. Mercedes felt the heat of his gaze on her as she walked back to the party. She smiled at her coworkers as though nothing was going on, but nerves were rioting under her skin.

Porsha raised her eyebrows when they found her at the dessert table.

"Later," she whispered to her friend.

Brent wound his arms through both she and Porsha's elbows, escorting them out of the ballroom.

Once she dropped off Porsha, they drove to his place, where Brent rushed to peel her out of her dress. In contrast, he took his time loving on her. Mercedes understood in his every kiss and caress that he was done pretending it was a casual thing between them. Her friends had been right. He was inevitable. She surrendered to it, their sweat-soaked bodies sliding against each other as they forged their bond tighter.

His teeth scraped against her neck, his power filling the room.

"I'm not letting anyone keep you from me," he whispered against her skin as he sucked and nibbled his way down her body. "You're mine, say you know that."

Mercedes arched her back as he pushed her legs up, his tongue lashing against her clit.

"Say it, Sadie. Say you're mine."

How he expected her to be able to talk at all as he devoured her pussy, was a mystery to her. His growl vibrated against her, and she moaned. He backed away, and she grabbed for his head to move him back.

He slid back up her body, gripping her chin so that she had no choice but to meet his eyes. "The words." He demanded, power saturating his voice.

"I'm yours," she whispered frantically.

His satisfied smile was the only warning she got before he pushed inside of her. He wrapped her legs around his waist, his hips pushing into her, his dick filling her.

"Mine," he growled against her neck before gripping the skin between his teeth.

"Brent, careful," she panted, though the reasons for him to stop were scattering with his every thrust.

His strokes were slow, and he swiveled his hips, pressing against her clit. Her legs tightened, and she scraped her nails across his back. She wouldn't last long, especially with him whispering in her ear. The only light in the room was from the moon shining through his sheer curtains.

"I love you, Sadie," Brent whispered, punctuating his vow with a hard thrust. "I want you to be my mate. Say yes."

A part of her understood that she shouldn't make that type of decision when she was two seconds from orgasm. Another part of her knew that once he was hers, no one could take that away. Brent lifted her leg higher, deepening his strokes until he hit a spot that made her see stars. Her orgasm rolled over her, and she screamed in pleasure. He didn't relent. His hips drove into her prolonging it. She chanted his name, canting her hips to take more of him. She never wanted it to stop. He burrowed into her neck, licking across her pulse, and she made a decision.

"Yes," she whispered.

His hips paused, and his head shot up so he could look her in her eyes. "You're sure?"

"I love you. We're inevitable."

He growled, kissing her, his back arching as he drove into her over and over. She pulled back and gasped as his power rolled over her. Her magic rose to meld with his, a heady feeling that filled her body until her skin tingled. Brent nuzzled against her neck, licking her skin until he got to her shoulder. His body shuddered on top of hers, his power doubling before he gripped her shoulder with his teeth. She went up in flames the moment his teeth pierced her skin. She came, screaming, her nails scoring his skin. His back bowed, and he stiffened on top of her. How long they stayed trapped in that vortex, she couldn't tell. Her body was putty by the time he lifted from her shoulder, staring down at her in wonder.

"I can't believe we did that," she whispered, understanding the gravity of what they'd just done. Had Brent even talked to anyone in his clan about her? What would his parents say?

"You can't imagine how happy I am about it." He whispered against her lips

She frowned because, actually, she could. "I can feel you," she whispered

He smiled. "Good, that means the bond is forming."

"Forming?"

"It won't snap fully into place until the moon is full. I got impatient." There was no remorse in his tone.

"So what we did?"

"I've claimed you, but my mark won't be permanent yet."

"What will your parents think?"

"With you in my arms, I don't care," he whispered, swiveling his hips.

Her body ignited all over again. Fevered whispers were the only sounds as night turned slowly into the morning. How had she ever thought she could keep herself separate from this man? If he was willing to risk a position he'd worked his whole life for, then surely she could do that as well.

He was worth the fight.

16...

Mercedes growled before pasting on a smile as she was stopped yet again on the way into the office. She was running late, her head was thumping, and she was highly regretting staying the night at Brent's. They'd barely left his bed the whole weekend. Besides checking in with her friends to assure them she was alright, she'd not even touched her phone the entire time. Sunday, she'd given thought to going home, but he'd talked her out of that. Not that she'd given him much of a fight. She enjoyed sleeping next to him. Of course, it meant she'd had to haul ass to her house to dress this morning. And now, she was late.

Mumbling a hasty apology, she moved around the paralegal who'd stopped her to ask a question as she entered the lobby. She waved to Terrell at the front desk and scrambled into the elevator before he could stop her.

She took a deep breath as soon as the doors closed. It was her first deep breath since she'd woke up snuggled against Brent. It was then that a hard truth had hit her. One, she should've seen coming. Well, *had* technically seen coming, and still, she'd been surprised and thrown off-kilter. She and Brent had only been 'dating' for a few weeks now, certainly not long enough for the feelings twisting her insides.

She was in love with him.

Full-blown, holy shit, he's the one, love.

One would think that thought would've crossed her mind when she agreed to let him bite her, but it hadn't. The whole weekend had passed with her basking in the bond she felt forming with him, but it hadn't been until this morning that the total weight of it all had crashed down on her. She remembered what Tasha had told her at brunch the other day about equating mating with love. Tasha had said it was more than that, more profound than that. Mercedes swallowed the lump in her throat and took a deep breath.

Insecurity was wrapping its way around her thoughts, and she didn't understand why. He'd claimed her Friday night and initiated the mating bond, but the anticipation of how his family would react was making her nervous. She thought back to his tea leaves. She'd seen his new position in his clan, but she'd also seen turbulence. Would she be the reason for that turbulence? Would he lose his position if they completed the mating?

Her grandmother had long warned her about putting her feelings and personal relationship into someone else's reading. Had her own feelings for him skewed her reading of his leaves? Her fingers itched with the need to touch her tarot cards. She started her mornings laying out a spread to get a read on what her day would be like and as a form of meditation. She hadn't had time this morning, and now all those pesky worries were trying to take over her thoughts.

As soon as the elevator doors opened, her eyes strayed to Brent's office. She frowned when she saw him lead his father through his door and close it. Butterflies started fluttering in her belly, a nervous feeling she associated with a coming change. She gnawed her bottom lip, spinning scenarios in her head. How far out was the full moon? Would that give him enough time to convince his family? She pushed out a breath and rolled her shoulders. She was at work, and one of her number one rules was only to allow work worries at work. She had plenty of time after work to worry about personal problems.

Instead of her regular rounds around the office soothing auras, she headed straight to her desk. She noticed all the stares and whispers but ignored them. She was sure by lunchtime she would have to answer about Friday night. She closed the door and flopped into her desk chair, closing her eyes. This was the reason she had routines. It kept her anxiety from spiraling as it was at the present moment. She reached into her desk drawer and clutched the Citrine she kept there. Taking a few deep breaths, she centered herself until her mind was clear.

She flinched at the knock at her door, shoving the crystal into the drawer and slamming it shut. She looked up to find Brent standing there, a smile on his face.

"Hard time getting in this morning?" He teased.

She blew out a breath and rolled her eyes. "Staying up half the night with you certainly didn't help."

He chuckled and entered her office, shutting the door. His wide body took up much of the space inside. She smiled, her feelings rearing up and overwhelming her.

"I need to talk to you," he whispered.

Her smile dimmed a little. "What's wrong?" Her thoughts immediately went to his father visiting him. Had something happened?

"Nothing's wrong per se." He sat gingerly in the chair in front of her desk. "Just talked to my dad about what happened at the Christmas party the other night."

She winced but said nothing.

"My father is ready to step down." He continued.

She nodded, "I remember telling you that."

"The tea leaves!" He snapped his fingers, "that's right."

"So…" she cleared his throat.

"So. Bears are old-fashioned."

She took her hands off her desk and sat back. "Ok, is this the part where you tell me they don't like witches?"

He shook his head, "What? No."

"That there is concern about what happened Friday night, and I'm not a good fit for you?"

"Babe, no." He frowned. "You're mine. Did I not show you well enough this weekend?"

Mercedes clutched her hands in her lap and forced herself not to give away her distress even as her body heated at his words. Knowing how strong his senses were, he probably knew, but she wouldn't give him the satisfaction of seeing her cry. He was breaking things off with her after what they'd done Friday night? Had his father objected? Would he have to give up the alpha position for her? Would she allow him to do that?

"So, like I was saying, old fashioned. Dad told me that the other bears were insisting that I mate before I take over." He wiped a hand over his face. "The alpha power can be unpredictable, and having a mate balances that out."

"Ok."

She didn't help. She wouldn't make it easy for him to tell her he needed to find a decent bear from a strong bear family. He could kiss her ass on that. He was the one who'd come to her, telling her she was his mate. No way would she help him break his promises.

"I know we agreed to keep this low-key while you considered the mating…it's only been a few weeks, which is fast. But I was hoping, after Friday night, that we could finally take this public. I want to complete our bond."

If Brent thought he—

Her heart stuttered and then pounded, her breath freezing in her lungs. Had he…he was asking her?

"I'm sorry, what?" She said after she could finally form words.

"I know we haven't been together long. I was hoping to have a longer time for us to get to know each other, but my father says it's time and so…" He trailed off, his face flustered, his bear flashing in his eyes.

"Your father gave you the okay to marry me?"

He swallowed, his hands shaking as he leaned forward. "Well, marry is…that's a human sentiment. But as for our mating, I wasn't asking my father's permission. I don't need it. I want to know here, in the light of day, when we're not in bed, will you fully bond with me?"

Her throat clogged, and she prodded his aura to make sure he wasn't lying to her. But there it was, same golden as always, no hint of deception. She probed that connection they'd forged from his bite last night and found nothing there as well. He was nervous but very earnest.

"But you did tell him about us?"

He nodded. "Of course, I share everything with my parents."

"And he's okay with it?"

Brent narrowed his eyes. "Sadie, you're making me nervous, babe. Put me out of my misery, yes or no on bonding?"

"You...can't possibly want to mate with me, already. We just met. You haven't even seen my hair out of these braids." She stood, pacing the small office, all her panicked thoughts from this morning rushing back. "We shouldn't have made such a rash decision the other night."

"I've wanted to mate with you from the first time I saw you," he answered honestly. "Shifters are just like that, babe. You're it for my bear and me." He frowned. "I don't know what your hair has to do with this."

"Oh, Brent," she whispered.

She didn't know what to say. It felt crazy to say, 'I'll mate with you after only knowing you a couple of months.' He didn't pressure her, just waited, his gaze patient if not longing. She nodded, not even sure she was letting her brain have any input.

"Ok," she said.

"Ok?" he asked excitedly.

"Yes." She still had some reservations, but she knew that she loved him and that he was meant to be in her life.

He rushed around the desk and grabbed her up, devouring her mouth. The sound of a throat clearing came from her door. She looked around and saw her boss frowning at them.

"Showing out at the Christmas party wasn't enough for you?" Trina gave a pointed glare at her brother.

"I'm sorry, Trina, Sadie just agreed to mate with me."

His sister's face transformed. "Oh. Oh my God, Brent, that's wonderful. I have to tell Mom."

"I should be the one—" he yelled after his sister, but she'd left, zooming to her office. Brent turned back to Mercedes. "So, that's going to spread quickly."

She gave a watery laugh, her legs shaky, not sure what she'd just agreed to. So many emotions were going through her.

"Will you come to dinner at my mother's tonight?"

She nodded.

"And you agree to mate with me?" He asked, his face unsure.

She smiled and nodded, a tear trailing her cheek. He kissed her cheeks, dabbing her face with his handkerchief.

His smile, so genuine and sweet, lit his face. "Is there anything I need to add to our earlier contract?"

She laughed and shook her head, pushing from his arms as she noticed her co-workers gathered around her office smiling. She waved as they shouted their congratulations. Brent shooed them away and pulled her back into his arms.

"Go, I need to tell my grandmothers, and I have work to do." She smoothed down his tie.

"You should invite them to dinner." He suggested.

She nodded, too overwhelmed to speak.

He smiled again and dropped a hard kiss to her lips. "You've made me so happy."

He left her office, and she fell into her chair, her legs no longer working. Oh shit, she'd just agreed to mate with Brent.

17...

She'd had plenty of time on the drive over from her grandmothers' to think of a thousand scenarios of what could happen when she got to Brent's house. None of them were good. As a matter of point, they spiraled with each new scenario. Would his family hate her? His sister had seemed excited when she'd learned about their mating, but what of the others? She gripped the steering wheel tightly and forced air in and out of her lungs. If Brent could handle her grandmothers, surely she could handle his family.

Her heart resumed its erratic rhythm when she pulled up and saw how many cars were in the driveway.

"Oh Lord, it's a party," Lisa grumbled.

"He just said dinner," Mercedes whispered, trying to reassure herself.

"Julian Hamilton has five kids, so it's probably more than likely a family dinner like he said," Bea soothed.

"Yeah, that makes sense," Mercedes said to bolster her confidence.

"Are you sure you want to do this, Pumpkin Pie?" Lisa asked.

"I love him, Nana, and I saw myself in his future." She squared her shoulders and used that to push the last of her nerves away.

"It's so fast," Bea said, fretting. "I know shifters are usually right about their mates, but I want you to be certain."

"When you know, you know," Lisa said her usual pragmatic self. "Especially with shifters. At least you know he'll treat her right."

"That's very true," Bea said, back to her normal bright self. "Okay, well, let's do this then. Into the bear's den."

Bea laughed at her own joke, and Mercedes let out a shaky laugh along with her. They piled out of the car, and she reached into the back seat and grabbed the two bottles of wine she'd brought. Bea was carrying a blooming lavender plant in a beautiful wooden pot her Grams had made as their gift. Brent opened the door before she lifted her hand to ring the doorbell and her heart fluttered.

She took her first easy breath in what felt like hours.

Just seeing him settled her nerves. He grabbed her and pulled her into his chest, hugging her tight.

"Sadie," he breathed out and then kissed her neck. "Gram, and Nana, I'm so happy to see you." He grabbed them both in hugs, and her grandmothers tittered and giggled like giddy young women.

He helped them all out of their coats, hanging them in a hallway closet.

His mother came up. "Mercedes, I'm so happy you could make it."

"Mrs. Hamilton."

"Catherine, please," she waved away the formality. His mother took a deep inhale, her eyes widening. "Oh my, Brent seems to have moved faster than we anticipated."

Mercedes sent a guilty look at her grandmothers before shooting Brent a nervous glance.

"Mama," Brent sighed and shook his head.

"I didn't expect your scents to start melding so fast, is all," Catherine said, a quick look of alarm passing over her expression.

"Ms. Catherine, these are my grandmothers, Lisa Stanford, and Bea Wilson," Mercedes interjected quickly.

"It's a pleasure meeting you both. Brent told me how you raised Mercedes together. I just love the thought of that." Catherine spotted the lavender, and her eyes lit up. "Oh my gosh, how beautiful."

"They're from our garden," Bea told her.

"Really," Catherine ushered the women further into the house. "You have to tell me about it. I fancy myself an amateur gardener."

Mercedes looked up and found Brent watching her. She was wearing a simple slip dress, the light jersey fabric clinging enough to show off her curves, but not to the point of indecent. Her Gram had simply raised an eyebrow at the spaghetti straps but hadn't said anything. That was a sign that she hadn't gone full hoochie to meet his parents formally. But, the way Brent was devouring her with his eyes, she was wondering if it had been too much.

"Too skimpy?" she asked. He turned her around, his hand skimming her waist and reaching around the rub her ass.

"You look amazing. Come." He led her into the dining room.

Her eyes took in every detail of the beautiful house. The two-story was elegant and warm. Large paintings covered the wall, side by side with portraits of the family. Her heels clicked along the wooden floor as they entered the dining room. Nerves attacked her stomach as conversation halted, and everyone turned to them.

"Marked and mated all in record time," Gabe said before grunting at his brother.

"Kiss my ass," Brent laughed and threw up his middle finger.

"Excuse y'all, we have company," their mother scolded.

She smiled at everyone sitting around the table and introduced her grandmothers to the rest of his family. Brent guided her into the chair next to him, across from her grandmothers.

"Now, isn't this nice!" Catherine said with a strained smile. "We're so happy Brent has found his mate."

"With the number of women you've thrown at him, it was bound to happen," Tiana said into her wine glass.

The rest of the table hid their smiles as Catherine glared.

"As I was saying, there is so much to do. We have to plan the wedding and prepare Mercedes to take on the alpha female role now that Brent's already started the mating process."

Mercedes choked on her wine. Brent rubbed her back, and she carefully set down her glass as she got her breath back.

Her grandmothers gave her serious looks. "I'm glad you've brought that up. What exactly would Sadie's role in the clan be?"

Never one to beat around the bush, Mercedes was glad for Lisa's question. She also wanted to know.

"Well, bear clans are easy maintenance as far as shifters go. I tell people that the alpha pair's role is no different from that of an HOA president. We're responsible for keeping the clan financially viable, emotionally and physically secure, and for the most part, we serve as a liaison for them between other shifters and humans." Julian answered.

"Will the clan have an issue with Sadie being a witch?" Bea asked.

Brent's parents shared a look. Catherine, taking a deep gulp of her wine.

Julian rubbed his chin, "There may be some initial reservations. Brent told me Mercedes doesn't have an animal to call, and honestly, that goes a long way to soothing fears."

"My granddaughter is powerful," Lisa studied the alpha. "Are you using her to bring power to your clan?"

It was Catherine who choked on her wine this time.

"Shifters value power above all else, but having seen the way she wielded her magic at our Christmas party, I honestly don't foresee that being an issue. I think your granddaughter can handle herself quite well." He smiled at Mercedes.

Her Nana sent her a narrowed-eyed gaze. "What happened at the Christmas party?"

Mercedes squirmed.

"Your granddaughter nicely broke apart an altercation," Trina rushed in to help.

"Hmmm," was all Lisa said on the subject, and Mercedes knew she'd have to explain later.

The table was quiet, and Brent shared a look with Mercedes. They needed to steer the conversation out of the murky waters it was currently floating in.

"Even though there could initially be some pushback about having a witch as the Alpha female, they have the family's backing. That will go a long way." Julian reassured them.

"I love Sadie, and not once has her being a witch entered into anything I've decided regarding the two of us." Brent looked both women in the eye, so they knew he meant it.

His bear stiffened as Lisa and Bea both prodded his power to test the truth of his words. He recognized the sensation because Mercedes had done it yesterday when he'd asked her to take his bite. It took a moment before they both nodded.

"Ok then," Catherine said, getting up and refilling glasses.

The conversation went back to more mundane things until his mother and Sadie's grandmothers started earnestly discussing the wedding. It was on from then.

Dinner passed quickly and a lot more congenially than it had started. He was glad both sides of the family could get along. Hours later, Brent walked Mercedes to the car. Her grandmothers were still talking to his mother at the door.

He gripped Sadie's waist as she opened the car door. "Come see me when you drop them off."

She shivered and moaned softly. "How do we complete the bonding?"

"Same thing we did last night, only under the full moon." His bear bucked against him in feverish excitement.

"That's it?"

"There is more to it since I'm alpha, but initially, yes."

She turned around to face him and smiled. "I'm excited about the wedding, I must admit."

He snorted. "Up until you realize how big it will have to be."

She lightly slapped his arm. "When will you take over as alpha?"

He rubbed the back of his neck, "Still debating that with my father. Now that we've made this official, he'll probably push for soon."

"Are you ready?"

"My bear is more than." He pulled her into his chest and inhaled her scent.

"If completing our bonding is just a matter of sex, I'm yours whenever you're ready."

He growled and kissed her, his tongue driving into her mouth, his hands tight on her waist. Her words were incendiary.

She was his 'whenever'.

Power and lust warred within him.

"Brent," his mother called.

"Fuck," he cursed and pulled back, keeping her in his arms. "I swear you make me lose control."

She kissed his cheek. "I'll see you later?"

"How much later?" he whispered.

"It's already late," she told him.

"Sadie," he pleaded.

Her eyes went soft. "Give me an hour to make sure they're settled, and I'll be there."

He kissed her, pulling back as he spotted her grandmothers out of the corner of his eye. "Call me as soon as you get to Gram's and then when you leave so I know you're okay."

"I will," she promised.

He clenched his hands as she drove off, reluctant to let her leave. They were still a few days from the full moon, and he couldn't wait. His bear bucked against his controls, and fur rippled down his arm. He needed to release his animal and calm down. He unbuttoned his shirt.

"Brent Hamilton, you better not strip in my front yard!" Catherine yelled from the front door.

His brother snickered, moving past their mother and inclining his head towards the side of the house. Gabe planned to run with him. Brent smiled. Wrestling with his brother was a great way to get rid of his bear's aggression. He whooped and raced to the backyard.

18...

Nervous didn't entirely cover the feelings roiling around Mercedes' belly at the moment. There was some fear in there and strangely, at least to her, excitement. The air was positively crackling around her, the woods filled with a mix of shifter power and magic. She shivered as it raised the hair on her arms. The full moon was adding to that.

She pulled her phone from her back pocket and pulled up Brent's number to call him and let him know she'd arrived. Her heartbeat sped, and her body heated before she got a chance to push the button.

Her magic rose, his presence calling to it and her. She felt him before his arms wrapped around her waist from behind her.

"My Sadie," he whispered, nuzzling into her neck.

She cupped his cheek, her head bending to the side. She turned and kissed him. He deepened the kiss, his chest rattling.

Mercedes smoothed down his sweater. "Don't start nothing out here."

His eyes went dark with his bear a moment before he came back to himself.

She cocked her head. "Why are you fighting your bear," she asked him quietly.

He rubbed a hand down his face. "His instincts are a little more aggressive at the moment because of the challenges."

"And what are you stopping him from doing?" She was curious.

If ever there was a time for him to let his bear run wild, tonight was it. Brent had been on edge for the past two weeks battling his bear's power. His father had announced that he would step down at the next full moon meeting, and Brent had been preparing ever since.

He leaned down over her, and his hands went to her ass, squeezing and bringing her closer. "You're getting too many looks, and he's of a mind to make a very public statement." He murmured.

She warmed, loving the thought. "So all these marks you left on my neck last night don't count?"

His growl was satisfied as he traced those marks with his finger. She had no problem with his animal wanting to claim her publicly. She splayed a hand under his shirt, scraping her newly sharpened nails down his back.

He growled, and his eyes turned again. "Why do you encourage him?" he asked in a deep voice.

"Fighting your nature is a losing battle, Brent, and I, for one, have no plans to let you do it for much longer. You'll especially need it tonight. Unless you plan to let someone else take clan alpha?"

His eyes lit, his bear chuffing against her neck, fur rippling beneath her hands. Glad that she and the bear were in agreement, she stepped back. Brent studied her, his brows furrowed. How had he expected her to react to his animal? They'd spent every night together, and she'd tried to show him that that part of his nature didn't scare her, so he shouldn't be surprised at her words.

She patted his cheek and kissed him lightly. "Show me around your clan, Brent. That's a compromise for you both."

He nodded and walked her around, introducing her. His mother saw them and came up and hugged Mercedes.

"You brought your grandmothers?"

"No, ma'am."

Catherine smiled, "maybe next time." She shooed Brent away and carried her over to introduce her to some of the older women.

Brent stepped back and watched his mate go with his mother. His bear was smug, the creature happy that Sadie understood his need even as Brent fought him. Mercedes had reassured him that she didn't mind his more aggressive tendencies, that she had no problem handling his bear. He was starting to believe her. He sensed his brother entering the clan land and walked towards the front to meet him. Gabe would help calm down his nervousness...maybe. If nothing else, his twin would for sure remind him of what was at stake tonight.

He smiled when he noticed Naomi and the twins bundled into the back seat.

"Are they bundled enough, Nay?" He asked, opening the door.

"Yes, they're probably sweating in the amount of clothes their father put on them." She grumbled, unbuckling the car seat for Brent.

His heart melted as he pulled the baby—seat and all—from the car. He cooed at his nephew and walked him towards the party. His nephew's serious eyes traced his face as he drooled on his fists.

"Is it too soon to have them outside?"

"Lord, have mercy," Naomi muttered. "They're hearty bear cubs. According to my grandfather, they are strong despite getting here early. I asked before I agreed to bring them out. I want them to have the new clan link."

"You're going to be bombarded," he warned her as he rubbed his nephew's cheek.

"I wish a mother fu—"

"Gabriel, you are not going to be mean to people wanting to see the babies." Naomi scolded.

Brent snorted because his brother damn well would be, despite her stern warning.

"Thank you for coming."

"Of course," Gabe grunted. "Where else would I be than beside you. You ready to take the clan?"

Brent nuzzled into his nephew. "I'm ready, and my bear is more than ready."

"Then let's do this shit so I can get my boys back to our den." Gabe walked ahead of them.

Brent followed behind them, and as he predicted, bears surrounded them, wanting to see the babies. His sisters pushed forward and snatched his nephew from his hand, cooing. He looked around for

Mercedes and saw one of the male bears talking to her. His bear pushed forward, power flooding his body. She looked up and caught his eyes. She walked over to him, the sway of her hips not helping one bit. She smiled as she got closer. Sadie put her hand on his arm, he thought to calm him, but his mate's magic wrapped around him as she stood at his side. It did nothing to suppress the riotous feelings running through him. If anything, her power boosted him, his bear filling him to the point of imminent change.

"When are the challenges starting?" Her voice was strong and soothing.

He grunted, unable to talk.

She brought his head down to hers, rubbing her cheek along his. "Let him do what he's supposed to do."

"I don't want to scare you," he managed.

"Brent, I'm not worried about you or your bear hurting me. I love you, and that means all your parts. Stay focused and do what you have to."

He nodded, lifting Mercedes into his arms. She accepted his rough kiss, her tongue tangling with his.

His father interrupted them, gripping Brent's shoulder. "It's time, son."

19...

Brent was thankful that Florida decided to join the rest of the world and cool down for winter. He removed his shirt, the slow breeze cooling his overheated skin. His bear was primed, ready for the fight or fights that lay ahead. Mercedes turned him to face her. She pulled down on his head so that their foreheads touched. His bear rushed forward at the first tendril of her power. It wrapped around him, and her warm, steady confidence soothed the animal. He smiled, kissing her softly.

"You worried?"

"Not in the least. You got this," she whispered against his lips.

He stepped back from her as his father finished laying down the last rocks that made their battle circle. Julian walked to the middle and took in the clan gathered and waiting.

"Tonight, I willingly turn over the clan to my eldest son, Brent." He pinned said son with a proud smile. "But, we bears are always governed by only the strongest of us. If there are any who wish to come forward and claim that title, then tonight is the night for it."

The crowd parted, and three bears walked to the edge of the stone circle across from Brent.

"Aw hell," Mercedes whispered.

His bear snorted in amusement, not worried.

"You got this shit," Gabe said low.

Julian turned to Brent and nodded. Brent stepped into the fighting circle in just a pair of loose pants. His cousin Cal entered first, and they both gave a short nod to the other. Julian stepped from the circle and called for them to start. For the first time in a long time, Brent gave his bear carte blanche. Power filled his body, and despite his cousin's skill, he made short work of defeating him. The animal took over, his jabs to Cal's torso quick, brutal. It wasn't long before the male showed his neck conceding defeat. Brent roared, and the next male entered the circle.

He barely let Justin into the circle before he was on him. Justin ducked his first punch, but Brent was ready for him. He kicked out at his knee, the sound of the bone cracking. Justin growled, changing into his bear and charging him with a speed that Brent almost didn't see coming. He took the brunt of Justin's body as the male rammed into him. He wrestled with him, turning over, his hands extending into claws that raked down Justin's back. They grappled on the ground, Justin's teeth gripping his arm and tearing. Brent hissed in pain, his bear pushing forward. He changed into his animal, the fight becoming messy as both animals grappled.

He lost track of time as they battled, but Justin matched him well. His bear stood toe to toe with Brent's. It took some maneuvering, but soon, Brent had Justin's neck in his mouth, his teeth pressing down, waiting on the male's submission. Justin roared and twisted his body for long minutes before finally going lax. The male extended his neck, and Brent released him, accepting his submission. Justin changed into his human form, the scrapes, and bites covering his skin, telling of their battle. He held out his hand, and Brent changed, gripping Justin's hand and standing. The crowd roared and cheered.

"Five minutes," Julian called.

Brent walked over to Mercedes, naked, blood and sweat sliding down his skin. Despite that, she stepped to him, her hand going to his cheeks. His chest was heaving as he fought to catch his breath. He was exhausted, but he had no plans to go down tonight.

"You good?" Her palms were warm against his skin, a woodsy scent wafting from her hands.

He nodded, in answer to her question, his bear still riding him. He knew talking would be out the question until the fights were over.

"Just one more," she whispered. "You got this, babe." She stood on her toes and nuzzled underneath his chin.

Her magic wrapped around him, and his body flooded with strength. He gripped her chin, bringing her mouth up to his. The kiss was hard but gentle was far removed from him at the moment. It didn't matter, though. His mate met his passion, her sharp nails digging into his shoulders, matching his aggression.

It pleased his bear.

"Mine," he managed in a rumble.

"Yours." She slapped his chest, hyping him more. Her eyes were lit with a combination of lust and bloodthirsty fire.

His chest rumbled. His first priority after the fight would be Sadie.

"Let's finish it, Brent," his father called out.

He gave Sadie one last look before turning back to his last battle of the night. Abram smirked and pulled his shirt over his head. Brent rolled his shoulder and stepped forward.

"I gotta admit, I'm impressed with the Placid Alpha," Abram taunted.

Brent ignored him, leaving his body loose, waiting on the other male to make the first move. Thanks to Mercedes, he had all the time in the world. The weariness that had swamped him after the second fight was gone. And in its place, a determination to finish this fight so that he could tend to the fire banking in his mate's eyes. Abram darted at him but backed away at the last second. Brent shook his head. It seemed his strategy would be to tire Brent out. Sad for him.

Brent rushed forward, a flurry of fists of which Abram was only able to dodge a few. He grunted as he took a couple of hits to his kidneys. Both men were moving swiftly, exchanging blows until the claws came out. Soon, his bear was fed up with boxing and ripped from Brent's skin, raking his claws down Abram's side. He then changed, and the animals were at it.

***

Mercedes winced as Abram, in his bear form, swiped at Brent again. Blood arched in the air from the wound, and she clasped her hands together. She prayed the power she'd imbued in Brent would help. The oil her grandmothers had helped her prepare earlier should also give him extra strength. Her hands still tingled from its power, so she hoped it gave him the strength he needed.

She desperately wanted to close her eyes and block out the violent sight, but she would be Alpha female. Hiding from this aspect of clan life would make her and, in turn, Brent look weak. So, she kept her eyes glued to the brutal fight. She swallowed as the two wrestled in the dirt, fur and blood flinging.

"Come on, baby, finish it," she called out.

She wanted to touch him, to help him heal. As though he heard her, Brent twisted and had Abram pinned beneath him. He wrapped his mouth around the other bear's neck, and the night stilled, the crowd going quiet as they waited. Mercedes could feel her heart beating out of her chest as the seconds stretched. Moments later, Abram closed his eyes, and his body went lax. He changed into his human form, Brent's bear still not releasing him. It wasn't until Abram tilted his head in submission that Brent released him.

Mercedes took her first deep breath in what felt like forever and rushed forward. She felt the power at the edge of the ring and stopped, waiting until Brent left the circle. Brent stood on two legs, extending to his full eight feet, roaring loudly. The crowd answered, and she fought the urge to cover her ears at the loud sound. The clan continued to cheer as Brent changed back to human, his eyes solely on her. He scooped her up and kissed her, a rough, possessive kiss that sent fire racing through her bloodstream. She pulled back, and she watched the cuts and scrapes knit right before her eyes.

"You're okay," she whispered, more to reassure herself.

"I need you," he growled.

He walked her through the woods until they found an empty shed. She barely closed the door behind her before he jerked down her pants and entered her. She rode the storm of his aggressive lovemaking, loving every second of it. She needed this as much as he did; she needed to know he was okay.

"My Sadie," he growled, his strokes relentless as he powered into her.

She clutched his shoulders, throwing her head back. He growled and gripped the front of her neck with his teeth, thrusting into her. Mercedes couldn't stop the orgasm that washed over her if she tried. It started at her toes, throwing her body into a vortex of fire. She screamed, squeezing on Brent to wring out every drop. He licked against his teeth marks, the rhythm of his hips stuttering until he too shouted and came.

"I swear I planned for that to take longer," he panted against her skin.

Mercedes couldn't answer his joke because she was too busy sucking in air. She clutched him so tightly she could feel the beat of his heart against her chest. She refused to release her hold on him, her arms tightening. She knew he would be alpha and trusted her power enough to know that what she saw would come true. She just hadn't been ready for the ferocity of the fighting. The logical part of her understood that she wouldn't have lost him, but her nerves were shot, all the same.

"I love you so much, Sadie," he whispered against her neck.

"Oh, Brent, I love you too." She finally loosened her hold around his torso.

They stood in each other's embrace for long minutes, the sound of their breathing loud in the quiet shed—the noise from the partying clan filtered in some, but nothing that disturbed their moment.

20...

Mercedes slid her legs down from Brent's waist as he pulled out, settling on the ground. There was power radiating from him, the adrenaline from the fight still flowing down to her through their connection.

"I'm alpha now," he murmured against her skin. "You need to bond with the bear so that your connection with the clan will snap into place."

She leaned back to get a better look at him. "You mean your actual bear."

He nodded. "Don't be scared. My mate can handle him."

He gave her a mischievous smile that was still the affable Brent that she'd fallen in love with, even though that aggressive alpha bear was there in his gaze and in the power filling the space between them.

She nodded and followed him from the shed on shaky legs. They stepped out into the moonlight filtering through the trees in the forest. Brent turned to look at her, his gaze asking her if she was okay. Mercedes nodded and took a deep breath.

Brent stepped from her, his body shifting, the sound of cracking bones loud to her ears. It took mere seconds for the whole thing, and before she could blink again, a fully grown bear stood on all fours before her. Brent stepped closer to her, and with shaking hands, she slid her fingers through his coarse fur.

She let out a small squeak when the bear went up on two legs. She clutched its fur, forcing her body to be still. The animal nuzzled into her neck, and though fear crowded her, she stood tall. She shuddered as its tongue lapped against her skin, and the first tendrils of heat started strumming through her body. She flinched when Brent bit down carefully, his teeth piercing her skin.

She closed her eyes as power inundated her body, the bond with his bear snapping into place, merging with the bond she'd already had with Brent. The clan link was also there now, solid and vibrant. She opened her eyes as the fur in her hands gave way to overheated skin. Brent was naked in front of her, licking at the bite mark. The more he licked it, the more it burned, a wave of heat filling her body. The heat changed from mild to a fire racing through her. Mercedes panted as her skin tightened.

"Ride it out. You have it. You're my strong mate," Brent encouraged as he gripped her waist.

Her stomach cramped, and she leaned forward, pushing him away to curl into herself. She dug her nails into the palms of her hands as she was inundated. But then, her magic seemed to meet the bear's power, and meld and strength flooded back into her body. She straightened, and her skin lit, her nakedness drinking in the moonlight. She bowed her back and raised her head, tears leaking from her eyes at the euphoria filling her body. It soon began to cool, and when she looked at Brent, he stared at her hungry, a feverish lust in his eyes.

"Run," he growled to her.

She took off away from the crowd, though with lust riding her, she didn't think she'd care if they ran into anyone. Brent was coming up behind her as she dashed over a downed tree. She could hear his bear rumbling as he got closer. He caught her a moment later, taking her to the ground, spinning so that he took the brunt of the fall. She straddled his waist, and he tugged on her hair, bringing her down to him, devouring her mouth. He drove his hips upward, and Mercedes moaned as he penetrated her.

Her body was on fire, her need for him overtaking her. His shaft was thick, stretching her most deliciously. He lifted his hips, and she took every inch of him. He grunted, pulling her hair until she was bent back, her breast exposed to him.

"Ride me, Sadie," he ordered, cupping her breasts, squeezing her nipples.

Pressure built in her core, ecstasy whipping through her. He cursed and gripped her hips, pulling her up and then down on top of him.

Brent was mindless with his strokes, his power wrapping around them, damn near drugging him. They were fully bonded, and Sadie filled every corner of his heart and mind. He could feel her pleasure, and it added to his. Her moans spurred him on until every word out of his mouth was unintelligible, barely rumbles. She rode him, her back arched, her neck exposed, and Brent didn't think he'd ever seen anything as beautiful as the woman on top of him.

Mercedes chanted his name, her magic winding and intertwining in his bear's power. He pulled her down, needing to feel her skin against him. His strokes were uncoordinated, his need for her overriding all finesse. She sucked on the skin of his neck, her teeth biting down on him. That was all it took for him to lose it. He reached down and strummed her clit, needing her with him. She tensed, her teeth releasing his shoulder as she screamed and came. He followed her over; his body wrung out.

He held her tight as his bear finally relented control to him. The fucking animal had ridden him all night, and now that they were both stated, their mate pliant and warm in their arms, he could finally relax. He took a deep breath, purring at their merged scents. Sadie was his, and the clan was his. Brent was the happiest he'd been in a long time.

Mercedes sat up and looked around, her eyes going wide. Now that the magic from their bonding was faded, she seemed to realize where they were.

She covered her breasts with her arm and buried her face in her other hand. "Oh shit, we just had sex outside in the dirt."

"Hey, you're not the one laying on sticks," he muttered.

She snorted and shuffled off of him. "Where are our clothes?"

"I have no clue," he said lazily.

He stretched his body, wincing at the sore muscles from his challenges. He was fully sated, power thrumming through his body. But nowhere near as uncontrolled as before. He could feel Sadie's magic within him, corralling some of the more aggressive instincts of his bear. The animal was content, stronger than ever, but secure, so there was none of the fighting for power from before. Brent took an easy breath, love for Sadie overwhelming him. He didn't know if it was mating with her or finally having the alpha position that made the creature easier to manage, but he was thankful either way.

"Oh my, God, your parents are somewhere out here." She tried to cover more of her body.

He snorted and sat forward. "Trust me, the clan ain't checking for us."

"No way am I going back."

There was a rustling in the woods a moment before Gabe, in bear form, walked out of the trees, carrying clothes in his mouth. Sadie squealed and dove to hide behind him.

Brent laughed and grunted his thanks to his brother. Gabe dropped the clothes, grunted back, and left. Brent reached out his hand and pulled his shirt from the bunch, and pulled his embarrassed woman around to help her into it.

"Want to see our new house?"

Her eyes widened, and she nodded.

He stood a moment later, not bothering with the pants his brother had left. The bears in the clan were used to seeing each other nude.

"Come," he held his hand out to Mercedes, who now wore his t-shirt like a dress. He grabbed her to him. "Can you feel the clan?"

She nodded, her face happy, her contentment flowing easily through their bond. She yawned, her hands gripping his tightly.

His eyes traced her face, seeing her exhaustion. A warm bath and cuddling was definitely on the agenda for the rest of their night. "Let's go see our house."

Excitement spiked, and he smiled, incredibly happy to have her in his life. He walked her over to the two-story house his father had built for him years ago. Her eyes widened, and she rushed up the steps of the front porch.

"Holy...Brent," she turned in a circle, her eyes taking in everything. "This is your house?"

"Ours, love," he said softly.

Her breath hitched, and her eyes shone in the moonlight when they met his. He cleared the lump from his throat, moved by her reaction. He put the code in the door lock and opened it, lifting Mercedes in his arms. Brent carried her over the threshold, setting her down in the foyer.

"Oh my God," her hushed voice echoed throughout the place. "It's a beautiful house."

"Nowhere near as beautiful as you," he said, pulling her back into his chest. "Let's go see the bedroom, break it in."

She laughed and kissed him, and he knew they would be happy here.

Epilogue

There were a lot of different things Mercedes could've been doing a few days before her wedding. There was an endless amount of details that needed her attention, despite there being a wedding planner. According to the text messages she kept getting from Catherine, there were at least a dozen things still on her to-do list.

Instead, Sadie was sitting on the living room floor in her new house, between Brent's legs. He growled for what seemed like the one-hundredth time, and she winced as her head jerked to the side.

"Sorry, babe, I can't figure out how to get the very top out without tangling it," he grumbled.

She continued her slow and steady unweaving of the braid she was holding and snickered. This was hour three of the whole process, and despite his growls, her mate had a lot more patience than she'd given him. She expected him to give up an hour ago. All the other times he'd helped, he'd given up hour one.

"Just unbraid them as far as you can. I'll take the top," Mercedes soothed.

He sighed in relief, "that's a good plan."

She snickered again and wiggled to get comfortable. Her attention went back to the t.v. show they were binging. She appreciated that he was helping her. Usually, it was her, and whatever show TV One had streaming on repeat. They were more than halfway done, so despite the occasional tugs and cursing from Brent, they were making good time.

"Will we have this all done before your appointment?"

"Don't worry, babe. With your help, we'll be done well before to-morrow." She tucked in her lips to hide her smile as he cursed again.

"There are only three days until the wedding. Should you have waited this long to take your braids out?"

"Tasha got me. I'm not worried."

"You picked up the—"

"Brent, babe, you in women's business. You get your tux and make sure that everyone gets paid; that's your business." She teased.

He snorted and tugged on her hair. "Fine, you can't blame me for being excited."

Mercedes smiled. She could feel his excitement. His bear, on the other hand, was merely tolerant of the whole process. She loved that she could feel them both. She and Brent could've married at any point during the year they'd been together, but she'd wanted to wait until the winter solstice. The winter solstice symbolized hope and faith; some-thing Mercedes wished to carry into their marriage. Aside from that, it was the same day her parents had been married. It satisfied her as a way to include them.

Her phone beeped with several text messages, and she sighed, al-ready knowing who it was.

He laughed, "I told you she would be like that. But no, you wanted to wait a year before we got married even though we were already bonded."

"Legal paperwork is different. You can't blame me for being cau-tious," she teased.

"Mmhmm, and what did your cautiousness get you? My mother, breathing down your neck to make sure you make it down the aisle." He chuckled.

She snorted. He was right. "It's all of them, my family and yours. They've been harassing me non-stop. Naomi is the only one with sense. I can't wait until the wedding is over," she muttered.

"Me either," he leaned down and nibbled at her neck. "We can spend our honeymoon completely naked. That'll make it all worth it, right?"

She turned and pulled his head down, kissing him. "More than," she said as they came up for air.

She smiled at the lust heating Brent's eyes.

Brent's chest rumbled in hunger as he stared down into Sadie's face. Although they'd been living together a year, he never tired of looking at her. She turned her back to him and resumed unbraiding as though she hadn't lit a fire under him.

He gripped her hair and exposed her neck, scraping his teeth down the column. "We should take a break."

She shuddered, and her body heated, the heady scent of her arousal rising. Her magic rose, melding with his power and sending electricity down his skin. Damn, he loved their bond. He closed his eyes, nuzzling against her skin, reveling in the intimacy of it. She pulled from his arms and stood. He settled against the back of the couch as she straddled him, sitting in his lap. She wrapped her arms around his shoulders, her smile warm and sensual. His bear moved under his skin.

"Why you need a break, you hungry?" The sultry tones of her accent wrapped around him.

"Something like that," he murmured, lifting her shirt.

Mercedes obliged him, yanking her shirt over her head and tossing it to the side. Brent hissed in appreciation, his hands cupping her breasts as they spilled free. He couldn't keep his hands off her, and he didn't foresee that changing anytime in the future. Every time Mercedes was near him, he wanted to touch her, consume her. Luckily for him, she never failed to match his energy.

She leaned forward and licked across his lips. "You have half an hour. I'm not finna be up all night doing my hair."

Brent removed his hands from her chest, pulling his dick from his sweatpants. "That'll do nicely."

Mercedes squealed as he ripped through her shorts and lifted her. Her laugh turned to a gasp as he worked her down on his erection. Brent's smile was admittedly smug as her lips parted and her lids dropped, lust suffusing her face. He lifted his hips, his smile dropping as her scorching hot pussy squeezed around him.

Her satisfaction flowed down to him through their bond, and Brent's grip tightened on her hips. He would never get enough of her, and that was a fact. Every moment they spent together cemented their bond tighter. Because of her, he and his bear were getting along better. Sadie refused to let him suppress the animal's urges, coaxing the two of them into a truce that strengthened his position over the clan. She added to his life in every way.

As he lost himself in her body, he could only pray he did the same for her. She told him daily how much she loved their new life. She was a great alpha female, and the women in the clan made no bones about telling him how lucky he was to have her.

Mercedes lifted, her back arching as she rode him, chanting his name. Brent pulled her into his chest, devouring her mouth, needing to taste her. They moved against each other, trading kisses and sweet love words. It wasn't long before they both crashed over the edge. He swallowed her moans, holding her against him as his hips jerked on final time as he came.

"Are you happy, Sadie?" He asked, rubbing their cheeks together while he caught his breath.

She sighed, rubbing the back of his head. "Insanely so, my Placid Alpha."

He snorted and smacked her ass cheek. "No respect for your alpha."

Her laughter was music to his ears.

Also available from Dria Andersen

About the Author

I am a full time photographer, and a mom of two. I've been writing my whole life, and after the birth of my first kid, I decided I couldn't very well bring up a fearless human without first trying the things that scared me. So, I wrote my first book, and then subsequently more.

I try to write stories I love to read: love stories that feature brown girls like me. Some of my stories feature gods and goddesses, and creatures I derived from old, African folk tales remixed and thrust into a modern world. Visit my website, www.driaandersen.com for more information on my other novels.